THE PURPLE ROSE

To Barbara –
Best wishes
Charlotte
November 2013
(Enjoy!)

THE PURPLE ROSE
Charlotte Gringras

Tollington

First published by Tollington Press, London, 2012
www.tollingtonpress.co.uk

A catalogue record for this book is available from the British Library.

ISBN 978-0-9560173-9-0

Cover design by jenksdesign@yahoo.co.uk
Typeset by Helen Sandler

Printed in Great Britain by the MPG Books Group, Bodmin and King's Lynn
on FSC-certified paper from well-managed forests and other controlled sources

L'dor vador
– from generation to generation
(Hebrew)

PROLOGUE

The rows of empty cars provided an attentive audience for Martin's rants, which was a good thing, since I couldn't listen to him any more. He'd moaned all the way here, so the moment he parked the car, I jumped out, slamming the door behind me.

'Nicki, this is bloody stupid!' His words bounced from headlights to bumpers and back, radiators grinning in approval. 'Why the hell are we seeing a complete stranger?'

I fell stubbornly silent, striding ahead of him, towards the office building and our appointment. He trudged behind me, kicking a pebble like a grumpy little boy.

'Hey, are we not speaking now?' Martin caught me up.

'What is there to speak about?' I asked. Arguing was pointless; I had to bring him round somehow and changed my tone. 'We made the appointment together, remember.'

'It'll all be psychobabble, like a women's agony page –'

'Of course, men don't "do" agony, do they?' I said, pulling my collar up over my ears in defiance.

'There y'go, feminist to a fault.'

'Just drop it, OK?' I hoped this exchange was over and, as we neared the office, I relented. 'Fancy a coffee?' I pointed to a café, opposite.

'Maybe after.'

'I'm dreading it too, y'know.' I rang the bell.

We checked in at the counselling centre's reception and sat down. I looked at the bare walls; decor was non-existent. I thought they could do with one of my murals. Of what? People, fighting? I'm such a cynic. Martin took my hand but his palm was sweaty – not like him. My pulse raced. Martin and me, at a counsellor's? We used to be the couple everyone else turned to.

ONE

It had all come to a head a few weeks earlier when Martin didn't come home for my mother's funeral – or for the seven days of mourning that followed. He said he couldn't cut short his business trip but I felt he should have been with me in that week that changed my life.

In a typically rainy February in 2005, it was our first Friday night dinner without Mum, Malkah Bamberg. Or at least, it was the first since her death six days earlier – she'd been in hospital for a while before that. I brought the *Shabbat* meal to Dad's, feeling Martin's absence deeply.

I lit the candles, so all the ornaments on the dresser across the dining room twinkled in the shifting light. Those familiar things were part of her: the old Toby jug, Dad's first present to her; that horrid, Venetian glass bowl they bought on their first holiday abroad and Grandma Freidl's china thimble. Then there was that black and white photograph of me and my twin brother, David, as scrawny babies wearing only nappies. The objects stood on little crocheted mats made by Freidl, Mum's mother.

That baby photo was a reminder of David's absence; he'd managed to fly in for the funeral – he'd been on standby – but then had to go straight home, as his wife had just given birth to their third child. I always missed him, but especially now.

Mum used to sew in this room; she made all my clothes, as well as many for poor children. She never used a pattern and she made cheap material look fantastic with smocking, hand-covered buttons and gigantic sashes, tied in exaggerated bows, 'Just so'. Her sewing machine, previously used by her mother, had already been silent for a while. On Friday nights, when we were children, David and I had to clear the fabric scraps, before setting the table for the Shabbat meal.

Memories like these floated around me and, although my hands were over my eyes while saying the candle-blessing, tears still trickled out between my fingers, making everything in the room swim, eerily. Dad tried not to break down as he hugged and blessed me, as fathers do every Friday night; he pulled Jake to his chest, too, in Martin's absence. It helped Dad that Uncle Ernie recited *kiddush* with him but his hand trembled as he passed round the wine he had blessed.

Ernie and Dad looked more alike than ever, merging, in their grief, into almost a single face. They were like brothers to each other, but were actually cousins, with similar thick, grey hair – Ernie's was curlier – brown eyes and a straight nose; one I envied but didn't inherit. Dad was the taller but that night he seemed to have shrivelled. Ernie was a smart dresser, never casual; even his shoe colour matched his suits. Dad had adapted to the times and wore a sweater with an open-necked shirt. That night, I missed their infectious laughter.

As a direct mourner, Dad hadn't shaved since Mum's death, which made his face look thinner; his beard was mainly white, now. Jake, my son, made the blessing over the plaited bread.

After a sip of wine and a piece of bread, he started: 'Grandpa, tell us a bit –'

'Jake, not again – leave Grandpa alone! You've pumped him and Uncle Ernie with questions all week. They're both very tired.'

'Yeah, I know, but my grandma's just died and when I'm sad, I need to talk.' Jake was nearly twelve and mainly a good lad but he was turning into an investigative reporter. Of course Dad, like

Mum, rarely criticised him. Jake looked good, that night – he'd really tried. His complexion had improved, after a visit to the doctor; his fair skin contrasted strikingly with dark brown eyes. His hair, freshly washed, for once, showed its auburn sheen and he wore a smart sweatshirt with an abstract line-drawing on it, designed by Ernie.

'Grandpa Joseph doesn't mind – you don't, do you, Grandpa?' Jake protested.

'Well, let's have our first course and then we'll see,' Dad said.

'I like you in that sweater, Jake,' Ernie commented, smiling for the first time that evening.

'It's a sweat*shirt*, Uncle Ernie, not a sweat*er* – and anyway, you would say that, wouldn't you?' Jake grinned.

Jake always helped Ernie in his lifelong quest for perfect English – even after a lifetime here, he still tried to rid himself of the last vestige of foreignness and German accent. As we finished the chopped-liver starter, Dad looked up and turned to Jake.

'So, what is it you want to know, now?'

'More about Grandma – and about her mother, too, Great-Grandma Freidl. We've been learning about the suffragettes at school – wasn't she one?

'Yes and no one knew, till after she died.'

'Wow! Well cool!' Jake spoke in exclamation marks. 'Tell me about her, Grandpa; school's into personal life-stories lately. Our family's one big history lesson. And Uncle Ernie –' He broke off, looking beseechingly at Ernie. 'Can I tell them?'

'Of course.'

'Uncle Ernie's writing his life story for me.' Jake stood up, did a drum roll with his cutlery on the table mat, then, using a booming, American voice, announced: 'Ladies and gentlemen, coming to a boy near you! The first ever... "A" in history!'

Dad and Ernie laughed; Jake could always lighten the

atmosphere. Ernie had never talked about his journey on the *Kindertransport* – or what it was like, leaving his home on his own. Odd, really, yet he'd always simply been part of our family.

'Lucky you, Jake. Ernie, how come?' I asked.

'I had to tell my story, before I'm too old – and Jake's project gave me a reason.' Jake could twist him round his little finger; I hoped it would be a positive experience for Ernie.

Jake carried on: 'So, about Great-Grandma Freidl. Did she go on marches, smashing windows, all that? Great-Grandma Vandal!'

'Jake –' I shouted.

'Leave him, Nicola. If he doesn't hear it from me, who will he hear it from?' When Dad uses my full name, not Nicki, something serious is afoot. I was lucky he didn't give me my full title: Nicola Taylor. No sooner had I served his favourite, chicken soup with kneidls, than Dad got up from the table, went to the bureau where he used to repair jewellery and took out some papers, tied up with frayed ribbon, which he put on the table.

'It's easier to tell you with these, Jake.'

'What are they?' Jake made as if to grab them, but Dad, with unusual sternness, stopped him.

'Your grandma asked me to keep them after she died. They're letters from her mother, Freidl, which she wrote in her old age. They're about her life.'

'Hold on a sec, how long had *my* mum had them?' I asked, bemused.

'Since Freidl died.'

'But why not show us before now? How odd.' I felt hurt, but Dad looked so sad, in the realisation that Mum wasn't coming back. I stroked his hand.

'The soup's getting cold, everyone,' Ernie said. We were quiet for a moment, then Dad began to explain.

'So. Freidl dictated the story of her early life, as letters to Malkah – and future generations – and they were typed up by an assistant in her care home.'

'Why would she do that for her own daughter? And couldn't she write?' Jake asked.

'Well, she was over ninety at the time. I suppose her writing was shaky,' Dad explained. 'Just wait till you read them.'

'Don't be so melodramatic, Dad. What's the secret?' Dad, being mysterious – why? 'For goodness sake –' I raised my voice.

'Just wait, Nicola – calm down – or read the letters. Here, Jake, you start reading them to us.' Jake took them and untied the ribbon.

So I had to calm down, but Jake could be as excitable as he liked? Nothing changed.

'Is it about the suffragettes?' asked Jake.

'They're about lots of things. You'll see.'

So Jake began. He read from Grandma Freidl's stilted but perfect English. I wondered how my late mother felt when she first read them. Sad that she, to whom Freidl wrote, was no longer here. We listened.

My dear daughter Malkah,

You know, the moments that change your life are rarely of your making, I'm convinced of that. So, I wonder why I worried about any decision I made, because every so often, forces beyond my control would suddenly alter things completely.

Remember, dear, I'm over ninety, so I know what I'm talking about. As I tell you my life story, you'll see what I mean. I didn't really plan to leave my family in Romania, alone, aged only sixteen. It was a twist of fate: my Auntie Sadie had the ticket, but fell ill the week before she was due to leave. It took only twenty-four hours for my parents to agree that I should use it but I certainly didn't know that one day…

'Like me!' Ernie interrupted. 'I only had days, too –'
  'And when do we get to the big stuff?' Jake asked.
  'Shush. Keep going,' Dad replied. Jake read on.

… Going to a public meeting, three years after coming to England, would be the night that changed my life for ever. Thankfully, I remember it – it's correct that, once you hit eighty, early memories are clearer than those of yesterday! I had read a notice in my workplace, inviting people to a public meeting about workers' rights. I already had a great interest in workers' rights, particularly those of women.

It was taking place in a public hall in Red Bank; my uncle Isaac lived there, so I knew it would take a good half hour's walking to arrive on time. Deciding what to wear wasn't difficult, as I still hadn't earned enough as a seamstress to have many smart clothes. That was ironic, to be stitching clothes all day, yet rarely having the time to make much for myself – nor could I afford my own sewing machine. Some girls made clothes for themselves, at work, but risked being fired for it; I thought that was a risk too great.

From my old chest, I pulled out my 'best' skirt. I don't know why I call it that, I only had two! This one was in black grosgrain, long and full. I ironed my one white blouse and put on my well-worn boots, hoping the soles wouldn't wear out on the way. Looking in the mirror, I realised that however much I'd brushed my frizzy hair, it would be better under a hat; it felt right and proper to wear one to a public meeting.

Jake looked up. 'Hey – there's so much, I can't read it all.'
  'You'll hear who my Malkah is – or was – quite soon, but why not take the letters home?' From the same bureau, Dad took another pile of envelopes, in a rubber band. 'Here – take your time. It took me days. Jake, this really is history.'
  'Brill, Gramps!'

We tried to finish dinner quickly, intending to have an early night. We all needed one, after the effort of sitting *shivah* – and all this. We wanted to ask more questions but Dad simply said, 'You must read Grandma's own words.'

So we just chatted about everyone who had come to see us after Mum's funeral, that week. People whom we had not seen for years came with memories, many bringing food – cakes, biscuits or whole meals. One afternoon, I arrived to find biscuits and cakes squashed, because containers of homemade soup had been piled thoughtlessly on top.

In fact, the main course we ate that night – chicken with *tzimmis* – had been made and brought by my friend, Ros. We would have a rest from visitors the next day, Saturday; Shabbat took precedence over everything, even mourning, so the last day of prayers would be on Sunday. After that, Dad would be properly alone.

I was loathe to leave him but was anxious to read more of the letters. We went for our coats; Dad hugged me, then pinched my cheeks, like Mum used to do.

'That's better, you looked a bit pale.'

'Thanks for that.' I was being sarcastic and I couldn't check my appearance as all the mirrors were covered. I grew up wishing Mum or Dad would compliment me sometimes. If not my looks, then just – me. By its very nature, my fair, freckly skin was often pale; my frizzy hair, often unruly, could hardly have looked its best, that week of all weeks. Yet I knew Mum would look immaculate in any circumstances.

Dad wished us all 'Good *Shabbos*' as we left.

'*Shabbat Shalom,*' I replied, using the modern Sabbath greeting. 'Night. Sure you don't you want me to sleep here tonight?'

'No, dear. With Mum in hospital these last weeks, I'm used to sleeping on my own,' Dad assured me. As I kissed his cheek I tasted the salt of his tears. We left him in a house that now seemed to engulf him.

Once we were back home, I made some lemon tea for us all, turned up the heating, and we took turns reading the letters – preventing our early night.

TWO

I rummaged in the chest and spotted the old red fabric flower my mother had pressed upon me as I left Romania. After wedging it into the hatband, I put the hat on at an angle, like the smart city women customers wore theirs. I was fortunate to have my father's height – five foot six, in those days, was tall for a woman – and luckily my mother's slender figure. I had never cared about appearances until that day, but felt quite proud of how I looked, except I wished I could have hidden my freckles, which I hated.

Being involved in political meetings seemed to demand not glamour, exactly, but a certain 'presence'. After all this vain attention to detail, I was running late and threw on my only jacket: at least its peplum was flattering. I grabbed the tapestry bag my auntie had made me and ran downstairs. The landlady's voice bellowed out through her closed front door: 'I hope you're not gallivanting, young Miss Friedl. I will tell your uncle, if you are out too late!'

'Good evening, Mrs Grossberger, I hope you have a good evening,' I answered – I should have preferred not to reply but knew, of old, that a lack of response from me would only lead to a full interrogation. What I never knew was how she recognised my footfall on the stair, when there were eight other people living in that rooming house.

I half-ran, half-walked, to cover the two miles to the meeting. I became puffed and hot but couldn't run any faster without losing my hat. Suddenly, on the slippery cobbled street, I tripped. I thought it was due to the worn soles of my boots, but then, looking down, I realised I'd run into something – a bundle of rags, perhaps.

'Oh!' I heard myself cry, though there was no one around to hear me. There, by my feet, almost trodden upon, was a bundle. Looking closely, I saw a baby – silent but moving, swaddled in an old blanket, of which the frayed edge had unravelled. I picked it up and cuddled it, though I had never before felt remotely maternal, much to the distress of my parents. But this was an abandoned baby, left on the street. There was no one in at any house nearby when I banged their door-knockers, so I began to panic, whilst feeling overcome with pity for the little thing.

Jake interrupted. 'Are you thinking what I'm thinking? Could that be...?' We nodded and listened again.

What should I do? The baby might be ill and, to be honest, the meeting ahead of me seemed more important. What's more, I dreaded being late. The police station! Of course, the police would help, but at 7 o'clock in the evening I doubted that police stations would be open. Anyway, the station was in the opposite direction and there were no telephone kiosks in those days. I had to take the baby with me and think later, which with hindsight was ridiculous, but I had to be quick.

I ran on, carrying the baby bundle, when, as I feared I might, I bumped into someone I knew. In that district of Manchester where most Jewish immigrant people lived, that was highly likely... It was Mr Klein who ran a hat factory nearby.

'Well, if it isn't Miss Levy! Why are you in such a hurry, young lady?' he asked, clearly wishing to ask many more question of me.

'What have you there?' he asked, his nose almost touching the baby.

'A baby.' I replied. 'I just found it. I – actually, I tripped over it.'

I had to tell the truth – after all, I had no intention of keeping the baby and certainly couldn't be thought to have stolen it or, worse, to have given birth to it myself. Yet the pressing need to be at that meeting overwhelmed me.

'Let's see.' Mr Klein looked at the baby. 'Boy or girl?' he asked.

Till that moment, I had not looked properly at the little mite, but with Mr Klein, I did so: the gingery wisps of hair, pretty, pursed lips, curled-up fingers and spindly legs; it was a girl. Just then, she started to cry. Mr Klein put his little finger to the baby's mouth and she sucked it, ferociously.

'She's very hungry. I wonder how long it is since anyone fed her?' I had not thought of that; I hadn't thought of anything but the meeting, until that moment.

(My dear, dear Malkah, this is what you have been waiting for, the moment I began to care about you.)

'Oh my God!' whispered Jake. We all sat there, spellbound.

'Mr Klein, what should I do? I have to attend a meeting in Red Bank that begins at 7.30. Having found this baby, I feel obliged to do what I can to care for it, until I find the mother – but this meeting is very important. Have you any ideas?'

'I know about that meeting,' he said. 'There are a few things we could do. Firstly, go to the Jewish Hospital or the Jews' Temporary Shelter on Cheetham Hill Road, to try to trace the mother. Then we could contact the local rabbis, who may be aware of someone who might have had reason to abandon their baby. All those will take time. Mm… My wife is still suckling our latest, little Shmuel, so she could give this baby a feed, at least until after your meeting.' What kindness! 'You go, but make sure to call at our house on your way home! We couldn't have another mouth to feed with the four children we have already.'

'How can I…?' I began.

'While the baby is being fed, I'll make some enquiries. Unfortunately there are many desperate women who will abandon their babies rather than end up in shame, in some hostel.'

I was moved by Mr Klein's caring and helpful attitude; bumping into him was the best thing that could have happened.

'What a story,' Jake said.

'Incredible!' Tears streamed down my face, not only at the revelations but also at the clarity of Freidl's description. I wondered what I would have done in Freidl's shoes – the same? I wasn't sure; this grandma of mine was certainly remarkable. We carried on listening, although it was after midnight. But how did my mum feel on reading this?

'Let's give her a name,' I suggested. Looking at her closely, I decided to call her Malkah, my sister's middle name. Maybe she would grow up to be not quite a queen – the name's meaning – but at least special and beautiful.

My late mother was both those things and more.

I felt such a pang, then, for my dear sister and all my family, left behind in Romania. Miriam was a good and loving sister to me but, over time, she and I had grown apart. She was only a year older than me, so in our childhood we were like twins. However, she was small, a bit chubby and with our father's gingery hair – we barely looked like sisters. People think that all Jewish people are dark-haired, but many around us had ginger hair and blue or grey eyes. This baby's hair was probably like Miriam's, as a baby.

At this point, we were exhausted and stunned. In Grandma Freidl's picture of herself, I saw bits of me. Yet that couldn't be. Nature or nurture, then? Part way through her letters, Ernie actually said he thought that I was like her. I was touched – assuming it was a compliment.

We all went to bed; Uncle Ernie had been staying with us, over that week, anyway. Before lying down, I texted David. I had to share all this with him, right then, impetuous as usual.

'HOPE ALL WELL. NOTHING WRONG. CALL ME BACK, DAVID, OK?'

I was woken the next morning, by David's call. I hadn't expected that.

'Yo, sis! First, how are you?'

'Alright. Sorry – I shouldn't text on Shabbat.'

'No worries – must be important.'

'Kind of, but how's everyone? Send hugs to Hannah and the children. Didn't think you'd phone back, today.'

'Seemed urgent. So – what's up?'

'It's not really urgent-urgent,' I began, then told him, briefly, about the letters.

'Hang on – they're from Grandma Freidl – not from Mum? I somehow thought...'

'Yeah, the timing's weird,' I agreed.

'Why did Dad bring them out, just then?'

'Jake was asking questions.'

'Oh. And...?'

'Well, one day when Grandma Freidl was rushing in the street, she tripped over something and – that was Mum!' I shouldn't have blurted it out; David's gasp was audible.

'What are you talking about, "That was Mum"? Oh! Y'mean she was a – a foundling? That's mind-blowing.'

'Isn't it? There's plenty more, just wait.'

'I'll have to. Can't chat for long right now, we're getting ready for synagogue.'

'Course! Forgot, sorry. And I'm rubbish at the time difference. We'll scan and send the letters, soon. Shame we can't talk to Mum about it.' I was fighting back tears – for Mum and, to be honest, for Martin.

'Hey, sis. It's tough for you.'

'You, too.'

'Not quite, Nic. The responsibility for Dad lands on you. But you're just like Mum.'

'Meaning?'

'Efficient, capable...'

'Don't feel it.' No one had ever said that to me before.

'And Martin's away, too. That's hard – when's he back?'

'Soon.' I didn't explain. 'Must go, bye.' I let David read my silence.

'Shabbat Shalom.' Our call ended.

On Saturday evening before anyone came again, we read more letters, intending to do the same on Sunday morning. I went to borrow the last pile of them from Dad and when I arrived at his house, he was in tears. I put my arm round him.

'Actually I'm happy-sad. David just called to tell me their baby son's name: Malachi, after Mum – a name almost like Malkah.'

Back home, Jake was waiting to read more letters but Ernie said he was going back home to check the house. 'Come over, later, OK? We'll read more before evening prayers at Dad's.' I declined, so he took Jake with him; he could scan the letters for David while Ernie sorted out his house.

I badly needed some air, so, in a local park, with hardly anyone around, I called Martin. It was extravagant using my mobile but at least, if Jake came back unexpectedly, he couldn't listen in. Business trip or not, I thought Martin should have appeared sometime during the week. The thing is, he's never felt comfortable in what he describes as the claustrophobia of a packed shivah house.

He wasn't Jewish when we met and fell in love. He converted at the local reform synagogue; he learned about Judaism there and from my family. However, he'd never caught on to the atmosphere of those Jewish events which are hyped with emotion, happy or sad. They're huge, actually, particularly the 'big' occasions. The crowds, the talking, the apparent irreverence, compared to the hushed formality in the Christian tradition, remain alien to him. He couldn't even relate to Jewish weddings at first, with the ceremony so *un*ceremonious but jolly and informal.

Those gatherings bring out the old sensation of rejection he felt when we first told the family of our intention to marry. Sometimes, he says he still feels a stranger, yet we've known each other twenty years – and been married for fifteen. My parents' early hostility to my marrying a non-Jewish boy, made Martin feel they didn't like *him*. I've tried to convince him otherwise, then and subsequently.

This was my turn to be hurt, by his refusal to be with me. We'd argued over it, when we spoke, the day of Mum's funeral. He couldn't have made it to that, the day she died, but he told me he couldn't shorten his business trip either. I was sure his company would have let him come.

No one knew about our row, though David had sensed it, of course: twins are extra-sensitive – another thing Martin finds problematic. He thinks I am closer to David than I am to him. That's a crazy accusation but if he doesn't believe me now, he never will.

As usual after a disagreement, I was the one to phone back. The only call he'd made was to Dad, with sympathy. How did he think I was managing without him? Shivah is exhausting, even though there are people around. Sitting there, on that low chair, the centre of attention, all afternoon and evening. It's unreal. Surreal.

I took a deep breath and called Martin's mobile.

'Nicki – hi! I'll text you my hotel number, phone me back, OK?' I did.

'Hi, love! How are you?' His tone was so upbeat, I wanted to cry. How did he *think* I was?

'Alright,' I muttered.

'Is that all? There must be more.'

'There is. But it's hard, without you…'

'Don't start that again.'

'Start what?'

'That blaming thing.'

'Blaming thing? What d'you mean? I've just finished seven exhausting days. I'm shattered.'

'Give me a chance – you always jump in with both feet!'

'Hang on – I called you, Martin, remember? I needed you, we all did.'

'Oh God. The usual guilt trip!'

'It wasn't –'

'All my fault, eh?'

'What –'

'– For not being your perfect Jewish husband.'

'Martin! How can you throw that at me?'

'Try thinking what it's like, being away, trying to make a living – for *all* of us.'

'I can't take this.' I wanted to ring off.

'But I thought…'

'Just get home to us. We need to sort things out.' I didn't know what I meant by that.

'And if we don't…?'

'Don't even go there. When does your flight land?'

We said an acrimonious goodbye and his flight details arrived shortly after, by text. But things were even worse than I thought.

I needed to talk to someone: not David, that would be disloyal and of course, not Mum, now. I had a thumping headache and tried to breathe deeply while walking back. Once home, while I ran a hot bath, I lay on the bed with a glass of white wine and decided to read more letters, to catch up with Jake.

Perhaps Freidl would help clear my head. I remembered she had just named the baby – my mum – after her sister.

THREE

My sister was a more understanding person than I, prepared to forgive more quickly. Perhaps my 'steel' was what I needed in order to leave her, my two brothers and my parents behind. Oh, Miriam how I miss you.

'Come on now.' Mr Klein's voice woke me from my reverie. 'We've got a lot to see to!'

I handed the baby back to him and, giving a little peck on the baby's cheek, ran off, shouting, 'Thanks so much – you are so kind!'

The meeting had been announced on a little notice at my place of work. It was not readily visible from behind our sewing machines, yet was clearly meant for us. After reading it, I moved it to the wall by our cloakroom so that more of us would see it as we took off our coats. It was mysteriously moved back to its original place, a day later. That made me all the more determined to attend, since our boss seemed to hope we would not see it. Enlightened women were seen as a nuisance.

However, women were becoming more aware, both about working conditions and women's rights. There were Jewish Unions and also the movement for women's suffrage. I never imagined that as a Jewish girl, I could become part of the wider world; my world seemed so contained and inward-looking, with so many people still only talking Yiddish.

Uncle Isaac encouraged me to learn English at night school, as soon as I arrived in Britain – and Miss Gertrude was a wonderful teacher, herself fairly new to the language and country.

(Now you can see, Malkah, how tied up your start in life was with the political movement of the times. You were bound to become a feminist!)

I became consumed by the women's movement – in awe of it, actually and, once my English was fluent enough, I had joined the Jewish Tailors' Machiners' and Pressers' Union – exactly a year before this particular evening. I never imagined that I would have enough in my savings box to cover the membership, but eventually I did.

As I rushed to the meeting, I felt so lucky to live in a free country like England but also in a city like Manchester, which had given birth to the very idea of votes for women. I was not quite like Eleanor Marx, sister of Karl, who was at the forefront of political action, but she was another Jewish girl, which gave me heart.

I suddenly stopped running. Little Malkah: how could I forget?

My mother often called me a butterfly brain because I never kept my attention on one thing at a time; tonight was certainly not for butterflies. Could I find the baby's mother? If not, would the baby end up in the Jews' Shelter? How responsible for her was I? I shifted my attention, flitting like a true butterfly to her future, wondering how her life would be.

The notice had read: 'People interested in equality and workers' rights, come to a public meeting at 7.30 May 12th 1913 at... etc.' It was just signed off with 'J. Weinberg, C. Kaufman'. Neither name was recognisable from any Union meeting I had attended previously. Outside the hall, a trickle of people moved like a funeral procession, disappearing through the door. What I failed to notice, initially, was the lack of women.

Rows of chairs faced a platform set up for the speakers. Thus far, any occupied seats were taken by men – mainly young ones. I cowered at the back; eventually, one other woman arrived so I had the confidence to move forward a little.

So there I was, more interested in meetings like this than in looking for a suitable husband, as most Jewish girls of my age would have been doing at that time. This hadn't been a conscious decision, yet I did feel grateful that the Almighty had allowed me time in which to involve myself in other matters. Three men arrived and walked up to the chairs on the platform.

I noticed that one of the three was – well, Nicola would call him 'fit', I think. Despite his distance from the audience, he seemed to look straight at me. I also realised – but could hardly believe it – that one was my boss. The man I thought did not care! Life is full of surprises.

I smiled. Grandma never liked using the diminutive of my name – but she was right, I did teach her that word. I found myself quite envious. I envied her ability to be part of something so important, so life-changing. I didn't seem to have any such challenges in my life.

She went on…

Oh! Sorry this isn't quite in order, but I forgot to tell you that I subsequently made contact with Uncle Isaac, my mother's brother. You won't remember him but you have heard about him. He had begged me to live in his house when I arrived in England; he was unmarried and wealthy, with a house all to himself. I had refused, wanting to make my own way. I didn't want parenting any more.

The advice I did take from him was about the WEA, the education service set up to help working people to study. I had learnt to speak English, yes, and basic writing, but I wanted more than that. I looked at London University's extension courses and my boss said he'd help pay for one. But the WEA was the answer to my prayers. I met other people in the evening tutorials instead of working alone and the Union paid for part of the fees. After various courses, I gained a certificate in dress design and pattern making. It all helped me improve my written English, as I had to take tests and exams.

To go back to Uncle Isaac, he kept asking me to visit, so when this crisis occurred, I did. How inconsiderate of me. I arrived on his doorstep, not having seen him for a month, carrying a baby. He nearly fainted, thinking the worst.

'Don't worry, Uncle, the baby isn't mine – well, at least, not yet!'

He was wonderful, sorting out all the legalities, contacting the authorities and taking you, Malkah, and me to live with him. Just like that. Within a short time, a report came through of a Jewish woman found dead in an impoverished rooming house. We assumed she was the baby's mother, the police found some second-hand baby clothes left by her bedside and a new feeding bottle. They traced the purchase and found the date to be a day before I found the abandoned baby. Poor lonely woman, giving birth and dying, alone. I wept for her, mourned her, really.

Uncle Isaac had a big house and a maid, too. That's where you began your life, my dear Malkah. He was a successful businessman in textiles and was also involved in local politics, inside and beyond the Jewish community, so he had contacts. Oh… I forgot! I must go back to that meeting…

At that moment, David rang again. He'd already read the first part of Freidl's story; he obviously read it the moment it arrived.

'All this, straight from Grandma's lips. D'you realise, there's a chance we're not Jewish, strictly speaking, Nicki – how weird!'

It was – and I wondered how Martin would react to that. I felt weepy, partly worrying about Martin.

'Sorry, I hate crying on the phone, but – you know, it's a shame to find all this out without Mum here to talk to…'

'She wanted it that way – I wonder why? Hey, are you OK?'

'Just a bit emotional. Freidl never stopped doing good deeds – it wasn't so long before they took in their next little "waif".'

'Ernie, you mean? I know. That was 1938, wasn't it? It's all stranger than fiction. But there isn't much full-on suffragette action, is there? It's all fairly genteel, so far.'

'Mm… It must come a bit later. But listen. Y'know Jake's not madly into studying, but he has to do a family history for school. He's got his great-grandma's story *and* Uncle Ernie's is nearly ready, too.'

'Can't fail.' David answered. 'Could be good – in the midst of this week, something positive to focus on.' I didn't feel at all positive. 'Nicki, I must go. I'll call next week, for Shabbat. Love to all.'

'And mine to yours.'

There was a quiet tapping on the door. 'You OK?' Jake whispered, peeping round the door. 'Hm... Drinking in bed?'

'Perhaps it's OK for the end of mourning? D'you think? Come in.' I patted the bed for him to sit on it – he'd cheer me up. 'I've just caught up with the letters and David wanted to chat about them.'

'Just got an email from Dad – he's missing us,' Jake told me.

'Of course he is, love.' I was shocked to the core that Martin had said that to Jake and not to me.

'Anyway – you think Freidl's story is amazing? Wait till you see what *I've* got.'

'What?'

'Aha. Tell you in the morning!' With that, he went out of the room, blowing me a kiss goodnight as he left.

The bath was cold by then, so I had a quick shower instead. I couldn't sleep; I tried to read, but that didn't help. Jake had gone to his room – his computer is always on and he would have gone straight to it. I heard a shrill noise and ran in there.

'Jake! What's up?'

'Nothing, Mum, I'm just excited. I've finished reading the first instalment of Great-Uncle Ernie's life story... look!'

'Is that all?' I asked, yawning.

'*All?* It's stunning, Mum, look.'

'Thanks, but it's been a heavy week, plus the Freidl stuff. I'd prefer it printed it out, so I can read bits whenever I want.'

'Not sure about using rainforests when we can read on screen. Statistics show that it takes 100 trees to make...'

'OK, I get it, but what about the electricity used to keep the computer running all the hours God sends? I care about the planet, Jake, but you know what? It's *my* energy I need to conserve... and I'm really going to bed, now. Are you?'

'Will do.' He added, as I was leaving, 'Mind you, it was kind of lucky – that Grandma died just as the half-term began. Well, no, I don't mean lucky, but I mean, February half-terms aren't fun, anyway.' He was wise beyond his years.

'True, but there are better ways of spending it. Still... Night, love.' I left his room and went to bed.

I needed reserves of energy, whether for the return to teaching or for Martin's return. The first day at school was a half-day Inset – in-service training – not yet the full onslaught of a full classroom, but nevertheless not the best timing in the world. Life isn't about timing, though. Grandma Freidl told me that.

I spent a while looking at the lesson plans for my class and the schedule for the literacy Inset, which sent me rapidly to sleep. In the morning my anxiety went into overdrive. I couldn't prioritise everything, and worried about Dad, as his only local child, although Uncle Ernie would support him as well.

Dad did have a lot of friends, two of whom went to see him the day after the week of mourning ended. They were the parents of my friend Ros. They had been on holiday when Mum died. I popped in after they'd left and Dad was quite animated for the first time in ages.

Apparently, when they handed him yet more food, he said, 'If I eat all that, I'll turn into a *plumpkin*!' He blushed as if he was going to cry. That pun, 'turning into a plumpkin', had been one of my mother's favourites. Her mother, Freidl, told her that while trying to learn English, long ago, she thought the words pumpkin and plump were related. So that, her first English pun, was passed through the family.

'Funny, the things that trigger emotion, isn't it?' said Dad.

'What else did you talk about, then?'

'They wanted to know what the rabbi had said in his eulogy, then Sue asked me how Mum and I first met, but I'm sure she already knew.'

Sue knew it would help for Dad to talk. I had *certainly* heard that story before – but could not stop him.

'Yes, I know. Dad, I –'

'I told her how we'd met the same day that Ernie and I found each other, after the war.'

I interrupted: 'You must be tired from talking so much.'

'Not really. Sue said she didn't know Ernie was only eleven when he came here and I told her how Malkah and Ernie called each other pest-brother and pest-sister – anagram of step, you see. They loved making up words to get over their language deficiencies.'

I'd heard that so many times. 'I know. But Dad, you talk about Ernie coming to Manchester – never about yourself. Why?'

'Because he had it much harder than me.'

'Why, exactly?'

'Lots of reasons.' He tried to shut me out.

'Which were?'

'I was older and spoke some English by the time I came here. Plus, I came with a crowd of kids from the same school.'

'But you still left your family behind, like him.'

'Yes, but we all went to the same hostel. So I wasn't alone.'

That was as far as we ever got with Dad's life story. He returned to his chosen subject: Mum. He was enjoying himself.

'Your mum was so tall and slim and... her amazing, greeny-grey eyes –'

I decided to humour him. 'What did you fall for, then, Dad?'

'Her whole manner, really – her self-confidence, her height. Sounds odd, I know, but I loved looking up to her, my first British-born, British-educated girlfriend – the first ever without a foreign accent. And she was very funny. But remember the one about the herrings? When I opened my jewellery shop and customers mispronounced "earrings"?' He smiled.

'I do love hearing these stories again, Dad, but I must get back. Sorry.' We hugged.

'She was a wonderful wife... just wonderful.'

'And person,' I added, as I saw myself out. He flopped into an armchair so I peeped through the window before getting into my car. He had closed his eyes, poor guy. But I felt he'd be alright.

FOUR

In contrast, I suddenly realised that my marriage might not be alright. I'd survived in some sort of cocoon and wondered how I'd cope with going back to work.

At least, with the help of half-term, I wouldn't have too much explaining to do to my non-Jewish colleagues. I loved teaching, when my own life was going smoothly. When it wasn't, thirty frisky nine-year-olds took their toll.

I thought I'd talk to my friend Ros, who was a counsellor. She said she had a crazy week but that she would call me as soon as she had a minute. I knew she would, she was dependable. How do we sense, when we meet someone new, that the friendship is special? Perhaps it's a girl-thing. Anyway, that's how it was when we first got to know each other.

We lived nearby when we were young and her parents met mine at a synagogue meeting. They'd moved to our part of Manchester – Prestwich – only recently, so didn't yet know many people. Our mums decided that Ros and I should meet to play, one Sunday afternoon, as she was finding it hard to fit in with local children. I'd spotted her at Hebrew classes on Sundays; we were about the same age but were at different junior schools.

She had thick, straight hair, cut simply; it always lay neatly to her head (and still did, in adulthood). I envied people with hair like that. When she let hers grow she could have plaits; if I let mine grow, it grew at right angles to my head, afro-style.

She had tiny features – fragile, somehow, with a wistful smile, as though she constantly had something on her mind. She held back in a crowd, a bit diffident, so it wasn't easy to get to know her.

The day came for my visit. Both families were quite formal and Mum and I had discussions about what to wear. This only happened because she made all my clothes, so she'd often rustle up something new in a few hours. For my first time at Ros's, I chose a kilt she'd made – a proper, half-pleated one, with a real leather strap at the side. To this day, I remember the bright red sweater I wore with it, the white, knee-length socks and black patent shoes.

It all seems so odd, now, that attention to detail, without a thought of whether Ros might be a tomboy and want to climb trees. I would go to her house on my own, with two main roads between us, but children were allowed to take risks, then.

As Mum waved me off, Dad called out, 'Have a good time, you'll like the family.' Odd, that. Surely they wouldn't have sent me to a family I *wouldn't* like?

Their house, at first sight, seemed massive. It wasn't simply that their older, higher house was detached and ours a semi. Ros showed me round: along narrow corridors, down to cellars, up to attics. I found it wonderful but scary. My imagination ran riot; I thought of *The Secret Garden* and hidden children in attics.

Their garden was amazing, too, with twisty paths and hidden areas under spreading, copper beech trees where shoots of spring bulbs were peeping through. As we were walking round, a little bell sounded and I was sure I saw someone running through some shrubs, off to one side. My imagination, again?

'Oh! That means tea's ready,' Ros told me. 'Mummy likes us to come in on time because she's usually baked something fresh. Come on.' This was weird and very posh. What's more, we hadn't even started to play, or even chat. 'Don't look so scared, it isn't that formal, it just saves Mum from shouting. We'll come out again, afterwards. I've got a box of scruffy clothes we can put on, so we can climb the trees and things. OK?'

I breathed a sigh of relief that she liked to mess about, too. Tea was homemade currant bread, still warm, and fresh scones with jam and clotted cream, all served at a big kitchen table. Much more of an English afternoon tea than my mum's kuchen and kichels. There was another girl at the table – but Ros hadn't told me she had a sister. Nor had Mum – how odd. I couldn't really tell her age; she didn't say anything, didn't look at me or even notice us come in.

I realised there was something wrong with her but she was treated quite naturally, though words were repeated to make sure she understood. She kept banging her cup and saucer on the table. I noticed they were Bakelite, not china like ours, and there was a thick table mat at her place. I wondered if she did that often.

'This is Nicki: Ni-cki! Can you say that, Gill?' asked her sister. She didn't respond but said, 'Gill, Gill!'

'What a nice name, how old are you, Gill?' I asked.

'Gill.' She didn't look up from the table when she answered.

'Good girl, now – how old are you?' her mum asked. She held Gill's hand to make her take notice, then with her other hand, held Gill's chin gently, to turn her face towards me. 'That is Nicki. Say *Hello.*' It didn't work but, after that, I helped butter Gill's scone for her. She just spread the butter round and round with her finger and then licked it.

Their mum told us to go off to play, when we had munched our way through the lovely tea. I wondered whether Gill would come with us. She didn't and hardly looked up as we left the room.

'I didn't know you had a sister,' I said, once we were out of earshot.

'Well, it's hard. Some girls won't come and play because they don't like her.' So that's why she hadn't made friends yet; Mum hadn't mentioned it.

'How can they not like her?'

'Well… you know…'

I was no angel but the thought that anyone would be bothered by Gill shocked me. I asked what was wrong with her. She told me she was what was called autistic. It was a fairly new diagnosis and even though there was a name for it, no one could do much to improve her condition.

'She goes to a special school. The thing is, she's in her own world; she doesn't notice people and she gets frightened a lot. That's why Mum uses a bell for tea: Gill goes crazy when people shout or call but she likes the bell.'

'Oh! So that's why…'

'And she can't be left on her own, except in the garden. She loves the garden.'

'How come?' I asked.

'Dunno. She whispers to the flowers and chases birds cos they don't talk back. She likes seeing things grow, too.'

'Does she ever play with you?'

'No. She seems to know me but she doesn't know what's dangerous – we never know what she'll get up to.'

'Gosh.' I thought it must be awful to have a sister who couldn't be your friend.

'When I grow up I want to be a teacher of children like that.'

Ros didn't exactly become a teacher; she became a psychiatric social worker. I was the one who went into teaching, but her skill as a counsellor came both from the training and from living with Gill, who had to go to live in sheltered housing once she was older.

That first visit to Ros's as a girl – when we eventually did some tree-climbing and made imaginary worlds under the trees – was the first of many and the start of our lifelong friendship. Mum told me later that she and Dad had not told me about

Gill beforehand, so that I wouldn't have the wrong idea. They liked leaving me to learn things my own way and told me they were pleased with me. For my part, I had simply enjoyed my afternoon.

Later, I managed a relationship of sorts with Gill, by showing her more about gardens, like how bulbs and seeds grow. At first, she would try to take them out of the soil as soon as we planted them. Eventually, she understood and we were both excited.

Ros and her parents still worried about Gill and would do always. All this went through my mind as I talked to Ros on the phone that day.

'Look – get yourself back in a routine and we'll catch up, I promise.' She rang off. Well, why should she have time, just when I wanted her? I called to check briefly on Dad who insisted he was managing well.

'Don't worry about me, I'm OK. Bye.' Dad read me like a book – even on the phone.

I'd have loved to talk to Ros properly, but decided to try Uncle Ernie. He had always played a pivotal role in my life, without interfering. Coming as a child refugee and living with my mother and grandparents, made him family – yet not quite – and, since he was younger than Mum, at times I found him easier to relate to.

He had never married but he'd lived so many lives, lost so much, yet found replacements in us, whom he watched, with affection, from a distance. I knew he was not hung up about 'Jewishy' stuff (as he put it), which might help.

I thought about the Ernie from all those years ago, when Martin and I were trying to find somewhere to live. We had both only been working for a year after graduating and were wondering how we'd ever afford anything.

There were standard semis around, in serried, suburban ranks from the 1940s; there were new, anaemic, integral-garaged properties; and there were older terraced and end-terraces with character, which needed fortunes spending on them. Some of those appealed to us, as they were on high ground near Rainsough Brow, looking out over the open space of Waterford Park and the River Irwell. Not quite the rural setting Martin had grown up in, but they were also near to the family.

We had been to see one, a couple of times. Out of the blue, Ernie phoned, asking whether he could come to see it before we made any decisions. We agreed, because Ernie was still a successful architect in the city and would give good advice. He met us there; he looked it up and down and we toured the house together. What he said took us completely by surprise.

'Listen, you two. This is a good, solid house, the open outlook can't be built on and what with the cellar, there's great potential. You could put a room in the roof and do up the cellar, which would make it a really good starter home.'

'I don't think we need to do up the cellar… and anyway we can't afford to.'

'I know. So listen. You're my only family here. I'd like to redesign it for you, free of charge, obtain all the plans and regulations, then, if Martin could help at weekends and evenings, I'd bring experts in at cost.'

We were open-mouthed. 'Oh Ernie, we couldn't…'

'Yes, you could. And I'll build in some bedroom furniture, as a wedding present.'

I hugged him, simply saying, 'Lucky us!'

'Look. I'm the lucky one. I'd have had no one if your grandma and grandpa hadn't given me a family. Agreed, then?'

We nodded, giggling. 'We love decorating, too.'

'The more the merrier,' replied Ernie, almost crushed by Martin's bear hug of a thank-you.

That's how we started out in a house that Ernie transformed. We put a dormer in the roof, which helped to make an en suite bedroom. There was just space for a shower cubicle, but the quaint, sloping ceilings gave the room character and it commanded the best views. They were green, even if they weren't exactly rural.

Ernie recommended stripping all the doors and did the same with the banister: exposing all the lovely wood transformed the house. Martin rolled up his sleeves each evening, and at weekends we worked together when the workmen had left.

We chose light colours for the hall and landings, and geometric-patterned wallpaper for one wall of the knocked-through living area. When the little cupboard-like cloakroom towards the back of the house became a study, we found a lovely old coat stand in a junk shop for the hall. (That curly coat stand, the first piece of furniture we bought together, would stay in use ever after.)

When the top bedroom was finished, it was so romantic, realising that would be our bedroom, that we tried to make love there and then, using the dustsheets as a bed. I immediately started sneezing – not conducive to sexual contact. Making love on dusty bare boards is not a good idea.

We refitted the bathroom on the first floor and the kitchen had to be done too. That came about through a call from our parents. Dad offered to buy the cooker and fridge as a wedding present – really good of them, since he and Mum had already insisted on paying for the wedding.

'You don't have to, Dad, it's very kind – but thanks.'

Martin shouted down from the top of a ladder, 'Thanks, Joe!'

Then Martin's parents offered to buy the bed for us, as *their* wedding present. Martin's dad died soon after our marriage but he did see the house and the bed, installed – just once, before he took ill.

We were lucky. We went out, there and then, to buy a bed to be delivered the following week. Later on I made two head cushions to match the curtains. My first-ever attempt at a mural appeared there, too, in the shower room in a swirl of blue seaweed and green fish, over the doorjamb and on any untiled walls.

We tried out the bed immediately, without sheets, in our bare bedroom with its cute dormer windows, through which the tops of the trees waved their branches at us in approval. All was right with the world. Certainly better than dust sheets on the floor.

I came back to the present with a jolt, after reminiscing about Ernie's uncomplicated generosity. I wanted to see him but didn't stop to consider how vulnerable he was himself, after that week. I sent him a text.

'R U IN? CAN I COME 4 A CHAT?'

His reply came straight away. 'OK. BRING A BAGEL OR 2.'

I laughed – and left, buying them on the way to his house. Why was I so impetuous? I had no idea what I was going to say.

I arrived at Uncle Ernie's but, as he opened the door, I realised what a rash judgement I'd made. He had obviously been crying and, almost ashamed, he wiped his eyes with his sleeve.

'Oh Ernie – poor you! I'm so thoughtless; I never thought of how you're feeling. Whatever the age difference between you, my mum must have been like a sister-cum-mother to you.' He nodded. He was clutching something to himself.

'What's that?' I asked.

He didn't answer, but handed me a photo which was familiar. It showed my mum standing, smiling, by the gate to Grandma Freidl's house, her arm round a little boy – Ernie. He sat on the concrete ball atop the gatepost; on the other side of the post was Grandma Freidl, her arm steadying Ernie. Mum and Grandma were smiling but Ernie looked very serious. What was there to smile about, having just arrived in a new place surrounded by a strange, ebullient family? My grandpa Jacob probably took the picture with the Brownie camera I played with as a child.

'I am glad I've at least got a photo of *this* family,' Ernie said. 'I have none of my family back in Leipzig. I never thought of bringing photos with me, when I was told the trip to England was "just for a holiday"... Anyway, where are the bagels, young lady?'

How could I thinking of using him as a sounding board?

'Come in. What's this all about?' Ernie asked. 'I suppose it's to do with losing your mum. I'll just pour the coffee. Settle down.'

He left me in his stunning living room. His architect's eye and artistic talent were obvious. I sat, curled up in one of the gorgeous black leather armchairs. He had transformed the ordinary house, showering love on it in the way one would love a family. It was his refuge and, although small, had a feeling of spaciousness. I was facing the amazing fireplace. Its chimney was like an upside-down copper trumpet, which hung from the ceiling, hovering over the flames. It was the hub of the house. He still lit coal in it, refusing to succumb to living gas.

The aroma of real coffee hit me – he was the only member of the family who would grind his own.

'Here you are – a cup of your favourite Brazilian – fair trade, of course. Jake gave me a crash course in fair trade. He teaches me so much about his world. At my age I have to keep up with new trends and all that conservation stuff and he's my contact with that generation.'

I didn't know how to respond.

'Don't put on that "poor Ernie has no children" look of yours, Nicki. I'm OK. It just didn't happen, that's all. So... why did you come?'

I started to tell him, tentatively. 'It's really hard, Uncle Ernie. I don't think you can help. It's about Martin.'

'What? Is he ill?'

'No, no, I mean it's about Martin and me.'

'Oh. That kind of Martin. Aha – when is he back?'

'On Wednesday evening and I'm back at work on Wednesday – just for the morning.'

'You look as though you are dreading it – his coming back. Aren't you delighted?'

'I am. Dreading it, I mean.' I'm sure I blushed.

'How awful – that you are dreading having your husband home after such a difficult time. You'll need him more than ever, now.'

'I needed him last week.'

'But he couldn't get back.'

'I didn't believe him. I thought he'd still surprise us and just arrive, after a day or two.'

'Is that fair, Nicki? Grieving goes on long after the first week, you know.'

'Mm – you know about these things – but shouldn't a husband be with his wife, then?'

'Says who? You, obviously. Perhaps he thinks it's more important to see through this business deal and be there for you afterwards – and for as long as it takes for you to feel strong again. Book publishing must be a worry these days.'

'True, but –'

'And he spent so much time with your mother when she was in hospital. I reckon he was there as much as any *son*, never mind son-in-law.'

I felt like a naughty child and he was right, to an extent. 'I am listening, Ernie, but there's more to it. When I questioned him – knowing he couldn't make it for the funeral – he threw the Jewish thing at me.'

Ernie frowned at that and thought for a moment. 'That's a shame. But angry people do find the weapon that hurts most. I bet he feels bad about letting you down. I don't think he's ever grasped all the Jewish stuff, to be honest.'

'Meaning?'

'Well... whatever he's learnt *about* Judaism, he hasn't mastered what *being Jewish* is – that's very different. I understand that, because before the Nazi regime in Germany, I didn't lead a

Jewish life at all. I only knew I *was* Jewish, not really what that *meant*, apart from candles on Friday nights at my grandma's.'

'I never knew that.'

'Mm, it was only when Nazi laws restricted Jewish life that my family took it all on board again – a kind of resistance. Then I absorbed more by living with Freidl, Jacob and your mum.'

'Aha.'

'But I was still a child – I had time – Martin didn't.'

I knew what he meant; I was in awe of him, he was so perceptive. He put his arm round me and hugged me. 'I know you inside out, my dear Nicki. You're like a daughter and a friend. I've watched you growing up and, really, I'm not sure that you and Martin make each other – how can I put it? – "joyously happy", but marital happiness varies so much. As your grandma Freidl used to say, "You never know what goes on behind closed doors."'

'True,' I answered, pensively. 'More of her wise words. I can think a little straighter, now.'

'And I wonder, why not try… try to think back to your first meeting him and what you fell in love with?' he suggested, wisely. 'I mean, what did you *both* see in each other? Is there anything left?'

'I think there is, actually.' With that I started to pick up my things.

'And there's Jake. He's a great kid and very knowing. Please try not to drag him into anything.'

'You're right,' I admitted. With that, I put on my coat, ready to get back for Jake. 'He wants me to read what you've written for him, Ernie. Thanks so much for this chat. It's difficult, delving into each other's lives. I won't use you like this again, I promise.'

'Why do you say that?'

'We're too close.'

'Maybe.' He kissed me goodbye. 'But I'd hate to think you

had no one to talk to. Your dad's far too vulnerable at the moment. See you, Nicki.'

'Will you come for Friday night dinner, this week?' I shouted, as I went down the path.

'No. Thanks. You look after your own family this week. That's what you need. I'll ask your dad here. Good luck.' Ernie waved me off. I left, more aware than ever that everything was up to me. But I wanted to read the rest of Freidl's letters before Martin got home.

Jake bounded down the stairs waving a sheaf of paper, the moment my key was in the door. 'Hi Mum! You look better!'

'Better than what?' I asked, giving him a hug.

'Better than you did. Bet it's cos Dad's coming home soon.'

'You're right. I must get down to some cooking before then and before you and I go back to school.'

'There's a little parcel on your bed that Grandpa dropped in for you.'

Jake nagged me to read Ernie's story but I only wanted to read Freidl's next letter. He had also loaded Ernie's story on to his little USB pen, for my dad's computer.

'Computers are fantastic for older people aren't they?' he said. I nodded as I opened the door to my room. 'I'll leave you to read, then,' said Jake.

Dear Malkah,

Here is more about the 'fit' man at the meeting. He was called Jacob – there's a clue – and at the end of the meeting, volunteers were wanted to form a committee. He particularly asked for women, since, like everyone, he was aware that the suffragettes were a force to be reckoned with.

I went to the platform and was introduced to them all. I already knew my boss, of course. He said, 'Ah, Miss Levy, one of our finest seamstresses. Miss Levy, may I introduce Mr Merton Weinberg and Mr Jacob Grupman.' (So the cat is out of the bag, Malkah.)

Of course – that was my late grandfather, Jacob, Jake's namesake.

That is when I first looked closely at your father. His eyes were what I looked at – or rather, into! Kind, big, brown and smiling. I melted when he looked back at me, proffering his hand saying, 'Miss Levy, I am honoured to meet you.'

'Why honoured?' I asked.

'Because you are the first woman to offer her services to this Union and I sense you have great enthusiasm.'

'I do, sir, but what I do not have is time – and I must rush back.'

There was to be a meeting at my workplace one week later. I couldn't wait.

So it was that I fell for Jacob. I had been determined to be an independent, politically active woman; since immigrating, I had been too busy trying to become English and earning a living to worry about a social life. Jacob seemed to like my fiery temperament and supported me in everything I did. The First World War was looming and it put an end to any suffragette activity; those who were in jail were released to help with the war effort. What kind of release was that? They were frightful times.

I continued with my job, but I was lucky, living with Uncle Isaac as I did and I saw Jacob whenever I could. He loved helping with the baby and he also found me fabric with which I made her clothes. He gave me the cloth with which I made the lilac hat and coat for suffragette marches. At least I had a flower for my hat: I dyed the red one purple.

I have just realised that I sometimes refer to 'the baby' and sometimes 'you', Malkah, but you will understand it anyway, I am sure.

Jacob would stand waiting for me in Piccadilly Gardens, blowing kisses to me from across the road. Quite inappropriate, while I was handing out feminist literature, but he said he loved me at my most strident! We had a quiet wedding just before the onset of the 1914– 18 war and Jacob was taking on a baby as well as me. That was a condition to accepting his proposal. He was such a special man.

There was no official method of adopting a baby in those days, but at the wedding we made an announcement to the witnesses to our Ketubah, *stating that we were the baby's legal guardians. Mr Klein was the godfather.*

We registered the birth, guessing the actual birth-date. It was all right then to put ourselves as 'parents', as there were many, many orphans and illegitimate babies as a result of the war. After that, organisations were set up to establish adoption legislation. Malkah, that is how you became ours. Since you were born before my marriage, I rarely spoke about your or my age, to avoid raised eyebrows.

There wasn't much guidance about how to 'make' you Jewish, in those days (although a boy would have needed a Brit*), so we signed a declaration to that effect, drawn up by a solicitor and witnessed by our rabbi. Then we named you Malkah in synagogue one Shabbos after the war. We didn't know whether you were actually Jewish at birth but you were ours.*

That was the last of that pile of Grandma Freidl's letters. They moved me more than any novels had done and it was real. I tried to imagine my mother reading or hearing this for the first time. What a revelation it must have been for her. I began to understand why she hadn't shared this account with us herself. And yet… Grandma keeping all this secret from her for so long still seemed strange.

I also wondered whether there was more to Freidl's story and why Uncle Isaac didn't feature more highly; however, other issues were consuming me.

I felt I hadn't breathed since seeing Ernie. Freidl's life story invaded my thoughts but I needed to clear my head. Ernie had hit on some good points and helped as much as anyone could. I busied around, tidying up a little, unable to decide where to put the cardigan I had worn for shivah, which had just come out of the wash.

It was torn at the funeral – an ancient custom to indicate my state as a mourner – and I'd worn it, on top of other clothes, for the whole week. And I felt like keeping it for a while. However, I left it hanging on the coat stand in the hall, wondering whether Martin would notice it, whether it would trigger anything in him. Or would it be a red rag to a bull? A real rag, I thought, almost giggling at my own cynicism. This quagmire of a relationship was sucking me down.

FIVE

I tried to imagine how Martin and I would greet each other and carry on. This consumed me but I had lessons to prepare and meals to make. The papers from Ernie that Jake had given me were there on the edge of the table, begging to be read, and there was that mystery parcel in my room. But this wasn't the time for those things. I felt better, cooking.

I chose a recipe for sweet and sour meatballs with red cabbage. While preparing the ingredients, I thought back to the time Martin and I met, as Ernie had suggested. I was a hippie student, arty and into acting. I happened to go to a drama society audition at university, not knowing Martin, or that he was directing the play.

He was gorgeous: tall, dark and handsome, like no Jewish boy I'd ever met. He had dimples when he smiled – aware of his own charm, yet not too full of himself. He had an endearing, Northern accent – Rochdale, I later learnt – and I was smitten as we started chatting...

I had taken my eyes off the meat, which had started to burn. As I stirred, I pictured Mum cooking. Consciously or not, I had chosen to make one of her favourites. Mind you, it was Grandma Freidl's recipe; she never used a cookery book. My sweet and sour never tasted quite as good but Martin liked it. How strange – it was automatic to make something he liked, in spite of everything.

Cooking was comforting, sloshing around the ingredients

and being creative. A drip of treacle, a drop of lemon juice, taste; a pinch of salt and black pepper, taste; more lemon juice. Memories wafted round the kitchen, enveloped in the steam: flavours and smells were so much part of human memory for me.

Mum and Grandma had managed to combine feminism and housekeeping, with far fewer kitchen aids. Mum ran her dressmaking business from home, never needing childcare, able to leave dishes stewing while she sewed.

I envied her talent for 'multi-tasking'. I loved her and I'd miss her – but I could admit to myself I didn't always *like* her. Like that time in St Anne's.

It was the last Thursday of our annual family holiday there, when I was about eight years old and very tall for my age. It was on a gorgeous summer day that I suddenly realised that parents – Mum especially – would not always carry me through life, making choices for me.

At the end of the pier stood the Floral Hall, where a full orchestra played regularly. Followers flocked to its glass structure and sat on deck-chairs, spread round like the petals of a dahlia. The sun's rays baked their way through the shaped windows, the sea swished beneath and nosy seagulls swooped down to peep. It was hot, steaming hot, and there was no air-conditioning.

Massive, artificial pink and blue flowers billowed out of mock Grecian urns. The orchestra always warmed up with 'I Want to Be Happy', a bouncy number which I found myself humming now as I stirred the meatballs. The orchestra was magical. The Hallé it wasn't, but it was definitely called an orchestra, not a band.

On Thursday mornings, there was a 'special'. Any child could come up on stage to sing with the orchestra, receiving a bag of sweets for the effort. No audition required, just the patience to wait in the queue, which was very long. I had waited to perform every year and never made it. That year, I was determined. I had a song prepared. Inappropriate, but prepared. I'd always longed to go on stage.

Every single child in St Anne's turned up. I knew that the queue of previous years wound round, out along the pier and back, like one of the local squirming eels. I felt it could be my last chance – maybe I sensed that I would soon grow out of my lack of inhibition. Mum sighed, resigned to my decision. That was the part of her I didn't 'like'. She never shared the thrill of her daughter going on stage – she seemed embarrassed rather than proud, which hurt – and I never understood why.

I joined the queue when the front of it wasn't even visible. I could hear each screeching little singer, keeping in tune more with the seagulls outside than with the music. Wasn't I better than that? I shuffled along, unaware of the time. That queue was an organic, living thing; it grew apace, puffing and sweating as it neared the stage.

Suddenly, Mum waved frantically. Pointing to her watch, she signalled 12 o'clock with her fingers. Dinnertime was always 12.15 sharp at Mrs Manning's boarding house and midday dinner, in Lancashire, was the main meal of the day. This wasn't like the casual timing of the protracted family meals in our family. I groaned and stamped my foot. Mum mimed eating, licking her lips, mouthing the fateful words: 'Bakewell tart and custard.'

Of course! It was Thursday! I started crying. I loved puddings, particularly Mrs Manning's. No one used the word dessert back then. That tart was the highlight of the week.

Mum came over. 'Well...? Are you coming?' Her tone was menacing.

'What do you mean? I'm nearly there – I can see the stage!' I could just catch sight of a curtain cord over all the heads.

'It's up to you.' How could she be so cruel?

I asked her to tell Mrs Manning to keep my tart for later. I really knew there was no way she would ask a favour of the formidable landlady. I had to choose between the stage and the tart. I decided by default.

'I've waited so long, I can't give up now!' I cried.

The thrill of my approaching moment of fame eclipsed the cloud of uncertainty that hovered over me. Every moment of the queue's shortening was agony, since at any point before 12.10, I could have changed my mind and run full pelt down the promenade to Mrs Manning's.

Mum had left – she wasn't even going to watch me. The boarding house was very nearby but the stage was there. I ran through the song in my head, all about 'holding me closer'... What a precocious song that was for an eight-year-old. Thinking about it now, it would have been embarrassing for Mum to hear those words from her little girl.

I heard bits of other performances, mindless songs of the time. Then, a man's voice: 'Right then, kiddies, we'll have to stop the line here. It'll be 1.30 by the time all these have performed. Too late, sorry!' He put his arm out in front of me. 'Those on this side will go on – those on the other side, come back next week.'

The queue turned into a roaring dragon as children bawled in unison. I sobbed that I wouldn't be there next week, but it fell on deaf ears. My tears fell onto the glistening curls of the tiny girl in front of me.

Mum had taught me to stand on my own two feet and at least I knew what life had in store. She was tough but also a little bit mean. However, her strictness was balanced by Dad's softness. Was this the right time to remember Mum's least redeeming qualities? A voice broke into my thoughts.

'Mum – you're going to ruin that food!' Jake had come back already. I had completely lost track of everything.

'Goodness, Jake, thanks!'

'Smells good, though.' His nose was right in the steam.

*

I went up to bed early, tired but happier, since at least some routine had returned. Tomorrow, Tuesday, I'd have to be ready for the onslaught. Then I remembered the parcel from Dad – just a crumpled, brown paper bag. Inside, there were two notes attached to another little package. I opened it in a rush. And there it was, in the bag – a frayed, purple fabric rose. Or maybe it was a peony. It was definitely a flower, anyway. How amazing. I was sure it was Grandma Freidl's! There were notes inside the bag, too, one from Mum, the other from Grandma.

I knocked on Jake's door. 'Are you awake?'

'I am now, Mum.'

'You think you have seen it all? Look inside this parcel. Read the notes first – here, keep it a while.' With that, I kissed him goodnight and went to bed. Just as I was nodding off, the phone rang. It was Martin.

'Hi, doll.' I was thrown by the lightness in his voice.

'Hi there. What are your travel plans? As arranged?' I wanted the call to stay businesslike.

'Yes – but – had you gone to bed? You sound kind of distant. I felt like a chat.'

'Oh!' I was taken aback. 'Sure.'

'Listen, I'll see you tomorrow anyway.' Was this upbeat manner real or fake? Martin the actor.

'I'm OK,' I answered. 'Anyway, tomorrow Jake will be talking non-stop, so chat now if your phone's topped up.'

'No worries. So how are you… and things?'

'A bit stronger, but anxious about going back to school.'

'And then I land back home. Not too well timed, is it? All a bit much, what with everything.' He sounded different, understanding. It was hard to take. 'Let's go out for dinner – on Thursday? Somewhere casual?'

'Great idea,' I replied, puzzled by his newfound sensitivity. 'See how your jetlag is.'

'Sure. Must see your dad on the way back from the airport. Can we?'

'Course, why not?'

'I just thought you might be too tired, after school and everything.'

'It's only a half day, in-service training on literacy – might be stimulating, with luck. Dad will be glad to see you. So, how's work? Stressful?' I tried to sound interested.

'A bit iffy. In book publishing, everyone's worried about the effect of electronic readers.'

'Mm. Tell me more when you're back, OK?'

'Will do. Look, sleep well. Read one of my sample pot-boilers, that'll help you sleep!'

'Might listen to the radio. Anyway, see you tomorrow.'

'Look forward. Love to Jake. And it's 1900 hours, Terminal Two. Usual place? Bye.'

This conversation was so different, I didn't know what to think.

SIX

It was a very rude awakening, being ready for school the next day, with Jake going back again, as well. I was giving him a lift to his bus stop. Only a half-term break, but so much had happened; I felt disoriented, detached from the world. Before I left, I called Dad and Ernie to make sure they were all right. They had to say they were.

I worried about how Dad was managing, sorting washing, preparing dinner... yet he was a practical man, for someone of his generation. During Mum's illness he had to look after himself. Uncle Ernie was a different matter. He had lived alone for years, but emotionally he was more alone than ever.

Jake nudged me: 'Mum, we're here – at the bus stop – we're here!' I'd nearly driven past the stop.

'Sorry, Jake.'

'Lots on your mind, Mum?'

'I'm OK. Have a good day, love.' I waved him off.

'Seeya!'

Jake's mature behaviour would soon run out, I knew. Some well-meaning people had told him to 'take care of me' after Mum's death – a weighty burden for a lad of twelve.

I carried on to my school. Since the school car park wasn't open that day, I parked alongside, on the street.

'Hello, Miss.' It was a little lad from my class; he ran up to me as I opened the car door.

'Hello, Jolyon. Have you had a good time? You do know

there's no school today, it's a day just for the teachers.'

'I know,' he answered, looking disappointed. He was one of those children for whom school was a good place to be – even if learning wasn't actually in his mind-set.

'So, how was half-term?'

'Didn't do much – Mum's at work and Dad's left us, so me and my bro went to stay at Gran's – boring – there's no kids nearby.'

'Well, I'll see you in class tomorrow. Perhaps you could imagine a different half-term holiday, in story hour? You're good at that. See you then.' I patted him on the shoulder and went in to school, thinking that I could do with imagining a different half-term.

The morning went in a blur: some good teaching ideas, some but not many condolences from colleagues, but I was glad to see Chris, the member of staff I am most close to.

'How are you, *really*?' she asked.

'So-so. Thanks for coming to see me last week.' She had never been to a Jewish house of mourning before but took it in her stride.

'No probs.' She put her arm round my shoulder, as we both left the room.

I always enjoyed decorating my classroom, to make it inviting. Maybe even Jolyon would be engaged. It was as near as I'd ever get to being an interior designer, my dream career.

It was past lunchtime when I arrived home, so I made a quick sandwich and coffee. For the evening, I put some rice in the microwave for speed, and made a fruit salad.

As I finished preparing the meal, I thought back to the time Martin and I first met; cooking always started me reminiscing. Ernie had suggested thinking about our early romance, so there I was, back at the Drama Soc at university, a well-known setting for meeting guys. Potential for romance between actors – or between actors and directors – was rife. Martin definitely had the charisma to attract people to his productions and to himself.

The last thing I had expected was that he would be attracted to me. I hadn't been around much before university; the odd social at the synagogue youth club was pretty much the limit of my exploits with boys. Yet here was someone who seemed so worldly, actually making a beeline for me after rehearsals.

His chat-up line was a good one: 'I just want a word with you about the character you're playing. Have you done much acting before?'

'A bit, at my local youth club and at school.' I was quaking.

'Great, but I see the character a little differently than you. Can you come for a coffee after the rehearsal?'

I gasped.

'Is something wrong?' he asked.

'No... nothing. I can come for a coffee but I have to be at the bus stop by 10.30. I go home with my twin brother.' I felt like a naughty schoolgirl.

'Home?' he asked. 'Do you mean *home*-home?'

'Yes, I still live with my parents. Are you shocked?'

'No, just surprised. Hardly any students live at home nowadays.'

I nodded. 'My dad's a bit old-fashioned in that way. He doesn't understand why, with a perfectly good home and bedroom, students should live elsewhere.'

'He's got a point. Is your brother into acting as well? We could do with more guys.'

'No, he isn't arty at all. He's a thinker – he's taking philosophy and politics.'

'Aha. Well, see you at Plantation, the veggie coffee bar, near the science block. I just have to sort out the stagehands and sets,' he said, with authority and that dimpled smile. I knew he probably wasn't more than two years older than me, but he seemed much more mature.

That was the beginning. Our conversation over coffee was

mainly about how to approach my stage role: a meek, mild woman. He said I still seemed too feisty. I told him I inherited that trait from all the women in my family. At one point he leant over the table on his elbows, looked at me with his wonderful, chocolate-brown eyes, and put his little finger through one of the curls which fell over my forehead. It stayed coiled round his finger for what seemed ages and made me squint.

'I've been dying to do that all evening. There was a little girl and she had a little…'

'Curl right in the middle, etcetera, etcetera,' I butted in. 'My family used to recite that all the time, when I was little.'

'And were you?' Martin had a twinkle in his eye.

'Was I what?'

'Very good and horrid when you were naughty?'

'Oh, that – I was never naughty!'

'I'll see about that. And next time we meet, can I try counting your freckles? I love them. I'd start with the ones on your nose.'

He was pretty forward but I couldn't wait for the next rehearsal.

That all seemed so long ago. I turned off the hob and then remembered I had to call David back.

His wife Hannah answered, so I switched to my faltering *Ivrit* – modern Hebrew. Then she turned to faltering English – that's how it always was. I felt close to her, even with the language barrier, because she was warm and understood the closeness of twins. David fell for her when he was in Israel on his gap year.

''Ow are you and 'ow is your father – and Jake?' she asked. 'Please talk English, it good for me.'

'We're OK, but how are *you* – and the children – do the older ones like the new baby?'

She said it was hard having three small children but David helped a lot. The two older ones went to the crèche just over the field from their house, so near that they could see them from their own front porch.

'Anyway, I called to tell you about something my mum left for me. It isn't valuable but very special. I'll attach a photo of it in an email soon.'

'*Nachon* – for sure, but what it is?'

'A fabric flower,' I replied.

'Fabric... what is fabric?'

'Material – stuff we make clothes out of, like silk.'

'Ah, I understand. You want to speak to David?'

'No, I wanted you – to tell you about the flower. I'll send a photo soon.'

'Good. I tell David when he comes back from training.'

'Are there problems?' I asked.

'Not really, but in the North there is training all the time – we must be ready.' At that moment, I heard the cry of a newborn baby.

'Hannah, is that Malachi? Go on, go to him. Just tell David I called. Love to you all.'

'Sure. I look at the photo soon.' And we rang off.

Jake would be home soon and shortly after, we'd be off to the airport. So, in case I forgot in the approaching frenzy, I took a photo of the flower and emailed it to Hannah and David with a brief note. It took my mind off the anxiety about seeing Martin, which was mixed up in my memories of being so in love with him.

In the meantime, I made a cup of tea, picked up Ernie's story from the table and began to read.

SEVEN

Dear Jakes,

So, you want my life story for a school project. Good – I'd hate to be buried with my story untold. Here are some more pieces of our family jigsaw. The fact that my cousin is your grandfather squared the circle – it made us a family again. You'll get to that, later on.

I want to tell you about my arrival in Manchester first, as I want you to know how I came to live with your great-grandparents and your grandma.

I travelled to England on the Kinderstransport. (I will tell you how my life was saved, but that is a painful story.) Manchester couldn't come quickly enough. As we slowed into the station, there was a big notice held up high with my name on it and, next to it, held by another person, was 'Hans'! He and I had travelled together. The thought that he might end up living near me was wonderful.

The person holding my name was a man, his arm round the shoulder of a young woman.

'Ernst?' she said. Her eyes smiled at me. I nodded, too afraid to speak, even in German. 'Frau Grupman?' I asked the lady, tentatively. The man explained, in German, that his wife was waiting at home and this was their daughter Malkah. He introduced himself as Herr Grupman, then said I could call him Jacob. (You were named after him, of course, Jake.) He was thin, bearded and gaunt. He seemed anxious, yet showed kindness.

Once he took off his hat, I took in his shock of black hair with grey peeping through. Meanwhile, Hans was being introduced to 'his' family. Amidst all the excitement (and fear) we managed to exchange the addresses we'd been given, then I left the station with Jacob and Malkah. She was really grown up but was able to be childish for me, somehow.

'Come', said Malkah, 'there's our bus.' Malkah was freckle-faced with an unruly mop of red hair; she spoke in English and gestured to what was the first double-decker I'd ever seen. Of course, she took me to the upstairs and it was from there I first looked at Manchester – so much like the Lowry paintings I later came to love.

I followed Malkah and Jacob off the bus and after a short walk they indicated their house. Malkah ran, trying to buoy me up, I think, to the house which was to become home; the home I thought was for a short holiday.

It has not changed much since that day in 1938, but my first memory of it is still clear. I noticed first the big, concrete balls on the gateposts, their white paint flaking in places and, above the adjoining low wall, the overgrown hedge onto the street. You will recognise one of those balls in that little photo of me on Grandpa's mantelpiece. I felt so grand, sitting on top of one, for my first photo with the family. Freidl's hand was steadying me, unseen, from behind. Malkah put her arm round me, standing on the other side. One copy was sent to my mother.

Of course! The photo Ernie had shown me the other day.

This tall, red-brick house was unlike anything I had grown up with in my country village. It towered over me, but seemed benevolent. Net curtains downstairs shielded the inside from prying eyes, making me all the more curious as to what lay behind. Upstairs, I made out the edges of a patterned curtain, swinging like a girl's skirt through a half-opened window. It seemed far too cold a November day for open windows.

I felt the door smiled at me, with its wide letterbox mouth and stained-glass eyes of every hue. I often used my imagination like this. Mutti (my mum) had taught me to do so, in order to escape from the terrible realities around us in Germany. When we saw the Nazis marching, she would point upwards, saying, 'Oh look, Ernst, that cloud looks like my feather quilt – don't you think?' and other things like that.

Anyway, the front door's nose was a fancy brass knocker, and there, two-thirds the way up the doorpost, was a mezuzah *– a bit like the one on our door at home. Its familiarity overwhelmed me; it welcomed me, but made me yearn for home.*

'Come on in, Ernst.' Jacob gestured kindly, sensing my anxiety and Malkah held out her hand, which I took, shyly. My first peep inside revealed a dark, dismal hallway, but the most amazing smell wafted through the house as a door opened and through it, wrapped in the aroma of baking, came a woman who was Malkah's mother, Freidl. Her presence lit up the hall.

'Ernst, you're here at last! I have been so worried about you!' Jacob translated as she spoke. How could someone worry about a person they had never even met? Freidl did. She bent down, put her hands on my shoulders and gave me a peck on my cheek (which I rudely wiped with my sleeve).

'Come in the kitchen and try some ginger cake, you must be so hungry!' Jacob spoke in German. I couldn't remember when I had last eaten, let alone home baking. Mutti hadn't baked since Papa disappeared six months ago. And my last memory of baking was on a distant visit to Oma (my grandma), who coped with the encroaching threat outside by focusing on her inner world of baking and cooking.

'Here, some cake will stop you dreaming. Do you want hot chocolate or hot Vimto?' asked Freidl, translated by Jacob. He explained that Vimto had been invented and made here, in Manchester. Its smell and that of the cake certainly woke me up, but suddenly the cake started to float away – as did the family.

Then, there I was in a chair, with Jacob's voice coming from the ceiling, 'You must be so exhausted, you nearly fainted! Sip this slowly. You'll soon be fine.' I drank my first ever cup of hot Vimto and nibbled at the delicious cake, but unable to do it justice.

Gradually, everything came back into focus, and I could make out their kind, worried faces. I took in the scrubbed, wooden table, the ginger cake, shiny and gooey on the top, and other things I had never seen before – toasted teacakes. I cupped my hands around the warmth of my spotted mug, drew in its fragrance and feasted my eyes on the family. I began to cry. Salty droplets landed on my sugary cake. I started to run out of the room, I was so ashamed but I had nowhere to run to – I didn't know the way round the house.

Freidl read my mind and told Joseph to show me round. 'Show him where the bathroom is, and his room. Poor boy, what will he think of us?'

Once I was shown the bathroom, I went in and locked the door, which gave me a valuable escape. I wallowed in my thoughts for a moment, then splashed my red eyes. The mirror showed me someone I nearly didn't recognise. I ruffled my hair and straightened my shirt collar, then went out to face them again.

'That's better,' said Jacob, 'now come and see your room.'

Across the landing, he pointed out one very tiny room, his and Freidl's room, and then opened the only other door. This was the one with the patterned curtains blowing and sure enough, the window onto the street was wide open. Malkah had followed us and ran to close it. I smiled, as though to say thank you.

'Freidl loves fresh air,' explained Jacob. My room had everything I could have wanted – except for everything I didn't have. 'We'll show you the downstairs and then I think you'd like a bath and bed.'

Their living room was cosy, all a bit brown, but there was a comforting fire in the grate. Glinting Shabbat candlesticks on the sideboard caught my eye and warmed my heart.

I went upstairs and spotted my special little suitcase on the landing. Jacob said goodnight and left me to bathe and go to bed. The next thing I remember was a knock on the bedroom door. I jumped out of bed, terrified, thinking I was in Germany and this was another dreaded midnight knock.

'Good morning,' Freidl said, peeping gingerly round the door. Then I remembered where I was.

'You say it! Good Morning – like Guten Morgen!' I repeated it and thus spoke my first English phrase.

I had begun sorting through my few possessions when Malkah knocked again, beckoning and tapping the watch on her wrist.

'Come on! Time for breakfast.' I followed her downstairs as she mimed eating. I knew what breakfast was when I saw it on the kitchen table and I ate ravenously.

'Good,' said Freidl.

Afterwards, Malkah showed me her room. It was tiny and didn't seem like a girl's room – no pretty wallpaper and the curtains were faded. Later, I realised that she had given up her room for me. I couldn't imagine having to do that for a stranger.

She arranged a game of chess and gestured: 'Do you play?'

'Ja.'

'You mean yes.' So time passed, with game playing and mimicking English words.

Jake, this is about my early days at your great-grandma Freidl's. Malkah was part-sister, part-mother to me as she still lived at home. Later she told me how she had always longed for a brother or sister and when I arrived she enjoyed doing those childish things with me and she always managed to make me laugh. Her job was to design and make clothes for local ladies, which she did from the house.

They showed me a lot of their city. They were very proud of it, even though parts still had traces of the industrial past. They took me as far south as Platt Fields, which I loved, and I adored the Museum of English Costume. It helped feed my interest in design and I went there often, while I was at university. Malkah showed me where there used to be a soapbox where anyone could just stand and make speeches. What a country! What a city! Manchester is in my bones, now, you know.

There is a lot more to tell you, of course, about life under the Nazis but that part is harder for me. For now, I will just tell you that I celebrated my twelfth birthday at your great-grandma's home.

Although it was awful having a birthday without my parents, the previous one, in Germany, had been unbearable. Mum had made special treats and invited ten friends from school. We waited and waited but not one child turned up. Their parents had forbidden them to come, just because I was Jewish.

Now, Jake, my wrist is aching. I wish I had learnt to use a word processor earlier in my life, when my fingers were supple. I'll continue when I can and explain how, much later, I met up with Joseph – my cousin and your grandpa. Also, I wrote a poem about these experiences that I have never shown to anyone – you may be the first!

My love as ever,
Great-Uncle E

I tried to picture the girl who was my mother in Ernie's description, though emotionally, it was all too much. I wondered if there was ever a right time to read such a memoir and knew that the earlier part of Ernie's life story would tell a more traumatic tale. For Jake's sake, I was glad to have read it when I did, but I needed to focus on the present.

EIGHT

Jake came home from school looking grumpy. The good phase was over, then.

'Hi there. I've finished Ernie's story.'

'Hm,' he grunted, dumping his bag and coat on the hall floor. He went and sat on the bottom stair, so I knew something was up. For us, that stair was never the 'naughty step' but the place where serious discussions took place between him and Martin or me.

'Well… they didn't like them.'

'Who didn't like what?' I asked.

'Great-Grandma Freidl's writing and Uncle Ernie's story.'

'How could anyone not *like* them?'

'A couple of kids in the class made sarcastic comments, like "It's alright for *you*, it's easy for *you*, we have to rely on books and the internet." Or: "You and your wonderful family – you're always going on about it, fussing about your grandma dying. Everything's such a big deal." And: "Bet half of it isn't true, anyway!"'

'How awful.' I was wondering what to say next.

'It was. I couldn't answer back.'

'They're just jealous.'

'Mm. They're always like that.'

'Is it the same boys each time?'

'Why d'you say "boys", Mum? It's always the same threesome – two girls and a boy, actually. I think they're…'

'What?'

'You know...'

'No. What?

'Anti-Semitic.'

'Hold on, Jake. Careful. People can be jealous – or they may even not like you – with no hidden agenda. I'd be jealous of you, if I were in your class, to be honest.'

'Thanks Mum!'

'If I were that kind of kid, I might. Look, if this is only in history and doesn't go further, I'd put it away, OK?' I reminded him he had work to finish if he wanted to come to the airport. We had a snack together before he went to do it. I felt for him but knew that, for now, he'd just have to deal with it and I could see that his real life stories could be a bit sickening.

Time raced on, so I put the dinner on 'automatic' and went to do myself up a bit. I wanted to appear fairly together for Martin, initially. As I looked in the mirror to brush my hair, I began reminiscing again, going back nearly twenty years – nearly half my life. The freckles were still there but the colour of my hair and my skin had changed. It was the freckles that started me thinking.

Our relationship was strong enough to deal with the hard time we had prior to marrying, three years after we met. First, there was Martin's conversion, then later, trying and failing to have a baby, then having Jake by IVF. All quite tricky, really.

And the freckles reminded me about the second time Martin and I met up after rehearsals. He went on about my freckles and curls again. It was so flattering, I'd never thought them attractive features before; he made me feel good.

He lived in a village near Rochdale but had a bedsit near the university during term-time, in that, his final year. It belonged to a relation, who let it to him at a low rent. When he heard I grew up in North Manchester, near Middleton, he thought it lovely that we didn't live far apart. Geographically, perhaps, but culturally we lived as far apart as opposite ends of the universe.

He told me how hard he had worked to get rid of his Rochdale accent but I couldn't imagine wanting to get rid of part of myself. With a family full of different foreign accents, it had never struck me as an issue.

'Well,' he said. 'I want to go into theatre or television and believe me, they're so prejudiced against regional accents.'

'You're kidding!'

'No – and the North–South prejudice is huge.These accidents of birth…'

I thought of how it was to be Jewish and the minority identity that gave me. Almost like Rochdale, really.

'Well, I like your accent.' I smiled at him, taking in his amazing, chiselled cheek bones and looking into his melted-chocolate eyes.

'Thanks,' he said, leaning over and kissing me on the nose. 'I kissed your thousandth freckle.' He winked, lent over again, squeezed my hand and kissed me on the lips – more than once.

'There are no freckles there, you know,' I said, pointing to my lips and leaning forward for another kiss. I couldn't believe I could be so forward – I had never been kissed before. This time he opened his lips to part mine with his tongue and a shockwave went through me. Suddenly, I understood the stuff in books and magazines. Keeping his hand on mine, he suggested we go for a walk.

We strolled through the campus, going from the concrete block of the Union through to the old, original university building. The quadrangle was so beautiful; we stopped to look around us and suddenly he held me and stopped, turning to me, putting his hands round my face. He lifted it up to his and kissed me again, passionately. We put our arms round each other and stood, hugging like that for ages, up against the well-used wall of the oldest building on the campus. It must have had tales to tell. Maybe Ernie had met girls there, when he was a student.

Martin pressed his whole body against me, including his lower body, in a way that no man had ever held me before. Dancing at the youth club disco had nothing on this.

Suddenly he pulled away, saying, 'Hey, it's nearly time for your bus, Nicola.' So considerate.

'Call me Nicki, by the way, everyone does,' I told him.

At that point there was a whistle and: 'Nicki, hi there!' from across the quadrangle.

Martin looked shocked. 'Who's that? A boyfriend?'

'No. It's David, my twin brother.' He ran over.

'David, meet Martin. Martin, this is David.' I worried that David would tell my parents, but I went on, trying to sound casual. 'Martin's the director of the play I'm in, remember? At Drama Soc.'

'Sure – hi, Martin.' With that, David shook Martin's hand, raising his eyebrows quizzically at me, then winking, as though to say, 'I won't tell.'

At that point in my reminiscences, Jake barged into my bedroom.

'Mum! You're daydreaming again. We'll be late! Nice hair-do, though.' My hair, at least, had benefited from the prolonged absent-minded brushing.

'Thanks, charmer. Let's go.'

At the airport, my heart raced as Jake and I sat in the car, waiting for Martin's mobile call to say he'd landed. Meeting Martin after everything was like waiting for someone I'd never met. Jake was obviously excited, as he would be. I wondered whether Martin was as worried about our meeting as I was.

In fact, he ran, grinning, out of the terminal, coat flying, and Jake went over, gripped him briefly and helped with one of his cases. Martin looked good in businessman garb; his tie flew as he ran, and he tried to smooth his unruly mop of hair. I stepped out of the car and we hugged. It seemed natural.

'Missed you,' he whispered into my ear. He cupped my face in his hands just as he had all those years ago. 'Lots.'

'Same here.' Did I mean that?

'Come – get me home, sharpish!' Jake had loaded both cases into the car and Martin wrapped an arm around him so he could hug us both at once. Then he sat in the front. He looked sideways at me. 'You look good you know, Nic, in spite of everything.'

I was glad I'd tried to look good for him. I cheered *me* up, too, after shivah. We both liked me in red and the bright sweater with my dogtooth-check trousers were a relief from the plain skirts and blouses of the previous week.

'New hairstyle?' he asked, patting my head gently.

'No – it won't be trimmed till the month is up.'

'The month…?'

'Twenty-eight days from Mum's death. Not long to go.' I wanted desperately to change the subject.

'Aha. Well, it suits you longer.' He turned to the back of the car. 'So, Jake, how're things? You seem to be going great guns on your history project!'

'Yeah, right – but I wanted to ask you about a physics problem after. Anyway what's with this "ebook revolution", hey?' Making quote marks with his fingers, Jake continued, '"The biggest thing since the invention of the printing press." "Bookshelves and libraries will be obsolete." What d'you reckon?'

'Slow down, Jake,' Martin said. 'That's too much to answer right now – give me time. I'd like to see Grandpa, now – Nicki, can we go via your dad's and see him for five minutes?'

'Sure.'

We stopped outside Dad's and I held Jake back. This was Martin's time.

'Martin! What a surprise!' Dad opened the door and ushered us in. 'When did you get back? Come in!'

'We came straight from the airport,' Martin replied. 'I wanted to see you.' They hugged emotionally. Martin held Dad away from him, looked him up and down saying, 'You look strong, y'know, Joe. But I'm not surprised. You've always been gutsy.'

Dad insisted on making a cup of tea. He obviously needed to chat and proceeded to tell Martin, yet again, about the early days of his jewellery business. How Malkah would joke about how his immigrant customers pronounced 'earrings' like 'herrings' and laugh at the thought of women wearing smelly herrings on their ears. It was the old, oft-told story that Dad had tried to retell me the other day. Martin listened as though he'd never heard it before.

'I'll miss Malkah's laughter more than anything, Martin.'

'You're doing OK, though, Joe, really you are.' Martin gripped Dad's hands. He was so good at saying the right thing – unless, of course, he was saying the wrong thing. He's good with words, my Martin, perhaps that's why he can hurt so much. We all needed to go home but, as we left, I thought of something.

'Dad, we read all Freidl's letters, but I think there must be more. More suffragette stuff – something. I mean, d'you think Grandma Freidl kept her account secret *just* because of the foundling bit? Or do you think there's more, somewhere?'

'Maybe. Where did you get up to?'

'Where they officially had Malkah – Mum – named in synagogue.'

'Oh. I think there is more, yes. I'll look around. May get me tidying my desk,' Dad replied.

'Nicki, let's go before jetlag kicks in,' Martin said.

'Sure. Good to see you.' Dad kissed us all goodbye as he saw us out.

Back home, I loved the smell of the meal in the oven that

greeted us as we opened the door, like when Ernie first arrived at my grandmother's home. Whatever had happened, I thought Martin deserved a good meal after so long away from home. Old-fashioned me.

He went to put away his jacket and shouted, from the hall: 'What's this ragged, grey thing on the coat stand? Is it for the charity shop?' I knew he meant the cardigan that I'd worn last week.

'It's what I wore for shivah. It has been washed, you know!'

All Martin said in response was, 'Oh.' Then, 'Food smells great, Nicki – can we eat now, before I fall asleep?' The cardigan wasn't referred to again.

He and Jake washed their hands while I put out the meal on the worktop. Martin peeped into each casserole and kissed me, whispering into my ear: 'Thanks for this, doll.'

I couldn't deal with the soft, loving way he was treating me. I was glad he appreciated the meal, but his voice of the other night rang in my head.

'Well, cooking gives me time to think and this took me right back to my childhood.'

Jake and Martin started the discussion about the effect of electronic readers. He thought it could seriously affect independent booksellers, since people with e-readers would buy ebooks through the provider. He conceded that there would still be writers – possibly more than ever – and readers as well.

'But it'll change distribution methods,' Martin explained, 'so we've a lot to take on board. The first e-reader may be out in a couple of years – I saw a prototype at this conference.'

'Cool, Dad! What's it like?' Jake asked.

'Amazing. So small and fantastic for travelling – just one item for all your reading. And you can change the font size… all kinds of tricks.'

I could understand the worries for publishers.

'But will bookshelves become obsolete?'

'No idea. But the company's trying its damnedest to be ahead of the game.'

'Hope they make sure there's still a life for agents and publishers,' I said.

'Me too.' Martin looked downbeat for the first time. 'Meanwhile, Jake, up you go. I need time with Mum before we go to bed.'

'Night, Dad, night, Mum.'

'Sleep well.'

'Jake's been great, lately, Martin. I'm proud of him,' I said when he had gone.

'Good. He was really perceptive in his emails to me. So... where do we start?'

I tensed up.

'With that flower?' he asked. 'Is now the time?'

I'd thought he wanted to restart the row. 'It can be,' I said. 'It's upstairs. When did you hear about it?'

'Jake told me in an email. Amazing. And Freidl's letters – wow!'

'There's Ernie's story too, you know.'

We cleared up together. Once finished, he put his arm round me and ushered me out of the kitchen.

'Come on, old thing. You must be shattered.'

'You, too.'

We went upstairs slowly and Martin undressed for his shower.

'Show me all the stuff tomorrow, before we go out. We are going out for dinner, aren't we?' he asked from behind the shower screen, as I cleaned my teeth.

'Sure.'

Was he really unaware that I remembered each word he'd hurt me with, last week? Or was he still a good actor? It seemed that neither of us wanted to touch the thorny issues just yet.

By the time I went back into the bedroom, Martin was lying

seductively in bed with the covers half thrown off, beckoning me into the gap he'd made.

'Come on in, love, come and keep me warm. It's always cold in an empty hotel bed, especially those king-size ones.'

I thought he would be exhausted but I immediately found myself folded into his arms, being kissed around my ears and neck in the way he knew would make me wriggle with pleasure. This was the last thing I had expected. He never wore pyjama tops but I realised that under the duvet he had no trousers on either. This was crazy, after everything. Yet I did still love him. He was so gentle, caressing and stroking me, whispering things like, 'You need to be loved, right now,' and, 'You feel good, silky smooth.'

We continued to make love after long and delicious foreplay, such that we rarely take time for in our usual, rushed routine. I could have been back in the rickety bed in his student bedsit, where we made love for the first time ever. And, just like that time, after a rest, we started again. I'd always thought jetlag affected men's libido in the opposite way.

'Hm… it seems to be an aphrodisiac!' I said, sighing, as we lay back afterwards, my head nestling in his armpit.

'What does?'

'Jetlag.' I stroked his chest with the tips of my fingers.

'Maybe, but I'm not going away again just to find out.'

With that he soon fell asleep, facing me. I lay awake for a while, admiring his features, his still-angular cheekbones and perfectly straight nose. I felt happy in a physical way but very confused. However, orgasms have a way of putting everything else to one side. They are also very good sleeping potions.

I woke to the sound of our clock radio and quickly turned it off for Martin's sake, as I had to be ready before him. I got dressed in the bathroom and started down the stairs, soon joined by Jake.

Martin called from the bedroom, 'Hey you, don't go without saying goodbye!'

'OK,' I called.

Breakfast was hurried, as usual. I picked up the pile of books and files from the hall floor, Jake took his blazer from the coat stand and we both shouted goodbye to Martin as we went through the front door.

The day passed reasonably well, although Jolyon, so keen to be there in the holidays, didn't turn up for school on the day it mattered. His sister called in to the classroom saying he was ill. I reminded her that a note was needed next day, without fail.

On the way home, I phoned Dad and Ernie. Dad said how glad he was to see Martin last night. 'He's a good person, Nicki. He always knows the right thing to say. How was your day?'

'Fine, actually – as though nothing had happened. I'm lucky I love teaching and it stops me from worrying too much.'

'Well, you worry too much about me. You've a lot on your plate. So Ernie and I are making Friday night dinner for *you* tomorrow, at his place.'

'I can't let Ernie...'

'It was his idea.'

'I'll make the dessert.'

'No, you won't. I've desserts in the freezer till they come out of my ears, left over from what people brought. Have a Friday off.' So it was settled.

'Great. See you there.'

Then I called Ernie to tell him I'd started his story and how much I admired him. He said he didn't really like being admired for the cards that were dealt to him. 'But you can admire me for being me, if you like. How's Martin?'

'Full of beans. I was surprised how energetic he was, after the long flight. We're going out for a snack tonight.'

'Joe was so pleased he came to see him, jetlag and all,' he said. 'You'll come on Friday night, won't you?'

'Yep.'

'See, you're not the only one to organise people,' laughed Ernie.

I smiled to myself, clicked off the hands-free and arrived home soon afterwards. I checked the writing my class had done that day and made myself a coffee. The phone rang – it was Ros.

'Hi, Nicki. Haven't spoken for a while. How are you?'

'Fine.'

'No, but how are you really?'

'For now, OK. Difficult over the phone. Martin's home, I'm back at work, Jake's back at school – life's taken over, really. Thanks for asking. Let's meet up anyway.'

'During our lunch hour? Can you?' Ros asked.

'Free lunchtimes are usually taken up covering for absent colleagues, but let's try. Say Thursday – a week today?'

'Great. Our usual?'

'Yes, fine.' I was finishing off my coffee when Jake burst in through the back door, dropping his sports kit and school bag, while he opened the biscuit tin, causing a cascade of crumbs.

'I'm starving!' He shoved a handful of biscuits into his mouth and took a smoothie from the fridge.

'I'd never have guessed. *Please* wash your hands and put the bags where they belong, and sports kit in the washing machine.' He did all that and came back in.

'I'll dish up your meal. Microwave it when you want – Dad and I are going out for an early meal at The Bistro.'

'Can't I come?' he moaned. 'There's not much homework.'

'No, sorry. Dad and I are going on a grown-up date for two. We need to catch up.'

'Hm. Like I don't? We've had no time, either – it's been tough being the man of the house.'

'I know, but you're not any more.'

'Thanks for nothing. You'll be treating me like a baby again, any minute.' Jake moaned on. 'You only treated me like a grown-up because you needed me.' He was right – but there was no room for negotiation.

'Jake. Just accept it, enjoy having the house to yourself and stop prattling on – and *please* pick up your things.'

He went out of the room, mumbling: 'Only leftovers in the microwave for little old me... enjoy your posh nosh and wine...'

I ignored him, carried on clearing up, then went upstairs to check that everything was ready for school. My mobile beeped. It was a text from Martin: 'Y NOT TAKE J 2 NIGHT?'

I was furious. 'HE BEEN BEGGING?'

'YES, HE SENT TXT.'

'I'M P'D OFF.' I clicked on the little angry face symbol. 'WE NEED TIME 2 GETHER.'

'He replied immediately, 'OK C U', with a smiley face.

Before I left, I knocked on Jake's door. 'Hello, in there.'

The music went even louder, then silent – he'd put on his earphones. I knocked again, partially opening the door. Jake's sulky face peered round. He grunted.

'I'm going to meet Dad but I'm popping into the late supermarket en route,' I said. 'Anything you want?'

'No. Oh, maybe some crisps to take to footie practice tomorrow?'

'Fine. You know we're all going to Ernie's for Friday night dinner, with Grandpa? You can look forward to that, even if you aren't talking to me any more. Night, in case you're asleep when we get back.' I blew him a kiss.

'Won't be. I want to show Dad the physics thing.'

'OK. Bye.' I went downstairs and left for the restaurant.

The passionate welcome home of the previous evening tempered our evening out. The issues between us were smouldering just beneath the surface. Martin told me how stressful his work had become, though he didn't exactly apologise for his anger. The book industry needed ways to cut expenditure and everyone was afraid for their jobs.

'So that's why you were so preoccupied on the phone that night?' I wanted to suck my words back into my mouth, the moment I said them.

Martin scowled. 'I knew you'd bring that up. Will it help to go over it now? Can't we leave it? You seemed happy enough to have me back, last night.'

'I was – but it's hard to forget...' I left it there. His job was a worry and anyway, his career was only second best. His main dream had been to write, plays or books, so he was frustrated at work at the best of times. An idea came to me.

'Why don't you sit yourself at a desk, with an empty pad and pen in hand – or with a laptop – and write?'

'What?'

'You heard. Write – something. A play, maybe?'

'I haven't time, Nicki.'

'That's no excuse.'

'It is.'

'I don't think I could, any more.'

'You could.' I wanted to humour him.

'We couldn't afford it, for one thing,' Martin was right, there. 'I can't ask you to be the main bread-winner.'

'Why not? You could start writing in evenings and weekends, couldn't you?'

'Weekends? There won't be much of a weekend as Jake's Bar Mitzvah gets nearer.'

I feared another Jewish-thing row was brewing and tensed up.

'I'll be going to synagogue every week with him,' Martin continued. 'He is nearly twelve.' I was touched that he'd thought of it before me. 'You didn't think I'd remember, did you?'

'Dunno.' I didn't want to rise to the bait. 'You're a good dad.'

'Thanks – and I can also be a good Jewish dad.'

Not that, again, I thought.

'It'll get quite hectic,' he said.

'Sorting out his extra lessons? I bet Dad or Ernie will help out and take him for us, sometimes.'

'We'll see,' said Martin.

We jumped from one thing to another that night, somehow, but covered a lot. It helped us avoid rehashing the row. Martin then changed the subject completely.

'I read the start of Ernie's story, before I went to work. It's hard to take in what he went through, isn't it? But when I called to tell him I'd read it, he said he had something to tell us. Wouldn't say what – sounded mysterious.'

'Didn't say anything to me.'

'Oh, and there was something peeping out of a bag on the dressing table. What is it?'

'Grandma Freidl's flower, remember?'

'Oh yes. Y'know, nothing much ever happened in *my* family.'

'Have you ever asked?' I said.

'No, but Mum isn't a talker. It's such a small family; tiny and uninteresting – only got one aunt, Dad's sister, who never married, and that's it. But I think we go back four generations in Rochdale.'

'I bet there's something.' I wanted to show an interest in his family for a change.

'Anyway – back to Jake's Bar Mitzvah. What are we going to do for it?'

'Do? What do you mean, "do"? Oh! That kind of "do". You keep changing the subject.'

'Well, we're catching up, aren't we?'

'Yeah, only... with Mum dying, I haven't thought about it. I mean, we do have a date, at least. We could have it in Israel if you like.'

'Why?'

'Lots of reasons. Lovely time of year, early spring – and it gets over the issue of where to hold it, here.'

'Reform or orthodox you mean? That old chestnut?' said Martin.

'That – and it would be lovely, that's all. Also, Jake's only cousins could be with us.'

'You really mean: so your David will be sure to be there, looking on from his lofty, devout position!'

'Nasty! He's never been superior about religion,' I reminded him.

Martin said nothing.

'What's your problem?' I asked.

'Dunno, sorry,' he replied. 'But let's ask Jake. He matters most.'

'Sure, but we two need to agree, first.'

'We're rarely together on Jewishy things, though, are we?'

'This could be a first, for Jake.'

'True,' Martin piped up. 'It's one of my "isms", crowds. Not in a phobic way, just too many people knowing my business. I've never got used to that part of Judaism. Converting doesn't teach you the togetherness stuff.'

'But isn't it good to have people's support? You're good at giving it.'

'I try. Were there crowds there after your mum died?'

'Yes. Crowds and so many people I hadn't seen for ages,' I told him.

'It seems so intrusive to me, when people are grieving. I'd run away and hide.'

I frowned.

'Hang on – don't get angry, Nic.'

'I'm not. It was wonderful... knowing how many lives she'd touched... people who knew different aspects of her. People just coming was, well, magical.'

'Honestly?'

'Honestly.'

'Well, I... Back to the Bar Mitzvah.' I was relieved. Martin went on, 'I'd love Mum to come with – her first visit to Israel.'

'We couldn't have it without her, wherever it is,' I said. I could see that Martin's jetlag was catching up on him and he read my mind.

'Let's go home now, Jake's waiting up.'

'Jetlag doesn't bother you much, does it?' I said as I kissed him across the table. 'Do you remember kissing me across a table, on our first kind of date, at university?'

'No and, yes, maybe.'

'Yes, maybe what?'

'No, jetlag doesn't bother me and yes, maybe I remember the kiss.' Martin took my hand as we went to pay the bill.

We were both eager to get home to bed but Jake accosted us as we arrived home; Martin went up to tackle the physics problem. I had a bath and went to bed.

Our sex life was fun; since Jake was an IVF baby and our only one, never having to consider contraception made life easier – the 'plus' side of infertility. I was almost asleep when I felt his fingers softly tracing a path round my tummy, over my thighs then between them, finger by finger. I turned to him, rolled onto him and we made love like that, our favourite position.

'I'm not surprised you had a suffragette grandma.'

'What d'you mean?' I didn't want to chat, just then.

'Feminists!' he whispered. 'You all descend from Lilith – lucky me!' And he buried his head between my breasts.

I looked down on his shock of black hair, with its few streaks of grey. Then I flopped down onto him and turned on my side, pulling him with me. We nearly fell out of bed. Giggling, we played around for another minute or two and then he fell asleep. Just before I dropped off, it struck me: perhaps Martin was a man who was better to have an affair with, than to have as a husband – we were better in bed than anywhere.

Oh my God! I hope no one else thinks… that he's good for an affair. I'd never considered that before. *Empty* hotel beds? My thoughts guaranteed a sleepless night.

As I woke, I remembered it was Friday. I nudged Martin in the ribs and asked, 'Who was Lilith, by the way?'

'Y'don't know?' he answered, half asleep. 'Adam's first wife. He left her because she always wanted to be on top. So they say.' We both laughed.

NINE

Thank goodness the new half-term started midweek. I used to think that was to make it easy for children; by now I realised it was as much for teachers. Some children took a week, at least, to remember what being at school was about: they forgot how to listen, respond, or produce a piece of work. I was at my most satisfied at the end of each half-term, when I had the measure of the whole class. Then it started all over again.

However, after work that Friday, I could go home and flop, since we would be out for dinner. Martin came home in a buoyant mood and started talking to Jake about the preparations for his Bar Mitzvah in thirteen months. Good one, Martin. Was he currying favour?

Jake was pleased, too. 'Which synagogue will it be in?'

Martin paused. 'Ours, the reform, of course. Why?'

'Just that I've been going with Grandpa to his, over this last fortnight. Enjoyed it. It's nice being with him.'

I could feel a row brewing.

'That's as may be,' said Martin, 'but this is with me. Ernie can come with us, if he wants, he enjoys it there. So can Grandpa for that matter.'

I stepped in. 'Fair enough. Perhaps Grandpa could take you to the orthodox one with him, sometimes?'

'If I'm away, sure. OK, mate?' Martin ruffled Jake's hair.

'Sure.'

'And there are other options of where to hold it.'

'What d'you mean, options?' Jake asked.

'Well,' Martin looked at me for approval. 'We wondered about Jerusalem.'

'Brill idea! Sam and Rob had theirs there.'

'That's what we were thinking,' Martin continued.

'And my cousins can be there! But isn't it very expensive?'

'We'll find out, but it'll be that year's holiday, too.'

'And we're hoping Grandma Taylor will come,' I said. We were trying to humour each other – a game we were learning to play.

'Listen,' said Martin, 'I'm really looking forward to the bit in the ceremony when I say: "I henceforth give up all religious responsibility for this young man." I've remembered that from the first Bar Mitzvah I ever went to.' He looked genuinely happy and I didn't like to tell him that fathers don't necessarily say that bit at the reform *shul*.

We strolled over to Ernie's, enjoying the companionship a walk allows. As usual, the smell of Ernie's food hit us as he opened the door. I took the coats to the cloakroom, partly to put them away but also because I loved the Ernie-feel of that little room.

It had a shower in it – his way of fitting a guest shower into his house – and there were original touches. Bits of driftwood were used as shelves, hung from the ceiling. Shells held the soap and thick rope held an old fishing net on the curtain rail; the tieback was an anchor. Ernie's own collage images of ships and fishing adorned the walls, which he'd lined himself in planking, distressed and lime-washed. The whole thing was like a sophisticated beach hut. He did it to remind him of the holiday camp by the sea, when he first landed in England.

I joined the others in the lounge where his wonderful fireplace was lit. I could detect curry – Ernie can add creative touches to familiar food, just as he does to his decor. Dad was already there, helping Ernie in the kitchen, looking well and animated. As we all kissed each other 'Shabbat Shalom' round the table after kiddush, I dared to think my worries were over.

When we started on the chopped liver, to which Ernie had added sherry and a pinch of curry powder, he told us his 'secret' news. He had received an email from a German woman who had grown up somewhere near his childhood home outside Leipzig. She was a volunteer in an organisation working with elderly Holocaust survivors in Israel. Something about ridding themselves of their past history by reaching out to Jewish victims of Nazism. So she was currently living in Haifa.

'But why contact you?' Jake asked.

'She's contacting anyone from my part of Leipzig. In her survivors' group, there's a man called Dreher whose late father was a photographer. She's looking for the people in his photos – well, as many as she can. Then she'll collate memory books for him and some of the other members. I suppose she'll use some photos and some other memorabilia.'

'Sounds fascinating. Did you ever meet this woman?' I was intrigued.

'That's the whole point! Why do you think I'm so full of beans?' he replied, grinning. 'She is Herr Lanzig's daughter, Blume. My name was on the back of one of this man Dreher's photos, but *I* didn't know *she* existed; she was the baby at that time.'

'At what time?' Martin asked.

'The time on the Lanzigs' farm.'

'I'm lost,' Martin said. 'I didn't know you lived on a farm.'

Jake said: 'Herr Lanzig saved Ernie's life, Dad.'

Seeing our bemused faces, Ernie said, 'I think I'd better tell you the story properly.'

'I wish you would,' Martin said.

'I've got my notes here to read from... Are you sitting comfortably? Then I'll begin,' he said, smiling.

We all settled down to listen.

In the early autumn of 1938, when SS officers 'knocked on the door', my mother managed to get rid of them somehow but already had plans for me. The very next day, she sent me off with a bag of bread and water and a hand-drawn map which showed the back lane to Herr Lanzig's farm. He was a non-Jewish friend of my father's who had agreed with Mutti to keep me safe. So off I went.

'Just like that?' said Dad.

'How old were you, then?' asked Martin.

'Eleven – but you know, to me, it seemed like a big adventure.'

Martin shook his head in disbelief as Ernie continued.

I knew that the path running along the boundary of our dairy eventually became a dirt track. It ran past Herr Schnitzler's abattoir (Schnitzler was another family friend) and along the edge of a copse which signalled the end of Shnitzler's land and the beginning of the Lanzigs'. Mutti had drawn some squiggles and two circles, like clouds. The squiggles represented an orchard, where there might be fallen fruit to eat, and the circles were two giant oak trees. I was to wait under them.

'Had she prepared you at all?' I asked.

'No. But I was a country child. I was used to wandering through fields on my own,' Ernie commented.

'Go on,' Jake said.

As I ran, I realised I hadn't said goodbye to Mutti, and I knew I couldn't contact her once I was in hiding. I found fruit and ate some as I waited for ages under the trees. I worried that something had happened to Herr Lanzig.

I must have nodded off, when I heard a loud whisper: 'Ernst!' It was Herr Lanzig. He took my hand and I walked with him, in silence, along the lane to his farmhouse. He held his finger to his mouth, 'Sh,' opening a door in an outbuilding beside the farmhouse and beckoning me in.

He indicated a pile of straw with a horse blanket over it – my bed, I realised – a box with a cushion on it to sit on, and a standpipe with a bowl underneath it – my washbowl. Outside, at the back, he pointed to a deep hole. I guessed what that was for.

We were listening in rapt silence.

'Shall we get on with dinner and carry on later?' Ernie asked, concerned that his immaculate cooking would be spoilt.

So we reluctantly continued with the meal, though we wanted to hear more and ate Ernie's divine *lokshen* pudding (with his signature treacle and bananas) quickly. Why did I take my problems to Ernie, who'd gone through so much? Maybe his story would put my own life into perspective.

Ernie read on.

He gave me a torch, whispering, 'This is your home for as long as it takes, Ernst. We will slip you food in when we can, under this bucket. You can tiptoe to the house only by night, without the torch, to say hello. Please tap five times on our side door. There.' He pointed to it. 'Once a week you can use our bath – only at night, please. Otherwise, I'm sorry but this is where you stay. I only wish I could have your help on the farm!'

'Thank you, Herr Lanzig,' I said.

'Just listen to the next bit,' Ernie said, as if we weren't listening already.

Herr Lanzig said, 'Ernst, to me, Jews are people, like any other. Your father once told me that it says in your Talmud, "Save one person and you save the world." I always remembered that. Your father was a good friend and since he is not here for you, I am.'

Ernie looked up from the sheet, paused and said, 'This Blume is his daughter... can you believe it? I just can't wait to meet her.' This was amazing news. But he had more of his story to read.

That was my life, moving around by night, lying low by day. The animals' noises nearby were comforting. Soon after arriving, I found something unfamiliar in a box, amongst my food, under the upturned bucket. There was a ripe, new season apple, with a note: 'Happy New Year, Ernst. I think the date is about right.' There was a little dish of his farm honey, to eat with the apple in the traditional way. Herr Lanzig had remembered it was around the time of Rosh Hashanah. I relished the sweet, scented honey, tainted though it was by my tears, as I thought of my family. It should have been so joyful.

I stayed until the November of that year, the time of Kristallnacht. Herr Lanzig heard from my mother, somehow, that people in England would give homes to German Jewish children. So she'd arranged everything for me. I was to travel without her, on a train specially for children.

'Of course! The Kindertransport,' said Martin.
Ernie nodded.

I had just one day to prepare. Again, it sounded like fun and I was strangely sorry to leave my life in the barn. I felt safe there. One night, Herr Lanzig took me to the railway station, where we waited till dawn. In the morning mist, I could hear crying before I saw anyone: crowds of mothers and children, pouring into the station. And in the crush, I spotted Mutti.

This is when I started to cry. Oh, Ernie, I'm sorry. But... imagine being her.'

He murmured in agreement before continuing.

Thin and old, she looked. Our meeting was brief, the train whistled in to the platform within minutes. We hugged. A bittersweet hello/ goodbye. As I went towards the train, she pointed to my friend, Hans.

'Look, Ernst, there is Hans. Stay with him!' She pushed me through the train door. I clung to my friend, who was older than me by two years and seemed so grown-up. We hadn't seen each other for ages. My mother found our compartment and blew kisses, tears streaming down her face, like the raindrops on the windowpane.

'Did you ever see her again?' Martin asked.

'No – that was the last time, though I didn't know it, then. Her expression haunts me still. But that's another reason to go to meet Blume. The photo she mentioned may be of my parents and I don't have a single one.'

He paused, wiping his eyes and blowing his nose.

'And it also haunts me that Herr Lanzig had gone before I could thank him. So that's what we'll try to do, in Israel.'

'What? Thank him? Is he still alive?' Jake asked.

'Don't be daft, Jake, a posthumous thank-you! Is that why you're meeting this Blume?' Martin asked.

'Yes, partly. I will just read this last bit before I get the coffee, OK?'

Our motley group of children eventually reached the coast of Holland and continued, by ship, across the English Channel. We were taken to an unused holiday camp on the South coast where it was bitterly cold, but I fell in love with the sight of the sea. There were kind people supporting us all, till eventually, we went by train to London's Liverpool Street Station, where people or families would collect us and take us to their homes.

While I waited, I was put on a table, because I was small and there weren't enough chairs, and I remember looking down at my feet swinging in my brand-new leather shoes. My mother had bought them, especially for the journey – really ridiculous, but a matter of pride on her part.

Many children had gone, while I'd been dreaming, so then I thought: What if no one came for me? Hans was called and I was terrified of our parting. But he called to me. 'Ernst, we are both going to Manchester!'

The people looking after us explained that we were to get on another train, and would be met in Manchester. I was to be met by a lady called Freidl Grupman. Which you know!

So we left London. The ladies wrote the word 'Manchester' on a piece of paper, together with the name Grupman, to help us at the station. We had identification labels round our necks which felt really silly. We enjoyed trying to read the names of the towns we passed; how wrong our pronunciation was!

It was so strange that we'd never heard all this before. We absorbed it as he went to make coffee.

'Ernie, I'm speechless,' I said, when he returned and handed round the drinks.

'That takes some doing.' Ernie smiled. 'You've already seen the bit about my arrival at Freidl's house, haven't you?'

'Jake and I have – Martin hasn't had time, yet.'

'Oh – but can we move to the present, then?' Ernie asked. 'Here are the missing pieces. Blume might have more evidence of the Lanzigs' heroism, so it might help us honour him, somehow.

'Have you tried to find her before?' Martin wanted to know.

'Not really, because, as I said, I didn't know she existed. I never saw a baby. I've often googled "Lanzig", but it wouldn't show her, because she took her husband's name.'

'Daft idea,' Jake mumbled. 'Changing your name.'

'Shush a minute! There's more,' Ernie interrupted. 'Last week, Blume's email arrived. She told me immediately that she changed surname on marriage, to Mannheim, and was the Lanzigs' youngest child. She proved that, by describing details about the farm, and she told me how Herr Lanzig kept the SS away by giving them food – that's how he stayed alive.'

'Lucky to have a farm, then, wasn't he?' commented Martin.

'And you'll be pleased to know that although he's now dead, he was never found out and lived out a good, long life.' We all smiled.

Ernie said that Blume had wanted to find him because of a photo with the faded word 'Bamberg' on the back, among a pile the photographer's son, Caspar Dreher, had shown her at the survivors' centre.

'You mean it was taken by his father?' Martin asked.

'Exactly. So, Joe and I are off to Israel soon. It's a pilgrimage!'

'Go for it, I say!' Martin responded.

'Are you up to travelling, Dad?' I asked, concerned for his emotional state on a trip like this.

'We both need to retrace some of our steps, while we have the energy. And there's little Malachi to see.' Dad grinned, clearly buoyed up at the prospect.

'True. It all sounds wonderful.'

'It will be,' he said.

'Well, we all might be going to Israel again in 13 months, for Jake's Bar Mitzvah,' Martin said, suddenly looking so happy. Ernie grinned and winked at me.

'That's terrific!' Dad said. He and Ernie had a lot to plan. Everything felt so upbeat, which was weird.

'Shall I include the Lanzigs in my history project?' Jake asked.

'Why don't you?' Martin responded.

'I'm having a bit of hassle.'

'What d'you mean?'

'Hasn't Mum told you?'

'What?'

'We haven't had time to catch up, yet. You tell him,' I said.

So Jake explained about the jealous kids. 'When I told the teacher, she said I should keep a low profile – that maybe I have an unfair advantage...'

'An *unfair* advantage? So have you got to hide it, then?' Martin snarled. 'Has everyone got to hide what they're good at? Ridiculous! So Ernie and Grandpa had to lose their families for –'

'Dad, calm down! I knew I shouldn't have told you.'

'Look, your testimonies help everyone, don't they? Who is this teacher, I'll –'

My dad interrupted. 'Hold on a minute, Martin. Jake, what's going on?'

'I've even offered the class some quotes for *their* projects but it makes no difference. They call me teacher's pet; but *please* don't go into school, Dad, I'll sort it.'

'How?' Martin asked.

'I just will.'

'I've an idea.' Ernie was at his most pensive. 'Why don't I offer to come into school and share my story with the year group?'

'What a great idea,' said Martin, looking relieved.

'Lots of schools invite survivors in, it won't seem so out of the ordinary,' I volunteered. 'It's the way history is going, now.'

'They want real life stories, I believe,' Dad said.

'Shush a minute.' Ernie interrupted us. 'Shall I write in myself, d'you think, Nicki? You know how schools work.'

'Can't see why not. But don't involve Jake.'

'I'll have to tell them who I am, though.'

'I mean, don't talk about anything else, you know.'

'Of course not,' Ernie replied. 'And it won't be only about

Nazism but about finding a new identity, here. I'll have to keep it as light as possible. And what's more, I can end by telling them about the family who saved my life.'

Jake nodded, beaming. A difficult situation defused.

TEN

Next morning, I stayed at home and had a lie-in, giving Jake and Martin time to chat as they walked to shul. They were so good together; any worries about our relationship were coloured by their closeness.

We had lunch afterwards and when Jake had left to see his friends, Martin turned and said, 'You know, I'm thinking very hard about your offer – your idea.'

'Which was…?'

'That before I am too old, I try to write – something. You look shocked, Nicki. You said it, remember?'

'Sure. What brought it up now, though?'

'Well, my company wants some of us to drop to a four-day week, temporarily.'

'God, things must be bad.'

'Not marvellous, but they'd pay us for four and a half days. I thought one day off a week to write, with half-pay, might be do-able. Not too tough financially, and I'd give it a go. What d'you reckon?'

'Mm, sounds workable.'

'And? You look worried.'

'Just thinking. I'll apply for the post of literacy co-ordinator. It's just been advertised.'

'Really?

'Sure. And there's an "enhancement" – a bit more money for more work.'

'Could you cope with it?'

'With you home a bit more for Jake, probably.' Perhaps we'd both be happier that way.

'And Bar Mitzvah lessons?'

'We'll sort it. So. Off you go and find a pen. Or a laptop, whatever...' I pushed him towards the door. He ran upstairs, two at a time. Our tiny study was also a dumping room, so he would have to start by finding the floor. It was the only room which was smaller than in our first house. We moved for more space, gaining a wider hall, a bedroom and a bigger kitchen-diner. It was so near to our first place that we had watched it being built, in a new development of link houses, still high up looking down at the Irwell.

We didn't use Ernie's ideas as much here, but all our DIY decorating and refurbishing was starting to look a bit sad. The wide, bright hall was still its best feature, with glass doors to the rooms off it. The carpet looked worn, though; we had discussed changing it for a wooden floor but it would have to wait.

Martin came down half an hour later, looking happy.

'Having fun?'

'Yeah. I'll try and get used to using my laptop so I can work anywhere.'

'Because the study's too much of a mess?' I said, giving him a peck on the cheek.

'No. I'll clear it eventually.'

Soon after, Jake came home.

'Da-da... drum roll, Jake. Introducing: your father, the writer!'

'Y'what?'

I told him the new routine.

'Good on ya, Dad.'

And so it was. Martin decided on Monday as his day off, so that, with Sunday, he'd have two consecutive days' writing each week, as well as evenings.

'But you'll have to pretend I'm out, incommunicado,' he declared.

'Understood.'

'What about homework?' asked Jake.

'Not even that!' Martin replied, tickling Jake in the ribs.

'And the washing?' I teased.

'Maybe I'll help with that,' he answered.

'Not fair,' piped up Jake.

'Well, I just lurve doing the washing,' Martin said.

It was a new start. Or maybe we were just playing Happy Families.

Life settled into a routine and the day for lunch with Ros came round... but it didn't happen in the end. The friend who had swapped playground duties for me was off ill.

The evening before, I had packed up the purple flower in an old vanity case to show Ros and, as I was wrapping it in tissue paper, Martin had seen me from upstairs.

'Just a sec, I haven't seen that yet.' He peered over the banister and I waved it at him.

'Amazing! How old d'you reckon it is?' he asked.

'A hundred years old, almost exactly. Freidl's mum gave it her before she, Freidl, left for England.'

'Wow. And where are her letters?'

'All the memorabilia's actually in the study,' I replied, 'but the letters are in Jake's room.'

'Can I read them?'

'Why ask? Anyway, they might inspire your writing. But I'm off – I'm seeing Ros in my lunch hour.'

'Send her my best, and to Howard.' He blew me a kiss goodbye.

'Will do.' I left for work, locking the vanity case in the boot of my car.

When I called Ros to cancel, ten minutes before lessons

started, I explained about the flower. I would have to show it to her another time.

'What is it? A rose?

'Not sure really.' I went on to tell her about it.

She was fascinated and told me she knew someone who had a way to preserve and display precious objects.

'In a block of acrylic?' I asked.

'Not quite. She takes a pretty picture frame and constructs a box behind it, deep enough to hold the object. It's airtight and she uses glass that filters out UV rays. Hey presto! Your memorabilia displayed and preserved.'

'Brilliant. I'll look for the website.' Later, Martin organised it for me.

When I got home after school there was an answerphone message from Dad.

'Call me. No worries.'

Of course, I did worry. But it was only about his flight to Israel so I told him what I could.

'Sounds good,' said Dad. 'I'll look into it. Bye.'

'Hang on, Dad, before you go away, can you see if there are any more letters from Freidl?'

'Will do. I think I have a couple more somewhere.'

I was glad Dad was going away. He might as well enjoy life while he was still fit.

When Martin came home, he suggested we call David to tell him about the Bar Mitzvah plans. I wasn't sure why it had to be just then but I was happy to humour Martin, who seemed so pleased with everything.

'Fine. So call.'

'Isn't it for you to tell him?' asked Martin.

'Good grief, why? He's your brother-in-law!'

So he did. David was thrilled that Martin phoned with the news and offered to look into hotels for a family 'do'.

'We can put on a good *simcha* here, you know,' he said.

'Whatever's going on, nothing puts off a celebration.'

Martin and I talked some more about his new work schedule. The idea had cheered him up. It offered him a possible escape route from book publishing. He said he would begin straight away and went up to the study. Then Ernie called – the phone was busy that evening. He was ensconced in the Lanzig project.

'It's very complicated, but if Blume died, God forbid, it would be tricky. As it is, I only need one other testimony, with hers and mine.'

'I bet you'll do it. Maybe her family saved someone else too?'

With that, I went to mark my books. While Martin was writing and I was marking, I wondered whether we might redecorate the study. Mind you, the whole house needed doing up. All that kind of expense would have to wait, now, unless I did it myself. But everything was peaceful – till Jake came in.

ELEVEN

I jumped up to say hello but suddenly felt dizzy.

'Wow! The room span, then,' I said as I sat back down again.

'You OK?' Jake asked.

'There's a 'dizzy bug' going round – hope it's not that.'

'Let's do DIY meals tonight. Can I eat now?' Ever-hungry Jake.

'Why not? I'm going for an early bath.' I saw the pallor of my face as I got undressed, although the dizziness passed off. I lit some perfumed candles and was falling asleep in the bath when Martin knocked and came in.

'What's this dizziness?'

'I thought you were locked in your garret,' I replied.

'Jake texted me.'

'But you were working.'

'Emergency contact allowed. Are you OK?'

'A bit weird. Jake's making his own supper –'

'Me too. No probs. Enjoy your bath.'

The next day, I decided to book a doctor's appointment.

'On the borderline of normal', the doctor said, ripping off the blood-pressure cuff.

'Well, I *am* on the borderline of normal,' I said, laughing nervously.

'Look, it's OK, but let's check it again in six months. Borderline is fine, as long as it stays there. If you want, I'll run a couple of blood tests. Are you alright otherwise?'

'I've had a stressful time lately, but things are back on track.'

'But losing your mother is very stressful.'

'Suppose so. I'll leave the tests for now, thanks.'

'Come and see me if you have any other worries, won't you?'

'I will. Thanks.'

Dad called the next day to tell me about their flight and everything seemed fine.

'Must be odd, planning a trip without Mum,' I said.

'Mm, but going with Ernie will be good. The last time we went to Israel, we were searching for evidence of our parents' survival. The only proof we found was that they'd perished.'

'I remember. That was ghastly.'

'Dreadful. But this is really exciting and I can't wait to see Malachi and the gang.'

'Wonderful! Oh – nearly forgot. Ros invited us all round for supper next week. For the end of the month's mourning and as a send-off for you two.'

'Great.' Dad said. 'Day?'

'Saturday evening, after Shabbat. Jake can go off to youth club from there – and she's inviting her parents, too. You haven't seen them since their visit after shivah.'

'Sounds good,' said Dad and we said goodbye.

I hadn't expected to see Gill round at Ros's, with her parents. The atmosphere was lovely and informal, even though Howard made a quick announcement that the evening was in honour of Dad and Ernie's trip, indicating a table decoration as he did so.

'Here's to a great trip for you both!' he said, and we all raised our glasses. Gill raised hers, too, a look of gleeful recognition that this is what she should do; what's more she said, *'L'chaim!'* Then she pointed to the decoration, which was her version of the Israeli flag: the blue Star of David on a white background, stuck into a plantpot of sand. 'Me, me!' she said, proud of her creation.

Ernie said, 'Oh, Gill, you made that for Joe and me, didn't you? Thanks so much.'

She smiled, looking at me in a way that showed she remembered me, somehow, but then her communication stopped. She had so many of her mother Sue's features: small mouth, big grey eyes, and tall slim figure, but it all missed, somehow. She wandered around the room, settled on a house plant that needed attention, and spent her time with that.

Dad and Ernie were ebullient, holding forth about their trip, Blume, and Malachi; everyone gave them complete attention. Howard, a quiet, studious guy of few words, grinned the whole time – I had never previously noticed his perfectly regular white teeth. He looked good, in a black v-necked sweater with peach shirt collar showing.

Ros had an expressive face, frowning to listen intently when Dad or Ernie told us something, laughing readily when they were funny. Whenever she laughed, Gill laughed with her, copying her response. Their dad, a serious, thin-faced, elderly man with rimless specs, smiled when they did that syncopated laugh. His smile transformed his gaunt face, so I could see his younger self again.

Dad and Ernie's plan had rejuvenated them both and their presence brought to life Ros and Howard's room, which I always thought so stark, a bit unlived in, somehow. It wasn't just that it was too neat and tidy – nothing was ever out of place – but I couldn't find a colour scheme to catch my eye. I often longed to see it with one or two scatter cushions, a mat – something. Brown dining-room chairs were at one end, black leather armchairs at the other with a wooden-edged settee. Her kitchen was the same: inside the cupboards and out stood serried ranks of utensils and products.

Still, Howard and Ros, cooking together, made us a lovely supper with an Israeli theme: hummus, falafel and various tasty salads. After we'd eaten, Jake's friends called for him so he left.

We all sat around chatting but I wished their lighting was softer, their furniture more squishy. It wasn't easy to relax but Martin and Howard hadn't seen each other for ages and chatted on regardless.

I fed a few questions about gardening to Gill, via Ros or her parents. Tidying the weeds didn't require any human contact, of course. Her love of gardening came from that special garden they had when she was a child. At least her parents could now feel that Gill was independent – to an extent.

I think it was because of Gill that Ros and Howard managed their lives without children and hence kept such an orderly house. They tried for ages for a family, but didn't want the IVF stuff or adoption. They did so much for Gill, perhaps she filled the gap. Or perhaps they feared a child of theirs might be like Gill. I never asked Ros and she never told. Sometimes good friendships depend on silence.

Gill's parents reminded Dad he had to complete the story about how he met my mum, which was left unfinished when they visited him, just after shivah. They couldn't work out how Dad's meeting Mum linked with his discovering Ernie. It amazed me that they didn't know already.

'It's easy,' Dad said. 'Ernie took Malkah with him on his search for *me,* that fateful night. Someone told him that a boy called Joe lived nearby, and they told *me* someone with the surname "Bamberg" wanted to meet me.'

'Didn't you guess it was your cousin?' Ros asked.

'We only hoped. Bamberg was a common name,' Dad explained. 'So, we arranged to meet at a youth group evening; I'd never gone to many Jewish clubs before. I lived with a non-Jewish family and although they did try to send me to those places, I didn't want to go on my own.'

'And the magic moment –' said Sue, egging him on – 'tell us more.'

'I agreed to go, but I didn't know Malkah would come with

Ernie, or who she was, of course. It was a *coup de foudre.*'

'I did have my nose pushed out,' Ernie chipped in.

Dad carried on. 'The electricity between Malkah and me relieved the tension that Ernie and I felt on meeting again. We had grown up, of course, but we did recognise each other.'

'So, miracles do happen, don't they, Joe?' Sue said.

'Except... soon after our reunion,' Ernie added, 'we realised we might be the only members of our family to have survived. We needed each other, but it was hard. Still – look what we have, now!' He gestured to all of us.

'And the day you two met up, Dad and Mum became an item!' I said to Ernie. I always loved that connection.

Howard was full of Martin's new career – well, everyone was interested. In our early days, his writing ambitions had been swallowed up by the bigger issues we faced: namely, the fact that Martin wasn't Jewish.

I recalled the day at his bedsit when I brought that subject up for the first time. We were in bed in the afternoon, between lectures. Funny – Mum and Dad could never have figured that these things could happen during the day. They thought that my going home each night kept me safe. Anyway, during our post-coital chat, it came up – that I was Jewish.

'So? You're Jewish. What's that got to do with anything – why throw it in, just when I offered to take you home tonight?'

I explained that if he were to take me home, it was best he knew. He couldn't understand that my parents would not be pleased that I was dating a non-Jewish guy.

'What difference does it make? We're just friends, aren't we?'

'Well...' I began – but didn't finish. It was up to me to clarify things but I was afraid of spoiling the best relationship I'd ever had. We had so much in common, books, theatre, art; I didn't only love Martin, I could ask his advice and I trusted him. The religion issue could topple it all and other changes were in the air, too. He would be graduating the following summer, a year before me.

'But I'd love to meet your parents,' Martin said. 'Now I have a car, it's mad not to take you home, sometimes. They met me at the staging of the play, didn't they?'

'Yes, but I introduced you as the director, not as my boyfriend, remember?' I replied, sheepishly.

'Never noticed. Ashamed of me, were you?' He was visibly crestfallen.

'No. You *weren't* my boyfriend, then.'

I knew I would have to tell my parents and take him home, one day. I knew David wouldn't interfere, but he said he'd be there for me.

Ros tapped me on the shoulder, bringing me back to the present as I helped with the washing-up, by saying, right into my ear, 'A penny for them?'

'They're worth far more than that.' I laughed her off.

TWELVE

Dad and Ernie in Israel were like two school kids at summer camp. They sent texts and emailed photos of themselves with Malachi, David, Hannah and the children. They phoned to tell us about their first meeting with Blume Lanzig and the people in her group, and sent photos of them, too. I had to warn them off their long phone calls.

'Please let's wait till you're back. Tell us everything then.'

'Yes, but we'd love to see the name Lanzig honoured in the Avenue of the Righteous Among the Nations there, one day, so we just told Blume.'

'D'you mean in the Holocaust Museum garden?' I asked.

'Exactly.'

'What are you talking about?' said Martin. Although I had the phone on speaker I turned to him to explain further.

'If you can prove someone risked their life to save a Jew, their name can be inscribed there,' I told him.

'Oh, yes I've heard of that, I think.'

Blume was naturally thrilled.

After that, we heard little bits but the rest was left for them to tell us when they came back. On the first evening home, Dad started the minute they came in.

'Blume's parents did harbour someone else and we're trying to trace them; we've told that to the verification department at Yad Vashem. We need three witnesses: Ernie is one, Blume another, so we're nearly there.'

I called Martin to come and join us.

Dad said, 'At the Holocaust survivors' centre where Blume is a volunteer, we met Caspar Dreher – the son of the man who had been a village photographer. They actually lived near our parents.'

'One coincidence after another,' Jake said.

'Listen,' said Ernie. We were all ears. 'We showed him proof of our identity, including the only thing I ever received from my mother after my arrival in England: a little, handwritten, regulation Red Cross postcard.

'You remember the one, Nicki?' he asked me.

He had shown it to me ages ago. It was totally unemotional, as it was censored and it just said: 'Be good, Ernst, don't forget your manners – say thank-you to the people who feed you. Do well with your lessons, you are a clever boy. See you soon, love Mummy.'

'That postcard was all the identification Blume and Caspar needed. They knew, then, that we were Ernst and Joseph Bamberg.'

'Oh wow!' I said.

'They were quite overcome,' Dad told me, 'and had the photograph copied and laminated there. Those little photos keep so many family memories alive.'

The episode was almost unbelievable.

'Fact or fiction?' I said. 'It's hard to believe all the coincidences.'

'It's balanced everything out,' Dad said, 'Know what I mean? And then there was the first visit to the Yad Vashem committee. David came with to steer us through the bureaucracy, but he was so excited to be at the centre of things.'

Their experiences in Israel could have filled a book and we knew there was plenty more to come.

*

I think Martin had heard enough about 'our lot' at that point and he suddenly suggested going to see his mum. 'Shall we go for the day, while the men are settling back home?'

'Sure,' I said, 'haven't seen her for ages.'

'We can tell her about the Bar Mitzvah directly – better than by phone.'

'Let's see when Jake has a free weekend day.' We arranged to go on the following Sunday morning.

'Your writing day out the window, Dad!' Jake said.

'Well, after that, on alternate Sunday mornings, I'll be teaching a couple of private pupils,' I said.

'Were you keeping it a secret?' asked Martin.

'It only came up last night – two of Ros's friends want help with their kids' English. Seemed like useful cash.'

'If you can manage it. But – well, thanks, doll.'

As we drove over to Rochdale on Sunday through the open countryside skirting the town, I clearly remembered our first visit there. Martin's dad was alive then.

What a difference from the first visit to my parents. The Taylors lived in a solid, grey stone house, set in the fields of their smallholding. Martin's dad was manager at the local mill but, at home, they kept chickens in the yard, a few sheep grazed on the hill and they grew vegetables for the local market.

They were so open, not exactly warm or effusive but they made me feel welcome immediately. They had a roaring fire and had made egg mayonnaise followed by vegetarian pasta for supper.

'Hope you like our home-growns, Nicola, and our eggs, of course,' he said, winking.

'Wonderful – but please call me Nicki.'

'But we've only just met, love,' he laughed.

We chatted easily; they asked me about my degree and what I wanted to do next. It was obvious they were proud of Martin and totally non-judgemental of anything he did or, clearly, of anyone he brought home. It must have been great, not being constantly scrutinised for what he did and with whom, as I had been. His mum seemed the kind of person I could turn to and it was a lovely evening.

Here we were again, so many years later. As we parked the car, Martin pointed to his mum.

'She's in the front garden as usual, pretending she's gardening when she's really looking out for us.'

'Hi, Grandma, what are you digging up for tea?' asked Jake, giving her one of his bear hugs.

'Hey there young man, y'nearly knocked yer old gran over! You've grown so big. Just look at you!' Edna's eyes gleamed as she held him away from her, looking him up and down, before giving him another tight hug.

We all kissed and went inside. She still lived in the house Martin had been brought up in. It was too big for her and in need of repair, but we couldn't persuade her to move, and we would have missed having such a place to visit. When we stayed over, it was like being on holiday, as we walked for miles behind the house. Over time, the village where they lived had grown, with many new houses occupied by people commuting to Manchester on the new ring-road system.

Jake told her about his Bar Mitzvah plans and cajoled her into agreeing to come to Israel with us. We had always tried to make her feel part of Jake's life and I was adamant that Jake should grow up valuing both families, Jewish and non-Jewish – I'd have hated Martin to feel that his upbringing didn't count. My parents had nothing in common with Martin's when they met, but they were respectful towards them and loved where they lived.

The four of them only met after many months of acrimonious debate over our deciding to marry. I don't know how we got through all that. I wouldn't have blamed Martin if he had called it all off, but we just couldn't be apart. We both visualised having a family and he felt happier once he realised that any children we had would be automatically Jewish, because I was.

In the end, he still agreed to convert, so that we'd keep a Jewish home. He couldn't face the rigours of orthodoxy, so we joined the reform shul. The reform conversion still meant he had to go through a circumcision, poor thing. I felt guilty; our falling in love had demanded so much of him.

All that was fine, on paper. In reality, Martin couldn't handle the gatherings around which Jewish life revolves. He would have been happy living a quiet life with me and hated the loudness of Jewish functions, even though it was well meant. When his father died, he told me how glad he was to be able to mourn in private without having to suffer what he called 'the indignity' of a shivah, which he thought intrusive.

Edna Taylor's voice brought me back to the present: 'You know what? I've only flown once, to Jersey.'

'No worries, we'll travel together anyway,' replied Martin, 'and it will be an intimate do, with a family lunch party. And sightseeing, too.'

'Well, I'd love to come – after all the effort my Martin has put into his Jewish life. It'll be great.' She put her arm round Martin, proudly. Turning to me, she added, 'And I'll see your David's children for the first time.' She had 'lost' Martin in a way, to our way of life, but accepted his choices with Lancashire stoicism.

'Great, Gran,' said Jake, grinning.

With that, we ate together and left for home, feeling more contented than we had for ages.

Two weeks later, a parcel arrived which contained the purple flower, looking lovely in its framed casing. I found a picture hook and hung it, temporarily.

'Love it,' said Martin. 'Brilliant idea. Now we have her flower, how can we make use of your grandma's story?'

'Dunno... Must be a way.'

'You know, my mum would love to read all her stuff – well, Freidl's *and* Ernie's. They're so far removed from her life but they're about Jake: his roots. And suffragettes acted for all women. Mum used to tell me some of what it was like for the women who worked in the mills. Talk about women's rights!'

'I want to call her about the flower, so she can tell me herself.' And she did.

'Women went back to the mills within days after childbirth – they had to turn up for work,' Edna said. 'So the bosses made a room with little holes in the walls. Women had to poke their boobs through the holes for their baby – well, they hoped it was their baby. They fed them that way, while someone else held them on the *other* side of the wall.'

'Imagine…' I whispered.

'My aunt told me about it, when I was feeding Martin. The alternative was a wet-nurse. That was quite common – costly, though. The mill owner wanted to keep the babies healthy – only don't get the idea they cared about them. Healthy babies meant the women at work. And if mums were breast-feeding, they wouldn't get pregnant again. So they thought.'

'I know.'

'Not dependable,' Edna continued.

'Mm. Anyway, we'll send you a photo of the flower and these two life stories to read, soon – one from my late grandma and the other is Ernie's.'

'Your uncle?'

'Yes. Well… he's actually Dad's cousin. They're the only members of their family to survive.'

'The Nazis, you mean?'

'Yes.'

'I like Ernie,' she went on, 'took to him as soon as I met him. So they were both refugees, then?'

'Yes. Ernie was eleven when he arrived, Dad was a bit older. But you'll read about it.'

'I'd love to,' Edna said.

'And I can't stop thinking of babies fed through holes. But I must go for now.'

'OK. Bye, love.'

'Bye, Edna.' I liked that woman. Everything seemed to be sorting out.

THIRTEEN

A few days later, when we got together again, Ernie and Dad were still like little kids, bubbling with everything from their trip. Malachi was 'gorgeous', Hannah and David were 'wonderful', the meeting with Blume and the group in Haifa was 'indescribable, surreal'.

We crowded round, as they showed us the laminated photograph of Ernie's parents' wedding, all trying to see at once. Ernie had inherited his father's straight nose, his mother's thick hair and broad smile. For her wedding, his mother wore a simple but elegant outfit – not a wedding dress, exactly, but a bias-cut, calf-length dress with a soft, floaty jacket and a side-tilted hat. There was a flower on her handbag, which probably matched the one on her hat.

'She had style, Ernie. That must be where you get your creativity from,' I said.

Dad pointed out the other couple on the wedding photo, who were holding a little boy, wearing a sailor suit that was far too big for him. That was him, my dad, in his parents' arms.

'The moment I saw the photo, I grabbed it – suddenly realised that little boy was me!' Dad shouted. The bridal couple were a handsome pair.

'It's certainly precious,' I said, moved by the significance of that tiny piece of card.

'And Aaron Dreher's were the first photos of *Kristallnacht* to hit the newspapers – so he was promptly arrested and ended up in Auschwitz.'

We gasped.

'He died there, sadly,' said Ernie, 'but of course, his son Caspar survived and salvaged a box of photographs which Aaron had hidden. Most of the group survived the camps; their experiences are way different than ours and Blume Lanzig does really important work there. She's a lovely person,' he said, blushing. I'd never seen him blush before.

What were the odds of meeting the one person who had the only remaining photo of their parents? The trip had filled so many gaps for the two cousins; they said they felt whole again.

'We'll hear the rest another time, OK, Dad?' I asked pointedly. I was exhausted. They went home for an early night, which allowed us one, too. In bed, Martin rolled over and stroked me. I was too tired.

'What a shame,' he said, 'you feel so warm and cuddly. Maybe tomorrow, OK?'

'OK. Night,' I mumbled. I was just nodding off when my stomach lurched. He'd said I felt 'cuddly'.

I felt groggy in the morning. I'd lain awake for ages and slept fitfully. School went smoothly enough, so I went shopping afterwards, having very little marking to do that evening. As I picked up some Gouda from the fresh cheese shelf, the smell hit me and I felt sick – really odd. I bought a few more things but felt too queasy to buy everything. I sat in the car with the window open for a few minutes before setting off home.

Next day, I called for another doctor's appointment which was for a few days' time. Maybe it was that dizzy, labyrinth virus after all. And my blood pressure had gone up a bit.

'So what's wrong?' he asked.

'I can't explain, really. I keep going woozy – sort of – not quite dizzy but not quite here, kind of floating.'

'Hm. Interesting description. Could be tension – it's not your blood pressure doing that, anyway. Let's run a couple of blood tests. Maybe you're anaemic – how are your periods?'

'Quite light, actually – and a bit irregular,' I replied. 'Suppose it's my age – I *am* nearly forty.'

'You're a bit young, but women vary. We'll see.'

With that, it hit me. *Late period, the last one or two very light, the 'cuddliness', the nausea. I must be crazy!* So I wasn't surprised when the doctor suggested a pregnancy test – but by then, I knew the result would be positive, even after all these years.

Could I be pregnant? Oh my God. Grandma Freidl was right when she said you can't plan your life – and things were just back on track… I went back to the doctor's room.

'It is positive. But you're not thrilled,' he observed, handing me a box of tissues.

I snuffled into one. 'Ten years ago we'd have been thrilled, but we thought we'd never have any more children. That's why I never thought – I mean, Jake's nearly a teenager! A baby would be so – difficult. Impossible, in fact. And we couldn't afford it – Martin's just cut his salary. Why now?'

The doctor sat there, patiently waiting for me to finish.

'When you say "impossible", what do you mean? Can you go through with it?'

'What – oh! I know what you're asking,' I said. 'Oh, God. Not that. But… I need to talk to my husband.'

'Of course, but you'll need to think fairly quickly, if you see what I mean.'

I couldn't believe the doctor and I were talking-about-but-not-mentioning abortion, yet I'd once been so desperate to have more children. I left the surgery in a daze. When I reached the car, I really cried. So life *was* too good to be true. I knew it. The hands-free rang.

'Hi, doll, just to tell you I've had a brainwave. I'm so excited – I've thought of a play!'

How could I wreck Martin's new life plan? 'Great,' I muttered.

'Are you OK? You don't sound it, were the kids awful?'

'Yeah, a bit... I'm nearly home. I went shopping straight from school. I need a drink. See you.'

Back home, I barged into his study, breaking his 'knock first' rule. I had other things on my mind.

'It's not fair,' I whined.

'How the...? Oh, I know *how*,' he said, grinning. 'But I thought we couldn't... Wow! Fantastic.'

Martin never ceased to surprise me – I never dreamt he'd react like that. So I didn't know him, after all.

'Fantastic? Our lives are getting sorted, you've taken a drop in salary, I took extra pupils, our fresh start's ruined!'

'But it's wonderful, a new life so soon after losing your mum.' I hadn't thought of that. He leant over, lifted my face in his hands and licked my tears.

'Oh, Nicki, why worry about what you can't help? I can be a part-time house-husband – twenty-first century man or what?' He had an answer for everything, my Martin.

'There is a way out...' I said.

'Of what? Oh no. You wouldn't, after all the... we couldn't – you know –'

'Abort it? We could.'

'No way. You don't mean it. You're just shocked. I couldn't handle that, morally or physically.'

'What's physical for you? It's not your body!'

'OK, OK, but I'd have to witness it. I don't really think you could face it either, Nicki. We'll manage somehow. Hold on. The baby will be due before the Bar Mitzvah, so those plans will change.'

'The least of our worries.'

'Listen, let's go down and have a quiet drink – not alcohol – and chill for a while. Don't let's mention it to Jake yet.'

'Course not.' I felt I was living in a movie, a story happening to someone else, like when I first heard about Mum's death.

Another nightmare. Martin brought us both a cup of tea; we sat on the sofa drinking it, holding hands like teenage lovers. I leant on his shoulder and closed my eyes. Jake burst in.

'Ah, how cute is that?' he shouted. 'Love birds!' So we couldn't talk properly until we were in bed.

'Listen,' Martin whispered, 'I'll come to the doctor's with you and we'll talk everything through.'

'Everything except abortion?'

'You agree, don't you? You couldn't do that either, could you?'

'Suppose not.'

'Could that be why you felt cuddly, Nicki? Already?'

'Could be – but it must be very early on.'

'Maybe passionate sex makes us more fertile?'

'Ha, jolly ha.' I turned over. Away from him.

The moment I woke up next morning, I bolted for the bathroom to throw up. I've often wondered whether morning sickness is as much shock as a physiological reaction to pregnancy. But that was that. Now I knew with every muscle in my retching and wretched body that there'd be no abortion. I called in sick to school and made an appointment at the doctor's for the evening.

We went together, as planned. Jake was at football practice. Since the last time we did this, it had become a different world, with a technological approach to everything.

'Well, what are you here to discuss?' asked the doctor.

'My pregnancy,' I said.

'And you, Martin?'

'A pregnancy, we're agreed.'

'OK. Can I just examine you briefly, then, Nicki?'

I went behind the screen and strangely, felt quite excited. He looked puzzled – I always watch the face of any doctor who examines me, searching for signs of potential bad news. His puzzled look gave way to a smile.

'Get up, everything's fine,' he said.

Back with Martin, he leant back on his chair, folded his arms in a self-satisfied way, saying, 'Well, that's a relief. According to my examination, I think this pregnancy is more advanced than we'd thought. The light periods were probably when Nicki was already pregnant.'

'So an abortion would have been impossible?' I asked.

'Ill-advised, certainly,' he replied.

Martin and I looked at each other, realising I must have conceived before he went away, not after his homecoming. Even when Mum was ill, our sex life had been as important as ever.

'Having said that, you need a scan, soon, to check everything out.'

'Why so soon?' Martin asked.

'Because Nicki is considered at risk, at her age.'

'Meaning I'm old?' I asked, smiling – I knew that was the case, anyway.

'Well, on the old side of normal, yes,' he said, grinning as he recalled our conversation about my blood pressure.

'Meaning?' Martin asked.

'It means we offer your wife amniocentesis, to check for major abnormalities in the foetus. At her age, there's an increased risk of certain abnormalities.'

'I knew that, but doesn't the test give us bigger quandaries?' I asked.

'It gives you information. It's not that people always consider aborting a child with problems, but it can help to be prepared for any eventuality. Better than a shock at the actual birth,' he explained, 'and doctors can treat some things *in utero*, nowadays.'

'Mm. When would I have the amniocentesis?' I asked.

'Between the fifteenth and twentieth week. That's why I'd like you to have a scan soon, to decide when we time that in. If you want amniocentesis, that is. It's up to you – both.'

'Aha.' Martin was obviously weighing it all up. 'What are the risks involved – in amniocentesis itself, I mean?'

'You know, the best way to find out is to look on the internet,' Dr Richards replied. 'Whatever I tell you, you'll do that anyway, although it doesn't help you make decisions.'

'That's the problem,' I said, nodding. Martin took my hand, reassuringly.

'In the meantime, you need a midwife, an antenatal clinic and a maternity hospital. You book your scan and I'll write the referral letter, now. I'll see you again soon. And congratulations!'

At home, the internet went on and all the conflicting arguments about amniocentesis flashed before us. We were both reading it at the same time, fighting over the computer, when Martin pointed out that we could have a certain prediction of the baby's sex with an amnio.

'How things have changed, since Jake was born,' I said.

'Yeah – and it's meant to be certain, this way, the gender thing. It's from the DNA,' he added. 'We wouldn't want to know, would we?'

'Of course we would,' I said. 'It'd be great to know, to organise things – the nursery, to know whether there would be a Brit – all that.'

'But why take away the mystery? It's not as exciting. Let's leave it to… fate… or whatever.'

'We're beyond that kind of stuff, with so many tests. Nothing's left to chance nowadays.'

'Well, I don't want to know.' Martin the decision-maker.

'*You* don't. And I do.' This was getting stupid.

I suggested we make supper and sleep on it. I'd only just got used to the idea of pregnancy itself, without all this clinical stuff thrown at me. I wished tests hadn't been invented… but then we would never have had Jake. Martin would soon come round.

We wouldn't tell anyone about the pregnancy until after the scan. The midwife said everything looked fine, so they'd send me an appointment for the amnio. I was about twelve weeks on already, she told me.

I went into Martin's study before we went to tell Jake and he hugged me, whispering, 'They are very curvy already, you know,' stroking my breasts.

'They always have been!' I knew that my bra was already tight. 'Let's go and tell Jake.' But we suddenly thought better of it and decided to wait a bit longer.

Life went on as normal for a while and I coped with the nausea, so I didn't need any more time off school. So much had affected us both recently, but we adapted well to our new routine. Martin's writing was going well and he'd found a writing circle to go to: the criticisms of his work were painful but helpful.

He and Jake were enjoying their trips to synagogue together. They had time for a good chat there and back, people were welcoming to Martin and he'd made new friends among the Bar Mitzvah boys' dads. Jake was proud as Punch to have his dad with him every week and I'd taken over the lift to midweek Bar Mitzvah lessons. Ernie was to take him the following week, on the day of the amniocentesis. Our garden grew a bit rosier.

FOURTEEN

We decided to share the baby news with Jake. He was over the moon, asking immediately whether it was a boy or girl. How ironic. We both fell silent.

'We don't know, yet,' said Martin. Then we told Dad, Ernie and Edna. Only Ernie sounded a bit hesitant, knowing so much about our problems. We called David the next morning; whilst he was thrilled, he realised it might prevent the Bar Mitzvah from being in Israel.

'Mind you, things are not too good on the Northern border, so planning would be difficult for you, at the moment.'

'What d'you mean?'

'There are skirmishes and I've been called up to the reserves.'

'Yuk,' I said. 'How awful.'

After the call, Martin said, 'Let's just concentrate on us for now, the amnio and us.' He could always compartmentalise things, focus on what mattered. He always had. Like when we were planning our wedding, sixteen years ago. At that time, there were so many 'ifs and buts', about food, flowers and so on, but Martin kept saying, 'We have each other and we've overcome the biggest hurdle of our lives – my conversion – so why worry?'

He enjoyed his studies for conversion and learnt to read Hebrew quite quickly; Dad and David helped him, in between lessons. He liked languages anyway and was determined to be able to say his bridegroom's piece easily on the day. And he did concentrate on us, looking to the future, not just the day.

'The wedding day is nothing to do with the rest of our lives,' was his favourite comment. True, to an extent, but I couldn't take my mind off the fact that this was his first foray into a Jewish life. I did want it this way, but I was actually anxious for him.

At the wedding itself, Mum, Dad and Grandma Freidl pulled out the stops, and David did his best to boost Martin's confidence. He was best man, with one of Martin's college friends, and that helped them through the minutiae of the ceremony. Those two, with Ernie, and Ros's future husband, held the *Chuppah* over us, while Ros and my friend Lizzie were matrons of honour. As I looked at Martin, framed by the canopy, I actually saw tears in his eyes.

He whispered, 'Happy, doll? I'm your Jewish husband now,' and he winked.

'So happy, but dizzy,' I whispered back, after walking round him seven times; I was sure I'd gone round more than that.

'Sorry, I meant to count for you – I think it's been eight! One extra for luck?' Martin was beaming.

Later, I asked him how he had coped with being the centre of that Jewish crowd. He told me that the canopy, with friends all round us, became a cocoon, so he felt it was just me and him together; the people outside were in the distance. He did manage to capture the moment, my Martin – that was the artistic writer in him.

My daydream ended suddenly, when Martin tapped me on the shoulder and asked again when the amnio was to be.

'In two weeks.'

'And...?'

'I still want to know.'

'How do we work this one out?' Martin said.

'No idea – you're just adding tension to everything.'

'I am? Why me?'

'I do all the puking, the getting huge, all that, and you want to take away the one fun thing – finding out the sex. I need something to excite me.'

'I'm not doing it to upset you; I just want to be kept in the dark. *I* find it exciting *not* knowing. We'll have to decide before you go. Think about it.'

'It's up to you to do the thinking.' I was stunned by Martin's intransigence.

Next day I called Ros. I hadn't told her the news, the friend who had shared almost all my life. She sounded shocked – an honest response, in the circumstances.

'Wow – are you pleased? Starting over, what with everything?'

'I've got used to it actually,' I said, lying.

'How far on are you?'

'About twelve weeks. I'm having an amnio in two weeks – it's a whole new, technical world out there.'

'You don't sound overjoyed.'

'We'll have to sort out the money side, after Martin took a cut. But he's thrilled, so we'll get there.' It must have been hard for her to hear this, having failed to have children herself.

The doorbell rang and I hung up and greeted my father.

'Hello, Dad. Nice surprise.'

'I want to see my pregnant daughter. But you look a little pale.' He kissed me, frowning. All my life, my parents had commented on my lack of colour. I was just naturally fair-skinned. Sometimes I had what Mum called 'rosy cheeks' but rarely. I'd have been happy with my colouring but this constant reference to pallor became a family 'thing'. I think Mum and Dad said it when they saw tension in my face.

'I'm fine, Dad, come and sit in the kitchen while I make dinner.' He put a paper bag on the table – a bundle of a few of Mum's books; I pulled one out of the bag. 'Gluckel!' I said. It was *The Memoirs of Gluckel of Hameln*, written in the late seventeenth century. On the flyleaf was a handwritten note:

Dearest Nicki, You know this was Grandma Freidl's favourite book. It became my favourite and now it's yours. If ever you think women are over-worked, read this diary again. With love from Mum.

How wonderful. Dad stood up to leave. I remembered Grandma Freidl reading that book when Martin came on his first visit to the family. She was in the sun lounge at Mum and Dad's, peered menacingly over her reading glasses at Martin, looked him up and down and said, 'So – you want to marry our Nicola? Brave man!' She held out her hand to shake his, then turned to me and winked. 'Hm. I see why you fancied him!'

'Tell me about that book over supper,' Martin said, as he took the hand proffered to him, helped her out of her chair and guided her into the dining room. She knew how to charm him, my sweet, terrifying Grandma Freidl.

She told him a bit about Gluckel's diary and helped break the ice that evening so long ago, deflecting the tension round the table, as Mum and Dad tried to chat easily with Martin but failed hopelessly. They had no point of reference; they couldn't ask what the name 'Taylor' used to be, who his relations were, which shul he attended, so they homed in on his theatrical aspirations. They made his ambitions seem like wanting to land on another planet.

'So – you want to work in *theatre*, I believe,' Dad said.

'After my degree, yes. I want to write or direct; acting isn't my thing,' Martin replied.

'He's expected to get a first in his degree, you know, Dad,' I added.

'Look, you're a bright boy, Martin, so how is it you want to marry Nicki and –'

'Thanks, Mum!'

'I mean, and the Judaism part. It's such a hard, uphill climb.'

'I want to marry her because I love her and we just can't be apart,' Martin replied in a way I had never heard before. And under duress. He continued, 'Even bright people do just fall in love. Nicki's fascinating, we talk and talk, never run out of things to say – in fact, we even argue well!'

'What about you, Nicki?'

'I know it's complicated. I love Martin and you, too. You know that. But he'll give up a lot to convert, so that we can be one family – not forgetting his, of course.'

Martin looked at me and winked. I carried on.

'Any children will be Jewish because of me, so that's OK. I admire him – and if he converts at the reform shul, so be it. That's *my* compromise. I hope you'll both accept it.' I sighed after this, the most important pronouncement of my life.

Mum replied: 'It's been a struggle for us, from when you first told us about Martin, but it's obvious you're in love and that you make each other happy, so we'll do what we can.'

'And we'll make merry at the wedding,' Dad said, looking strained, for all that.

'Thanks, Dad – thanks, Mum. Grandma Freidl, what about you?'

'I just watch from the sidelines, Nicola, but I'm there for you. And if I were younger, I'd fancy Martin myself. Come and give me a kiss, both of you.' We did, and kissed Mum and Dad too.

'By the way Martin, I love the way you speak,' Grandma Freidl said, tweaking the conversation cleverly, as usual. 'It must be good for stage work.'

'In fact, it isn't. I work hard to get rid of it – I probably won't be accepted in London with a Rochdale accent, you know.'

'That's crazy!' Dad chipped in. 'This family has so many accents, it could open a training school. We've got a German accent, a Romanian one, Russian / Mancunian, and a Russian / Mancunian / Yiddish one. You want it, we've got it here!'

'That's as may be,' said Martin,' but there's a North–South prejudice. Northern equals "working class, ill-bred", all that.

Look at *Coronation Street*. That's about as much as you get on TV about Northerners. The characters are OK but you never see any *cultured* Northerners, do you?'

'And we think anti-Semitism is a prejudice. There's a whole other world out there isn't there, Martin?' Mum said, kindly. 'I thought society was becoming less class conscious.' At least the conversation had become interesting and less tense. Things did change and of course, now, in the twenty-first century, regional accents have become the 'in' thing on stage and on TV. That was all so long ago.

The amniocentesis came and went. It wasn't pleasant seeing a large needle going into my slightly swollen abdomen but a curtain prevented my seeing too much. The gynaecologist asked us whether we wanted to know the sex of the baby. I didn't answer. Martin said no.

'Mrs Taylor?'

'We think alike.' I could tell the doctor knew I was lying. 'We don't want to know.' Until that moment, I had thought Martin would change his mind. I should have realised after all our time together that wishful thinking changes nothing.

The results of the test would come by post in about a week, he told us. He described in detail the chances of abnormalities – but we couldn't consider abortion, anyway.

While we waited for the results, our difference of opinion preyed on my mind. I felt better physically, however, so I managed to teach. My class was a good one and we enjoyed the cash from my fortnightly one-to-one teaching. Our routine returned and Martin wrote for two days a week, as planned.

Ernie phoned one evening to ask us round with Jake, for an early supper.

'I've got some news,' he said. We needed some good news and he greeted us with two bits – as well as a delicious home-made quiche and salad. The first was about Jake's school, the second about the Lanzig issue.

The school had sent him a proper invitation to speak to two groups of pupils; he was pleased but nervous. He said it would be quite different, sharing his traumas with young strangers, but we all encouraged him. He and the teacher had decided to hold a pre-planned interview, based on his written story. A bit like on a TV chat show.

'Sounds great, Ernie,' I said.

'And what's your news about Herr Lanzig?' Martin asked.

Blume had told him that the survivors' group had some new members. One of them had helped on a farm – the Lanzig farm – for just a month, which saved his life.

'Did you ever meet him?' I asked Ernie.

'No. It was before I arrived. And they pretended he was a farm hand, since he was blond and old enough. Still a big risk, having him there. Blume told me that boy didn't have the good luck to get on a Kindertransport. He went home for a while, until the whole family were deported. He was the only one to make it.'

'Blume must be so thrilled, finding the people her father had saved,' I commented.

'She is but it's so sad to know the rest of the story,' Ernie said.

This man's recollections meant there were three eye-witnesses. This mounting evidence of Herr Lanzig's courage would certainly qualify him for a plaque in that special garden.

'I feel I've achieved a life's work in a few weeks,' said Ernie. 'I'm so lucky.'

Luck is relative, I thought.

'Oh and I've passed the police check to say I am a safe person to talk to school pupils,' he laughed.

'Well cool!' whooped Jake. 'Can't wait.'

Martin suddenly piped up, 'Now that Ernie's story will go into the annals, how does everyone think we can we best use Freidl and Malkah's story?'

'Use it for a story – or a novella,' Ernie suggested.

'I had thought... maybe a play?' replied Martin. '"A Manchester Tale"...'

'Yuk, Dad,' Jake said.

'Well, you think of something better, then!'

Martin seemed excited by the idea, but then, Jake piped up with a classic: 'Hey – if this baby's a girl, it can be a kind of saga of the females of one family. "Four Women and a Flower"?' He laughed.

'Not keen – but we won't know anyway till the baby's born,' Martin said, no longer smiling. How suddenly his good features could change: his dimples became wrinkles, his high forehead a deep frown. Jake went on, like a dog with a bone.

'I don't get it. Steve's mum knew what she was having, you can find out everything, these days... *and* you don't even have to... have a wife... or even... I mean... babies can just be made in test tubes!'

'So...?'

'So, what about Four Women and...?'

'Don't like it – and anyway, it plagiarises that film. Hey – do I need permission to use Freidl's story?' Martin asked, neatly diverting the conversation. I suggested he asked Dad.

'I'll call him now.' Dad was thrilled and said it was fine. The evening had been such a tonic, till Jake started his baby interrogation. The topic changed, though, when we had coffee, because we talked about the design of the vintage cups.

Next morning, the postman arrived just as I was leaving for work. I took my own mail, amongst which was one from the GP, asking me to 'pop in and see him' for the results. I panicked. Was this usual? There must be something wrong. The letter said I could gatecrash his surgery. I did that without telling anyone, after school.

'What's wrong?' I asked, as I went into the surgery.

'Nothing. The baby looks perfect, thankfully.'

'Phew!' My relief went counter to the early reactions to being pregnant.

'I wanted to see you because the hospital doctor asked me to. He said you and Martin didn't seem to agree about knowing the sex of the baby.'

'Hm...' My tears started. I reached over for the familiar tissue box.

'What's the problem?'

'I want to know and he doesn't.'

'So can't I just tell you?'

'I'd be betraying him.'

'Really? That must be tough, considering that the baby will soon be kicking inside you. And she's well and truly there,' he said, looking me straight in the eye.

'*She!* You shouldn't have said that, Doctor.'

'It was for the good of my patient. You are my patient, Martin is not. I've known you so long, Nicki – and not knowing was churning you up. You can keep it a secret, can't you?'

'I'll have to. How lovely, though, a daughter...' I dared to dream for a second.

'Take care of yourself now. See you in three months. Now I leave it to the midwives.'

I left the surgery, happy but anxious, and received a text from David: 'CALMER NOW – CALL ME 2 MORROW?'

When I got home, Martin was waiting on the porch for me. Of course! I hadn't told him I'd be late.

'Really sorry, love. I took the doctor's letter with me to work and he fitted me in this afternoon.'

'But why didn't you – ?' Martin looked worried.

'Look: the amnio result was fine. I won't be seeing him for a while – and I think I felt it move!' I looked at Martin, willing him to relent on The Issue.

'Great – what a relief.' He hugged me and stroked my tummy with no other comment. I'd have to go on with the subterfuge.

I called David back the next day. We talked about silly things, avoiding his army training. We talked about the children and I said how much they'd all enjoy meeting this baby in six months' time.

David said, in Ivrit, '*Hatinoket?*'

I gasped. 'How did you guess?'

'I didn't. It was a question,' David said.

'Oh God, I can't believe what I've done. Don't say a word to *anyone*! Martin didn't want to know the sex but I found out. I shouldn't have told you – or anyone. Please, please, don't let this get out.'

'You didn't actually tell me. Why the big deal?'

'We totally disagree on it,' I said.

'Well, it's been said. That always happens here, cos words for "baby girl" and "baby boy" are different. But I don't know why I said it in Ivrit.'

'I did wonder. But d'you always know in advance, there?'

'Yeah – and it helps the family to plan for a Brit or not.' I was panicking. 'Nicki? You OK?'

'No. And please forget about this.'

'OK, I promise.'

'I must go, David, take care. Have you been in the shelters at all?' I asked, changing the subject.

'Only for a practice and it's not good for the soul, taking three little ones into a shelter, believe me.'

'I bet. Listen, I'm off. Lots of love.'

'Love to all.'

I felt I was guilty of betrayal and dishonesty. I couldn't decide which was worse: Martin preventing me from knowing something I deserved to know, or my reneging on an agreement. I was as bad as him.

I felt so low and Jake kept going on about it – he sensed we differed seriously. But Martin, happy in oblivion, was doing well with his writing, having definitely decided to tackle a play about suffragettes. He would include snapshots of some real, famous suffragettes and was fleshing out the characters of Great-Uncle Isaac and Grandpa Jacob. The contrast between Jacob's devout Jewish life and the revolutionary women's movement could be interesting, but it still needed a good, dramatic twist from somewhere.

One evening I was suddenly overcome with nausea. It didn't happen often but when it did, it knocked me for six. The phone rang as I ran to the cloakroom.

'It's David,' Martin shouted, recognising the number on the receiver.

'Can you answer it?' I asked weakly, doubled over.

As I sat on the toilet with my head in my hands, I heard Martin shouting.

'What did you say, Hannah? I understood that word! Can you get David for me?' After a short but definite silence, he said, 'I see. Sorry, I must go.' The conversation ended abruptly, and Martin stamped his way across the wooden hall floor. I looked at him and was scared.

'Oh no! There's going to be another war isn't there?' I cried. 'David said there'd been skirmishes!' I ran to puke some more.

I just about heard Martin saying, 'It *is* war but not the kind you mean.'

'What? You look ghastly! What is it? Are his children sleeping in air-raid shelters?'

'It's not that. How did they find out, Nicki – Hannah and David? How did YOU find out? What happened to trust, Nicki? How could you?' I had never seen him so angry. Then it dawned on me what he meant.

'It just came out,' I whimpered, crying from being sick and from fear of the row to come.

'You've betrayed me!' Martin shouted. 'You knew it mattered, so you tell your precious David... of course, who else?'

'You're right to be angry, but it wasn't on purpose, truly. I'm sorry! Maybe I should have...'

Jake barged in. 'What's going on? Why are you two shouting? Mum, you're crying *again*. For goodness sake, stop it!' He was almost crying himself. I hugged him.

'We're having a row, that's all, Jake.'

'I'm going a walk,' Martin said, leaving without a coat – and it was unseasonably cold. He'd be back.

'I just don't get it,' Jake cried. 'Is it about the sex of the baby? Why is that such a deal for Dad?' he asked.

'I can't answer that – ask him yourself. But can you get yourself something to eat and I'll make a snack when Dad gets back.'

Martin didn't come straight back. Over half an hour later, my mobile rang. He asked me to meet him at The Bistro for a cup of tea. I didn't want to leave Jake while he was upset.

'Well he's a big boy, he'll have to be upset for a bit longer.'

'I'll see if he'll go to Dad's for a while. I'll drop him off en route.'

'Up to you. You do baby him, you know,' Martin said.

'Oh, something else I do wrong?'

'See you in half an hour,' he said. I told Jake that we needed to talk. I caught Ernie in and dropped Jake off there. They both looked bewildered.

I sat down gingerly, facing Martin in a romantic red leather booth in the coffee shop, feeling anything but romantic.

'I can't deal with this,' he began. 'I can't go on shouting at you, but I can't accept what you did. I don't know where your priorities lie – with me, or with the family.'

'Give me a word in, I –'

'I don't understand you any more. Just imagine, hearing it from Hannah and David?'

'Awful, awful. I had a shock too, when the doctor let it out.'

'I'm going to sue *him*,' Martin said, menacingly.

'Why? I'm his patient. He was worried about me.'

'But he was mixing it. And you didn't keep our promise.'

'It was impossible to keep – totally unreasonable.'

'But you promised.'

'I was under duress.'

'You see. It's an impasse. So I'm moving out to Mum's during the working week, for a month or so… Clearing my head. Then we'll see.'

'We'll see – we'll see what? You're *leaving* me?'

'No… I'll come back at weekends, take Jake to synagogue and write in the study.'

'You've got it all worked out! Have you had this escape route all lined up, Martin, hey? Going back to Mummy? What does she say about it? Good God! I should be the one to leave!'

'Mum's angry, actually. She said she loves you and Jake so much. She said she'd call you.'

'You're totally out of order, Martin. Absolutely. And where do you think you are going to sleep at weekends? You can't have everything you want, orgasms one day, Mummy's apron strings the next.'

'So would it be OK to sleep at Ernie's at weekends?'

'Ask him. I wouldn't think he'd want to be involved. But hang on. What the hell is all this about?'

'You betrayed me. You know –'

'Call that a betrayal? It was a slip. A real betrayal's far more sinister and you bloody well know it. And you're leaving me in a huff? Grow up, Martin.'

'I told you. I'm not leaving you. I just need space.'

'You read too much psychobabble in mags in the office or something. Space, as you call it, isn't available right now. There's been no space round here for weeks, since Mum died in fact.'

'I meant…'

'Hang on. *I* meant, you aren't looking for space, you're running away, Martin.'

'No, I'm trying to sort out my head.'

'Where will you go?'

'Weekdays at my mum's and weekends at Ros and Howard's.'

'How sweet is that, hey? OK, well you know what? When you come back, with a lovely, clear head, you may well find your son and your wife at odds with you. You'll have a damn hard time winning them back. Remember that.'

'I didn't expect that reaction.'

'What the hell did you expect? Oh don't answer that. My God, I feel I'm in a TV soap or something.'

Martin went quiet. After a moment and a deep sigh he said, 'I can't find another way through everything, the way I'm feeling. Basically, I can't fathom out whether you still care about me. And that's it in a nutshell. Everything's out of kilter.'

'We may all be off our heads, by Friday,' I said. I knew I was being cruel.

'But maybe you'll find you need time without *me*, at the moment.'

'I've no idea. Problem is, I don't see how I'll be able to take you back again,' I said – and I meant it.

'But we may find we love each other again by then,' Martin said. I could see that he meant that, as well.

I looked at him directly for the first time in this conversation and said, bitterly, 'What if you're having an affair or something? This won't help in that case, will it?'

'But I'm not!' he shouted.

'So go then, for goodness sake. Let's start this experiment in separation.'

Martin leant close to me and whispered, 'Will you kiss me goodbye when I go?'

'You're crazy!' I said. Yet, as he came closer and kissed me lightly on my forehead, I did kiss him back. 'That makes two of us.'

'What?' Martin asked.

'Crazy people,' I replied. 'Do we need counselling?'

'Maybe,' he said. 'After the baby?'

'That's too far away. I need to know if I'm going to be a single mum,' I replied. I had never considered that till then.

'You do have a vivid imagination Nicki, it wouldn't come to that!' How was he so sure? 'But OK, let's see a counsellor. Yes.'

'When? And how much will it cost?' I asked.

'Let's try for Friday afternoons or Sundays… we'll find time.'

'And money?' I wondered where all this would end but we decided to try for an appointment with a counsellor at the place where Ros worked, on her day off.

Our coffee stayed untouched in the little booth and I drove Martin back in silence.

FIFTEEN

'I must tell Jake myself,' he said, as I turned into Ernie's drive. 'I'm the one leaving. Oh God.' He looked as though he might cry, yet he sounded so cool and calculating. What made Martin tick?

'I'm such a failure,' he mumbled, 'and I love Jake so much. I dread hurting him.'

'That's happened already. We'll tell him together and we can tell him the baby's a girl at the same time.' He didn't answer. Why did I feel sorry for him? I didn't need to help him tell Jake. In spite of everything, he suddenly seemed so vulnerable.

We picked up Jake and threw trivial comments to him along the way. We then sat round the kitchen table, for the most depressing family chat ever. Martin aged by ten years as he told Jake what was to happen; I probably did, too.

Jake rose to the occasion with unusual aplomb: 'You know, I've been in a minority at school till now, *not* having separated parents. Most of my mates go back to different homes each weekend. I've felt quite deprived!' A good actor, like his dad, but then tears began to roll silently down his pre-teen, greasy cheeks.

Mine joined his, in the last of our paper hankies. And my baby girl began to move properly, in silent protest, as if to say, 'Whatever's going on, I'm right here.'

The next morning Martin packed a small bag and left. He did kiss me goodbye.

'I still love you, you know,' I said.

'I love you too,' Martin replied, tapping my tummy. 'Look after our baby. See you Friday.'

Four days was a long time. The family were told and I called in sick to school, making an appointment to see the head the next day. I hadn't even told her about my pregnancy yet. Jake said he didn't feel like going to school, though I felt he should.

'I'll take you later. You can say you woke up with a headache. You probably did,' I said, hugging him. We arranged to see his pastoral care co-ordinator about the situation. After he'd gone, I emailed Ros to ask for any other good counsellors she could recommend. She suggested the name of someone at her place. She allayed my concerns by telling me he always worked on Fridays, when she wasn't there.

'We're the best group around and he's great,' she added. I duly phoned for an appointment with him.

In the middle of the week, soon after I arrived home, the doorbell rang. It was Edna.

'I – is Martin OK? What's wrong?' I said, shocked to see her.

'Typical Nicki, always worrying. I'm here about you, silly. Can I come in?' We kissed.

'Of course, sorry, how rude.'

She marched purposefully past me towards the kitchen, made straight for the kettle, filled it and switched it on.

'Er, d'you want to come and sit down?' I asked.

She opened the fridge for milk and made the tea. She knew instinctively where everything was: mugs, spoons, plates, biscuits. I wasn't sure whose home we were in, for a moment.

'I am doing,' she said, as she plonked herself on a chair at the kitchen table. 'Join me?'

And so we sat, looking everywhere but at each other.

'What can I do?' she started.

'Meaning?' I asked.

'To help. You and Martin. I may be giving him a bed, I wouldn't refuse him that. But I'm not taking sides. You're a great couple – too much to lose,' she said, leaning over the table and putting her hand on mine. She looked straight at me and there they were: Martin's eyes, seeing into my soul.

Jake arrived home just then and they hugged.

'Hi, Gran. Just popped in, have you?' he said, cheerily, not appearing surprised to see her.

'I was shopping in Manchester and came up for a cuppa,' Edna replied, nonchalantly. Jake took a yoghurt and went off to his room.

'So...' Edna began. 'We'd best talk quietly,' she said, gesturing towards the stairs and Jake. 'Can I help, d'you think?' She sounded desolate.

'I've no idea. I can't see how you can – and stay detached,' I volunteered. 'I mean, whatever's happened, you'd be bound to have an opinion?'

She nodded. 'I know. If I... kind of... tell you what Martin was like to bring up, would that help?'

'We met twenty years ago, married for fifteen years – I should know him, but...'

'But suddenly you don't. Is that it?'

'Partly,' I replied, afraid lest I say something offensive about her son. 'We've had some disagreements.'

'And...?'

'And then he said I'd betrayed him, but I –'

She interrupted. 'You don't have to tell me the details. Did he think you'd been disloyal?'

'What's he told you?' I asked.

'Nothing. Nothing at all. But that's my Martin. He has such a strong sense of loyalty, it's been his downfall before.'

I was relieved.

'His dad thought it was cos he was an only one. But I think

it's just how he is: loyal to a fault. Expecting the earth from people.'

I nodded and said, 'I do think being an only child has something to do with it, actually.'

'How come?'

'Because he reckons I'm too close to David.'

'Aha. Thought as much,' Edna said, wisely.

'There's more to it,' I commented.

'Of course, but he never understood siblings, even when he was little. He'd go to a friend's and come home so stroppy, if the friend's sibling was there. He wanted the friend to himself.'

'Really?' I replied.

'Yep – couldn't get it through to him. And something else.'

'Yeah?'

'Don't be offended, but he did a lot for –'

'To convert?' I knew she'd get round to that.

'I've been with him all the way. But it's somewhere in his mind. It must be.'

'I know that, but it's so long ago,' I sighed. 'I can't keep going back.'

'No, love, but in a crisis it rears up again. And I reckon losing Malkah will have got to him.' Edna could get to the nub of the issue.

'And what about me?'

'Obviously! But, since Martin converted, Malkah was more than most mothers-in-law,' Edna went on. 'She was the only Jewish mother he had, y'see.'

It was my turn to put a hand on hers. 'Did you feel rejected?'

'He still loved me,' she answered. 'That's what mattered.'

'Suppose so,' I said. 'It's all a bit much.'

'Life is that,' she muttered. 'A bit much. Sometimes.' We were both quiet for a moment. Our thoughts reached across the table.

'I think you'll be OK,' she ventured, suddenly stopping as Jake came in.

'Cheer up,' he said, 'it may never happen.'

I blushed. 'You're right, it may not. Come here.' I put out my arm for him but he wriggled away and sat down with us. Jake and Edna chatted lightly and she left soon afterwards. It did help to know a bit more about my enigmatic husband.

School, meanwhile, kept me alive. We taught around themes and, with wheels or circles for that term, the children and I could let fly. We covered the maths of a circle, we looked at latitude and longitude, and wheels took us round the world. History introduced revolutions and science was taken over by life cycles. The thematic approach let me go off at tangents but they were all instructive and fun.

People in wheelchairs came in to school, so they learnt about life on wheels. The pupils behaved very well towards the visitors and learnt a lot. Accounts of the visits filled the walls. My problem lad, Jolyon, even got to grips with circumferences and he received a star badge at assembly. Life away from home was going well.

But Friday came. Martin sent a text when he was on his way. I showered after school; I was looking quite but not too pregnant and I liked it, so far. Martin arrived at four and we hugged – a threesome hug, as Jake came home at the same time. It felt good. How odd.

Martin felt my tummy and the baby kicked, just then. 'Oh, that's so lovely,' he said. 'I remember the thrill, now – it's coming back to me. Jake, feel it – he can, can't he, Nicki?' *How could he be so jolly-jolly?*

'I've felt it lots of times, Dad. It's brill.' Jake wanted to show Martin his schoolwork and they were glad to be together. It seemed so natural. Later, Martin went to take his night things round to Ros and Howard's; better there, than at Ernie's, though he had dinner with Ernie. Jake stayed with me.

Ernie was right. What was the point of Friday night, if the family wasn't together? Once I had blessed the candles and Jake made a quick job of kiddush, we took our meal into the living room and ate it on our knees – something we never did on Fridays. It was wrong that Martin wasn't with us but he came round later and we watched TV together.

Jake looked at us, scathingly, his arms folded.

'I don't get it. I can tell you're glad to be together, so why aren't you? You're like kids. Just make it up! Hey, I sound like a parent,' he sniggered.

He didn't really find it funny and he was right. Neither of us answered. As Martin left, we kissed goodnight at the door. If it hadn't been so different it almost felt like those courting days, when he took me back home after uni. Then, the kiss was the subterfuge; Mum and Dad thought that was all we did.

This time, the subterfuge was internal. Neither of us felt passionate yet we couldn't *not* kiss goodnight. I longed for a cuddle but wouldn't show it. Martin revealed nothing.

The following Friday, I was ready when Martin arrived in time for the counsellor's. I told Dad we weren't sure about dinner, but that Jake would come. Martin sat with Jake for a while, to hear the ideas for Ernie's day at school. I looked at Martin across the table and could have fallen in love all over again, just by looking at the intensity with which he listened as Jake talked. *This love thing's so confusing.*

Yet Martin looked strained. I wasn't sorry about that – I wanted it to be hard for him, away from me. Surely he'd soon change his mind?

'Come on Nicki,' he said, suddenly, 'time for our appointment.'

'Coming. Jake, you go to Grandpa's whenever you're ready.'

'OK, see you there.'

'Are we all going?' Martin asked, looking a bit concerned.

'Depends how we feel,' I replied.

Charlotte Gringras

So we left for that appointment at the counselling centre. As a pleasant, bearded guy came into the waiting room to greet us, I hoped Martin was feeling calmer than he had on the journey here.

SIXTEEN

'You must be Mr and Mrs Taylor,' he said, holding out his hand to each of us. 'I'm John Baker. Pleased to meet you. Do come in.'

He gestured us through an open door to a tiny room, then left us for a moment to collect something from reception. We pushed two of the three chairs together and sat down. I wondered how he worked in such a claustrophobic space.

He came back in and immediately asked if we'd like the window open. He'd read my mind, then. He was about forty, sandy haired, his beard neatly trimmed. He was dressed casually, in scruffy cord trousers, a check shirt with a sweater over it, which had leather patches on the elbows. He didn't give one of those 'I can help you' smiles; I was relieved. He started by asking if he could use our first names, to which we agreed, then went through the confidentiality clauses.

'So. Who's going to begin?' he asked. We said nothing. 'OK then, I will. OK?'

We nodded in unison.

'You've cheered me up, actually,' he said. We frowned. 'You moved the chairs together. Most couples move them apart, you see.'

'Never thought of that,' Martin said.

'Nor did I,' I responded, wanting something to say.

'The fact that you moved nearer was a good thing, I think.'

'Aren't you reading too much into it?' Martin asked. 'We don't cheer up many other people.'

'Well forget about those "other people" while you're here, then. I mean, just concentrate on yourselves for now. If you can, Nicki.'

'I'll try, there are so many people involved with us, it's hard.'

'Yeah,' Martin said, nodding.

'So let's talk about you,' John continued. 'Can you each tell me why you're here, in a couple of sentences – and also, whether you're here to help save your marriage?'

We answered differently, of course, but we both said we wanted to save it.

'But Martin's left me, five days a week,' I pointed out.

'She studiously avoided telling you why, John. Because she betrayed me.'

'Lots went on before that,' I said.

'So tell me about the "before" bits. Nicki first, OK?' John said. 'Crises usually start long before people come to see me.'

So I began, not knowing how clued up he was about Jewish practice.

'Well, Martin wouldn't come home during the seven days of mourning for my mother,' I explained. 'They immediately follow the funeral.'

'And the funeral is the day of death, isn't it?' John asked. We nodded. He wanted to know how serious it was that Martin wasn't at prayers.

'It's taken for granted that a mourner's spouse would be there,' I replied.

'Hang on,' Martin said. 'She's being selective again. She didn't tell you I was in Hong Kong on business, at the time.'

'Please call me Nicki, not "she", Martin, OK?'

'Nicki's often more demanding than Judaism itself, John,' Martin went on.

'He could have come back. I think he chose not to,' I added.

John interrupted. 'What's your take on that, Martin?'

'I could not have come back. But I visited my mother-in-law every day during her last illness. I couldn't have done more when she was here but –'

'He *was* good to her,' I acknowledged, remembering Edna's words. I took a paper hankie from a box handily placed nearby. I couldn't help crying when I pictured Mum in that hospital bed, almost strangled by tubes and drips.

Martin continued. 'Look, John, one to one I'm good with people, but of all the Jewish observances I can't handle, shivah comes top of the list. Even so, the only reason I wasn't there was my business trip.'

'You could've fixed it,' I said.

'Whatever,' Martin said, rolling his eyes.

'I've been listening,' said John, 'and it seems to me that whichever culture we come from, our nearest and dearest don't always come up to scratch. Life's fraught: too many plates to spin, if you get me.' I did. 'But also, everyone is vulnerable after losing a mother, particularly daughters, if that's not too sexist.'

'Mm,' Martin mumbled, looking at me for the first time. 'Suppose so.'

'And now you're pregnant, to add to it all. Not easy,' he said, looking concerned.

'Not for either of us,' Martin said. 'But she did betray me. I couldn't handle that, so I had to get away.'

'Again,' I responded.

'Nicki, tell me more about the baby's sex. How you learnt that the baby is a girl – and how your brother found out. You mentioned it in your first statement.' After I explained how the doctor had told me, John thought for a moment.

'Hm... Even if the doctor was worried about you, he must have known it would cause trouble. Odd one, that.'

'You see. He had no right to interfere, did he, John?' Martin said.

'But he knows me well and saw I needed to know,' I said.

Martin looked angry. 'John, don't you think he overstepped the mark? It wasn't up to him.'

John took time to answer. 'Well, he is there to care for his patient in every way, so he took that literally. But I'm trying to imagine having amniocentesis. It must be scary. Maybe knowing the sex is a kind of reward, something exciting, you know?' He looked at Martin.

Martin frowned. That had made him think. John put things very tactfully; I liked his approach.

'What about letting David into the secret, Nicki? Tell John about that.'

John said nothing but raised his eyebrows and looked straight at me, willing me to answer.

'I didn't tell him on purpose.'

'Oh no?' Martin interrupted.

'No! You know that.' I explained for John. 'In Ivrit, modern Hebrew – and in lots of languages – there are two words for "baby", girl or boy. David switched to Ivrit – so it came out. And no one keeps baby gender secret over there.'

'Not five months ahead, surely?' said John, with a wry grin.

'Yes, so people can prepare to travel for the Brit – the circumcision ceremony – if they know it's a boy,' I told him. 'Say, if family lives abroad.'

'But you should have kept it secret,' Martin said.

'I didn't mean to tell him,' I insisted.

'John, she just won't admit that David is more her confidant than me. She's really in denial about that.' Martin sighed in exasperation and John read our mutual frustration.

'Hold on there, both of you. I get the picture. Just let me think a minute. You've been together for twenty years, married for fifteen. Right? Martin, Nicki's always had this twin brother, you've always been an only child. Right? So what's new?'

This veiled criticism was a new tack. We were both quiet. He turned his gaze on Martin.

'Has anything changed between Nicki and David? I mean, they don't exactly live round the corner, so how can they be a problem?'

'Well, I...' Martin didn't finish.

'She told your secret. She was excited, surely?'

Martin blushed, saying, 'She told David our secret.'

'"Nicki", not "she", please,' I said.

John went on. 'I'm sure Nicki didn't say, "Who cares about Martin, here's our secret."'

'Of course I didn't,' I said.

'So, Martin,' John continued. 'Did David give you a hard time when you two first met, over that Jewish stuff? I hope that isn't disrespectful, but issues can linger for years.'

'Don't worry. Actually David was great,' Martin admitted. 'He even helped me with my Hebrew.'

'So where's the problem?' John asked.

'Must be me.'

'What do you mean, love?' I suddenly felt a bit sorry for him and instinctively put my hand on his. Weird, that. John noticed and smiled.

'If David isn't the trouble-maker, I *must* be wrong, then,' Martin mumbled.

'It's not about rights and wrongs,' John came in, protectively. 'We're human – and you're an only child. It's hard to "get" sibling relationships, particularly twins. And it won't change. Any more than you will.'

'I see that, but Nicki has to realise...'

'I do,' I said. 'But you have to trust me again,' I said.

'Good point,' John said. 'And – can you go back home again, soon, Martin? Living apart can become a habit.' The session was winding its way to a close.

'But can you see that we don't agree on anything?' I asked John.

'No, not really. I can make observations, not judgements.

I see that you are both fairly demanding, but couples do demand a lot of each other. Perhaps you need to accept it sometimes, when the other says, "I can't do that." We all have limits.'

I nodded. Martin looked serious.

'Does that make sense?'

'It does, actually,' Martin said. 'We can't always get what we want, can we?'

'Is there any hope?' I asked John, not expecting a good answer.

'I think so, if you want it. You are really interesting people with high aspirations. I enjoyed meeting you, whatever happens. If you want another appointment, I look forward to it.'

We shook his hand and left, undecided about seeing him again.

Over a coffee, put off from earlier, Martin said, 'He was good – no psychobabble, actually.' He looked sheepish.

I agreed, adding, 'Will it help?'

'Well, he was really sound... made me think.' We both fell silent, exhausted. We called Dad to say we'd arrive in time for dessert, as we tried to let it all settle.

Martin slept at Ros and Howard's and collected Jake to go to shul in the morning; I decided to go with them, in a togetherness move. In the evening, Martin went back to his mum's. He promised to read the first draft of his play to me soon. We thought of meeting up for a 'date' one evening to talk about the play and leave our marriage crisis out of it.

Lots of people told us that Rabbi Lever, at Dad's synagogue, might also help. I suggested seeing him instead of going back to John. Although he wasn't 'our' rabbi (there was a new minister just appointed at the reform), he knew us and was experienced. Surprisingly, Martin agreed and we made an appointment for the following week. The rabbi had an original approach: he asked each of us to send him, in advance, a brief résumé of why we wanted to see him. Seemed a good idea, so we wrote and sent them. No doubt they would differ quite a lot.

SEVENTEEN

In the midst of all our angst, Ernie's visit to Jake's school came round, but it wasn't bad to have a new talking point. I had permission to go along with Ernie, even though I had wondered how Jake would feel about that. In fact, it worked out fine, as I sat at the back quietly the whole time. It took my mind off other things.

The teacher in charge ran the morning session like a TV chat show. She interviewed Ernie, bringing out his story bit by bit. He described how it had all begun, trying hard not to upset the youngsters. He showed photos of notices banning Jews from public parks and other places, and told them how he was then banned from his own school. They couldn't believe that teachers would turn against their pupils.

Ernie was good at telling the story, even though it must have been painful. He has an expressive face and used his hands in a way I hadn't noticed before. The pupils were fascinated by his hiding at the Lanzigs' and didn't latch on to the horror of it, because Ernie made it *sound* like an adventure – he may have thought of it like that at the time – and didn't relay every fear he had to the children.

His journey on the Kindertransport itself did shock them. The very thought of a train full of children without their parents was anathema to children with fairly cushy lives... but again, Ernie made his arrival and his new family in Manchester sound exciting. I was so proud that this was my family. They hung on his every word when he told them about the little suitcases children had to use for the journey.

Ernie explained that some children brought their musical instruments but the border guards immediately tossed every violin, clarinet or music case out of the train. I saw that a few children were visibly upset.

Then they went into groups and enacted little scenes about travelling alone, or being unable to speak the language in a school playground. And then he brought out a ragged little book which I had never seen before. Ernie explained that it was given to all refugees settling in Britain.

'Imagine,' he told the children, 'I sat on a park bench, all alone, struggling to *read* all the rules, let alone understand them. One rule said, "Be quiet and polite."'

'Why give a book like that to a child?' a boy on the front row asked.

'They were probably mass-produced for adult refugees; no one expected children to arrive here alone, I suppose,' he said.

The visit ended with Ernie describing how he found Blume and the family photo. He took the school group right up to the present day and a happy ending.

The best thing was that he was asked to submit his story, with some of the pupils' work from that day, to the school magazine, which would remain in the school library in perpetuity. As we drove home, Ernie said, 'I was so chuffed about that.'

Dad came round to hear how the day had gone and I knew he and Ernie were itching to ask about Martin and me, but for once they resisted. Before they left, Dad invited us for Friday night dinner.

'And that includes Martin – please tell him, Nicki,' he said, astutely.

Martin continued to phone every day. Chatting on the phone was good – one step removed. I told him briefly about the school day with Ernie, trying to keep him in the loop. For his part, Martin had read Rabbi Lever's website and saw that he had a secular law degree, as well as rabbinic qualifications.

'Quite impressive.'

'If we see him, there'll be lots of: "On the one hand, this… on the other hand, that,"' I told him. 'It's all about reasoned argument. Most law students – in secular universities, I mean – study Talmudic debate, to see how it works.'

'Aren't you inflating Judaism's part in everything?' Martin asked.

'Remember Lizzie from university? She was studying law. She told me,' I replied.

'Oh yeah, Lizzie. Wonder how she is these days?' Martin said, not expecting an answer. 'Anyway, I can't imagine the rabbi being worldly enough to address our problems, however bright he is.'

'Well, just let me know what you decide. OK?'

'Will do, must get on with writing. I'm up to Act Two.'

'Great, see you.' We rang off.

A couple of days later, I went for my appointment with the midwife. My blood pressure was up a bit; my ankles weren't swollen but my legs ached. She told me firmly to take two or three days off work, preferably on either side of the weekend.

'And you must rest,' she said. 'Not necessarily in bed all day, but don't stand up unless you absolutely have to. OK?'

When Martin heard this, he wanted to come home to be with me but I insisted on keeping the status quo. He'd be home early on Friday afternoon anyway; the appointment with the rabbi was for the following week.

Dad and Ernie came to drop off some meals to help me rest. Sweet guys! While they were there, Ernie took a look at the room that would become the baby's, to help with decor. We decided not to use pastel shades, but Matisse colours, vibrant and clashing: bright magenta with scarlet, royal blue with mustard. He would prepare a mood board – a collection of colour and material samples – and draw a scale plan of the room with furniture. Very professional. That cheered me up, as I stayed put with the papers, a good book and mindless daytime TV.

Poor Jake was worried about me but went off to school as usual. I walked round the garden once he'd left and then Ros popped in.

After helping herself to a coffee, she sat at my feet, waiting to hear everything. She sounded like a mother. How long had it been since Mum had been well enough to be motherly? A long time, certainly. Initially, Ros said little, but what she said was forthright.

'You're both wrong – and right. I mean, it's pretty drastic, for Martin to move out.'

'I told him that.'

'Hang on! There must be something more to it,' she said. 'I mean, when he moved out, so much had been going on – your mum's death and your pregnancy. Maybe he couldn't cope.'

I said nothing, thinking about the row.

She went quiet too, then said, 'You know, maybe you're both a bit childish.' No one but Ros could have said that to me. 'But it's your childishness that I love.'

'Yeah, right.'

'No, really. But shall we go to a café? Get you out of the house.'

'OK, fine.' Just as we were leaving, I found a big envelope in the porch which had been hand-delivered and I peeped into it.

'Jake,' I called to him, 'feast your eyes on this. Ernie's mood board for the baby's room. Bet it's fantastic.' I handed the envelope to him as we left.

Over a fruit tea, Ros and I chatted, mainly reminiscing. She recalled another time, ages ago, when Martin and I clashed.

'One Saturday, Martin had booked theatre tickets but you'd invited people to eat out at a local pub.'

'I can't remember it,' I said.

'Selective amnesia, old girl,' she said, laughing. 'You both dug your heels in, stubborn pair.'

'What happened?'

'Martin went to the theatre alone, and you went out with friends. Everyone thought it was curtains for you both.'

'How awful.'

'But we liked you both, too!'

'Sure?'

'Course,' Ros said, stroking my arm. 'But you must have made up. Try to remember how, OK? I'd hate you to... Oh God! I've gone too far again... I...' She was tearful.

'We've not separated for good,' I said, without conviction. 'But look, this baby kicks like mad when I'm tired – can we head back now?'

'Sure. Is it a boy or a girl?' she asked, nodding towards my tum.

'We don't know, we want to keep the mystery,' I said, looking down, 'a surprise... I know most people do know, these days.' I could tell she didn't believe me. She drove me home but I was too tired to ask her in.

'I'll call you in a few days. Keep your feet up,' she called through the car window. 'And sort out the mess!' Typical Ros. I waved her off.

Later on, Martin arrived to see me. He was worried about the midwife's orders. Living away, but worried about me? I didn't know how to take it. He made us a cup of tea and sat next to me on the settee, asking about the nursery. Did he deserve to share that fun, if he was living elsewhere? Then Jake came in and asked me to show Martin the design, so that was that.

'And I've sketched ideas for a crazy mural.' I showed him the animals I'd sketched out, in surreal colours – a giraffe in peach with royal blue patches, a zebra in lime green and pale blue, parrot-like birds in lemons and limes. Jake then snuggled up on the settee between us, like he did as a little boy.

'I love it – I never knew you did that sort of thing.'

'You won't remember the one I did in our first bathroom. We moved out of that house when you were little. Trouble with murals is you have to leave them behind if you move,' I said.

'Can I help paint it?' Jake asked.

'Sure.'

He continued to sit squeezed between us and said, not looking at either of us, 'You coming back home then?' nudging Martin.

'Not yet,' I said. 'He'll be here on Friday as usual.'

'I'd better shift, now,' Martin said. 'Jake, why not have a few days in Rochdale during Whit – or summer? Grandma would love to have you.'

'Sure, but we can't leave Mum on her own. I'll go when you come back here,' he said, threateningly. 'Cos you've gotta come back.' He looked at us sternly. He had turned into a parent – or not quite, his lip quivered.

Martin saw him back to his room as I went to get ready for bed and he came into the bedroom shortly after. It felt strange. We hugged as though nothing was amiss; he caressed my growing belly lovingly.

'I can't stay, can I?' he asked.

'We're not sorted, yet. We'd enjoy a romp and think that solves it all but it doesn't. Let's see if the rabbi helps… Only a few days.' We kissed goodnight and he left.

There was a text message on my mobile: 'WANT EDNA'S PHONE NO PLS. MUST SPEAK 2 M. IT'S THE ONLY WAY XXX DAVID.' I sent it immediately. Unless those two spoke directly, we'd never get out of this mess.

On the next day of my enforced rest, Dad came round in the morning with a parcel. He had been to his friend's cloth warehouse, which was about to shut down. Almost all vestiges of Manchester's textile trade had disappeared, most of the warehouses becoming cafés and bars around Canal Street; this was the last to close.

He unravelled two massive rolls of cloth which he had on approval. One was blue with white, scudding clouds across it, randomly placed. I hated it. The other was of leaves, all clustered together like a Henri Rousseau painting. I hated it a bit less.

'I thought that either would go with your fantasy jungle theme. You choose,' he said.

I didn't want to upset him and the baby wouldn't care. 'I'll go for the leaves. I'll paint animals and birds on the walls, the floor will stay as it is, earthy – so the furniture will have to be neutral,' I said.

'Good. I'll measure up and have them made up for you, with a blackout lining. Short or long?'

'Short, please.' I didn't fancy too much of them.

'Great, I'll do that, love. You OK?'

'I'm fine Dad, really rested.' He left, smiling.

I put my feet up again and watched a TV programme about house decor. Not much could beat this nursery. I dozed off and was woken by the home phone but I didn't recognise the voice. It was Jake's year group supervisor from school. I gulped, sat up and straightened my hair, as though he could see me.

'Yes?'

Apparently, Jake had been to see him on several occasions, lately.

'Our actual discussions were confidential,' he said, 'but I called because I think Jake is more disturbed by your separation than he appears.'

'Oh.' I felt sick. 'Why?'

'He's getting into fights. Whether he picks them or others pick on him, I can't be sure. He certainly thinks the world's against him at the moment. He knows I'm making this call and I've told him to share his problems with you as he still needs parental input. I know you'll both take it on board.' I thanked him, grateful for his common sense.

I was worried. I texted Martin, who suggested waiting till Jake approached us – but that we'd talk to him by Friday. In the meantime Ernie called to look at the nursery again and to tell me some news.

EIGHTEEN

'Blume is coming to stay for a while,' Ernie said, as he sat beside me. That was news, alright. 'She wants to meet the family and see England – she's never been. But she's a culture vulture and doesn't believe that Manchester and Salford have art galleries or theatres, not to mention countryside.'

'Must have read a Londonist guide book,' I replied.

'Probably.'

I was intrigued – I thought Ernie's relationship with Blume had been quite formal. In fact they had been emailing and skyping ever since they met.

'Ernie, is there a twinkle in your eye?' I asked, grinning.

'What? For a blonde, German woman? She's just very interesting and good company. She arrives on Friday. I must get ready, I hardly ever have people to stay. But I want everyone for lunch on Shabbat after shul. Will Martin be here?'

'Think so. How lovely, Ernie,' I said. 'But won't we all be a bit much for her?'

'No. She wants to meet my family.'

I texted Martin to tell him, as Ernie and I went to look at the baby's room again. He'd brought lots of tester tins of paint to try. He was buying wood for the wall furniture he'd designed, which included a drop-down changing table over a built-in cupboard with shelves and drawers. Clever Ernie!

Jake came home from school soon afterwards, quieter than usual. I chatted about Ernie, the nursery and also Blume. He was interested, but he didn't sparkle or add any cheeky remarks.

'Hungry?' I asked.

'Not really.'

'Wow, must have been a good lunch.' I tried to sound upbeat.

'No, veggie slops, as usual.' I tried to persuade him into a slice of currant loaf that Dad had brought from the local deli; as it didn't work, I let him be.

Next morning, he said he felt sick. I called school to tell them and at about ten o'clock, I went in to him, intending to broach the problems at school. I didn't; he looked sickly and pretty unhappy so I gave him some lemon water and promised him a turn at painting the mural when he felt better. His eyes opened at that.

'Good one, Mum, ta.' He wasn't much more than a child.

I sketched very large, simplistic outlines of the animals and birds, on the wall of the baby's room, knowing, as I did, where the furniture would go. I was interrupted by the district nurse's visit, to check my blood pressure, as arranged. I didn't tell her I was decorating – but everything was fine. She said she'd keep an eye on me once I returned to work.

Martin called to check on us, saying he'd come back early the next day, Friday, to have time together before Jake came home.

'And I'm bringing a surprise, too. From my mum,' he said, before ringing off. Then Dad called. I felt like a receptionist.

'Have you heard about Ernie and Blume? Do you realise, she's over seventy and he's over eighty!' Dad said.

'So?'

'Well, I mean... she's *German* for goodness sake.'

'Dad, I can't believe you said that! Coming from such a special family, all the work she does – I'm glad Ernie's having a guest, his house deserves to be used.'

'Mm. Suppose so. I am glad you'll all meet her, though. When are we going there?'

'Shabbat. See you there, Dad.'

'In the evening? Martin's coming too, isn't he?''

'He is – but it's for lunch, Dad, not evening.' I was sure I'd already told Dad when we were going to Ernie's. He was nagging a lot.

I went back to the mural. It was relaxing, designing something fanciful. If only we could earn enough from my designs and Martin's writing. I was happy, painting, when Jake came in, looking awful. He wanted to help and in the circumstances, sloshing away together could be good.

He'd put on some old clothes, so I spread newspapers out on the floor, putting all the different paints on them. I explained my plan: that the animals could have their usual spots or stripes, but the colours were to be outrageous.

'For example, this parrot will be lilac, pale blue and lemon.'

'Yuk, Mum. Being different is OK but that's, well, daft!'

'Suck it and see!' I said. 'Trust me.'

'So, here's a zebra. What colour are the stripes going to be?'

'Your decision – scarlet and peach? Up to you. Tell you what, let's write initials of the colours on everything, in pencil, to help divide them out. Make sure there isn't red next to red, you know.'

Jake dabbed a bit of each colour as a guide, mumbling to himself, 'Mm. It's hormones that make pregnant women do crazy things...'

'Sometimes pregnant women eat weird *food*, they don't do weird things.'

We made good progress. I told Jake about his grandpa's curtaining and about Blume's visit. He was a bit bemused, as we all were.

Then he suddenly stopped painting and asked, 'So where will she sleep when she's at Ernie's? Unless they're up to stuff, there isn't room. He made that big en suite where there used to be a third bedroom and then there's only his study workshop. Ho, ho, ho!'

'None of our business,' I replied.

We went on painting, smiling at the thought, but after a while I couldn't resist asking, 'How's school?'

'Bearable. It's home that's shit.'

'Language! But I get the drift. I know it is. I could say it's OK, but it isn't. We're really trying to sort things out.' I sounded pathetic. 'Does school take your mind off it at all?'

Jake said it didn't, because he was worrying all the time about whether his dad would come back home before the baby and the Bar Mitzvah.

'And the bullies are still at it,' he blurted out.

'Oh. Have you reported them?'

'Yeah, but the teachers say I'm too sensitive.'

'It's in the genes,' I said, unhelpfully.

'Apparently, I'm "reading too much into the antics of a few kids who are best ignored".'

'That's a bit glib, sorry. People used to say that before there were anti-bullying policies. I'm not really satisfied, Jake.'

'What can we do? They start on about Ernie again, even though they really liked his visit to school. I got in a real temper yesterday and lashed out at one of them.'

'Not a good idea,' I said. 'Well, Dad looks into any school problems, you know that. I don't want to play the heavy-handed teacher/parent.'

'If Dad were home, I wouldn't get into fights.'

We went on painting, not realising how late it was. Jake suddenly felt hungry, after a day of nausea, so we made a snack together.

'I'm glad I was at home, so you weren't alone today,' I told him.

'I love painting,' Jake replied, steering away from emotional issues. 'When does a baby first sees colours and animals and things?' he asked.

'Quite early. They see black and white easier than colour,

apparently. And with an older sibling, babies mature faster.'

'You're just trying to get round me.'

'I'm not, it's true. Babies are mimics and this one will mimic you even more than Dad and me.'

'Oh yeah.'

'I'm not shmoozing you, honest!'

'Mum, don't use Yiddish, I hate it!'

'Lots of Americans use Yiddish nowadays.'

'We're not Americans.'

NINETEEN

It was Friday again. I was sure there were more Fridays than usual these days, but I felt stronger. I did some lesson prep for my class and prepared dinner just for the three of us. Shabbat lunch at Ernie's would be eventful – a stranger in our midst would be good.

I stuck to the usual roast chicken but made a vegetable soup with sweet potatoes and butternut squash, sloshing in some coconut milk and chilli powder at the end. What would Grandma Friedl have made of that? And rhubarb fool for dessert was simple, too, using soya for the custard. Cooking with Jewish *kashrut* rules was easy, now – unable to use milk after meat, we had options.

It was only two o'clock in the afternoon when Martin arrived. I hadn't heard him come in but he peeped round the kitchen door and then his arms encircled my baby bulge from behind.

'Come and see what I've got!' he said, grinning as he twisted round me.

'Hi! You *are* early!'

'Hope you're glad,' he replied, taking my hand with one of his and covering my eyes with the other. He led me out to his hatchback car and there he revealed a beautiful, old-style rocking crib, painted in the palest acid-yellow, with white ribbons threaded through the wicker. It was gorgeous.

'Mum did it up for you,' he said. 'It used to be mine. When

Jake was born, she didn't think we'd have room for it in our old house, what with his room doubling up as a study. So she couldn't give it us. I suppose she hoped for another baby, one day.'

'Didn't we all?'

'Of course she doesn't know we're having a girl, but it is a bit girlie, don't you think?'

'Maybe. I must phone her.'

'Not right now, let's have some talk time. Sit down and have a drink.'

'And the toast is…?'

'To my new play. I've finished Act One.'

I was disappointed. I'd have preferred to be drinking to us but I said, 'Great, can I read it?'

'D'you want to? It's very much a first draft,' Martin answered.

'No worries.'

I liked reading drafts. But I hoped to hear more from him about coming home. Reading my mind, he asked if he could stay the night, platonically. Ros's husband was away so he wouldn't stay there.

'How would we square "platonic" with Jake?' I asked.

'He doesn't know what goes on in our bedroom.'

'But it'll confuse him even more.' I moved on to the news about the school fights. Martin already knew, both from Jake's text and from the teacher – who had sensibly contacted both of us.

'So, what do you think?' I asked. Martin said he'd go in to school, perhaps with Jake. I was fine with it either way.

'But, you know, Jake's behaviour may have more to do with his genes than our problems. I was fiery as a lad, always took a strong line. And I had a fair share of bullying. Not anti-Semitism, of course, but plenty of other stuff. Bullying usually just fades away.'

'So, what about tonight?' I said.

'We'll have dinner, I'll stay and say as little as possible.'

'OK. A platonic night, then.'

Once Jake came home from school, I asked Martin to read us the play so far. Jake and I huddled on the settee and Martin came from behind the curtains, like a child pretending to be on stage.

'Presenting: Act One of *Four Women and a Flower,* by Martin Taylor,' he read.

'Great, Dad,' said Jake.

'But the title's a bit twee, to be honest,' I said.

'Mm. You're right,' Jake grumbled.

'It's a working title,' Martin said.

The play read well. He had turned my grandfather, Jacob, into a cantor in the synagogue, which worked nicely. It opened in their early marriage and then flashed back to the suffragette time. Martin had depicted Freidl's personality much as he remembered her. In the play, she would appear (under a different name) in three different stages of her life. It was good, but we all thought it lacked real dramatic punch.

Whatever was going on between us, Martin's play made emotional reading. As I was finishing off the dinner, the phone rang and Jake answered.

'Mum,' he called, 'it's Uncle David. He wants to speak to Dad!'

'So get him. He's upstairs, getting changed.' I was quaking. Had they not spoken yet? I closed the kitchen door so that I couldn't even try to eavesdrop but Martin came into the kitchen a few minutes later.

'That was David.'

'I know,' I mumbled.

'He wanted to apologise. Big of him, that. He'd left two messages on my mobile during the week which I ignored,' Martin admitted, looking sheepish.

'And?'

'He insisted that, although you told him the secret, it *was* an accident because of the Hebrew for baby girl.'

'I told you that, over and over,' I replied.

'And he said you never normally talk to him about us.'

'You didn't believe *me*, though.'

'Well, that call took guts.'

'The Bamberg twins have got guts – they take after their mum,' I replied, smiling.

'Must be. And he wished you and Jake Shabbat Shalom, of course.' He kissed me and then went upstairs. I heard noises but didn't know what he was doing. I hoped he wasn't moving the duvet, in order to sleep alone. When I went up to change for Friday night dinner, I peeped round the nursery door to look at the crib again and noticed something different. Nestling at the feet of the zebra was one beautifully painted purple flower. Martin stood there, brush in hand.

'Like it?'

'Love it, thanks.' He came up and encircled me and my pregnant belly with his arms; I leant my head back and he kissed my neck. 'That feels good.'

'Mm, tastes good, too,' he said, nuzzling me. 'And it's going to be a gorgeous room for our daughter to sleep and play in, Nic. I bet there are loads of people who'd like a mural like this.'

'Hang on – what if Jake heard that?'

'What?'

'Talking about our *daughter*.'

'Let's tell him, now.' Nothing if not impetuous, my Martin. 'You like my flower, don't you?' he said, as though nothing unusual had happened.

'I love it. One day our daughter will have the actual flower,' I said.

'Isn't that sexist? What about Jake?'

'Mm,' I replied, 'but the flower must pass down the female line. He can have the Gluckel book. That's important, too.'

'And he can have my play script,' Martin said.

'And the first night programme,' I added.

'By the way, the little Oldham theatre's considering it. They think people in a traditionally working-class town like that will be interested in the suffragette stuff. Mind you, they want the second act before deciding.'

'Then we hunt for funding,' I added. 'Can they get enough bums on seats?

'Who knows? There's a regular clientele and Jewish people go there quite often – it's not far with the ring road. But it's not just for Jewish people, anyway.'

'Course not, that's why it's a brill idea,' said Jake, who had joined us.

'By the time it's finished, your little sister could be with us at the opening night!' said Martin.

'Sister? Sister! Who's... what?'

'You heard. And you're the first to know.' Martin hugged me as Jake absorbed the news.

'Wicked. A girl... cool.' He grinned at me. All was right with my little world.

I suddenly realised I hadn't seen Dad for Shabbat, and with Ernie having Blume at his, Dad might be feeling lonely. Martin suggested bringing him round for dinner, so he got changed and went to fetch him. I added a place at the table and another wine goblet. Only ten minutes after he left, Martin called me on my mobile. He was whispering.

'Listen Nicki, I'm a bit worried. Don't let Jake hear your side of this conversation.'

'Really?' I said, carrying out his subterfuge.

'Your dad's place is a real tip. I mean, unnaturally messy. Everything's been just – left, somehow – and he's usually so particular.'

'So – ?'

'There's more. That curtaining is still lying there in the hall.'

I wished the curtaining was nowhere to be seen. But it wasn't like Martin. To *say* he was concerned like this. My dad, a mess? This was totally out of character. My earliest memories of him were of an immaculate man who, like Ernie, wore socks to match his shoes, which were not just black and brown. And he knew how to tidy up better than Mum.

Once, when I was about ten, Mum had to have an operation. While she was in hospital, Dad took over the household with an iron rod. He inspected my bedroom and David's and gave us both the vacuum cleaner to do carpets with, making no distinction between us. He did the washing and, seeing my embarrassment when he handed me back my clean panties, he said, 'Don't you think I have seen these before, Nicki?'

So, what was happening? As I opened the door now, Martin winked from behind Dad's shoulder as though to say 'Look'.

'Good Shabbos, Nicki,' Dad said, kissing me. He didn't smell fresh, that familiar Daddy-clean we all knew. *My God! What was up?*

'You look smart, Dad, I'm not used to seeing you in green,' I said, looking at his gardening sweater, which he never wore on Friday nights. He took no notice and went into the dining room, with his arm round Jake. Jake looked back at me, wrinkling his nose.

Dad wasn't as talkative as usual and hardly laughed all evening. Martin asked him to come and see the nursery, telling him, on the way upstairs, that the baby was a girl. Dad's lack of response was weird and he hardly commented about the room. He seemed to have forgotten about the jungle theme and his curtaining.

Martin and Jake took him home. When they were back, Jake said, 'Whatever's wrong with Grandpa?'

'Maybe he's depressed. He's got good reason. We'll keep an eye on him, but he said he was OK to walk to Ernie's tomorrow.'

The phone rang – it was Ernie. 'She's here!'

'Who? Oh, Blume! Fantastic, Ernie,' Martin said. 'Look forward to seeing her.'

'Hey listen. I just spoke to Joe and he'd forgotten she was coming.'

'He's tired – maybe life on his own is catching up on him. See how he is tomorrow. Shabbat Shalom.'

'Shabbat Shalom. Listen, I did a full Friday night dinner for Blume, and she knows all about everything, from her survivor friends. She's so easy!'

'Great, Ernie. Enjoy.' Turning to me, Martin said, 'He sounded ten years younger.'

By this time, we were all so tired that Martin coming up to our bedroom was no big deal and we fell asleep almost immediately. A platonic evening by default. The next morning, I had a lie-in; Martin and Jake said they could walk by for me after shul, but I said I'd meet them at Ernie's.

I was nearly there when I spotted Dad walking quite firmly – with his stick – from the other direction. It was as though last night hadn't happened; he seemed his usual self and excited to be seeing Blume again.

She was by Ernie's side as he opened the door. We all hugged. Martin and Jake were already there: Jake gave a thumbs-up sign behind Blume.

'Joe – you remember Blume don't you? Blume, this is Joe's daughter Nicki.' There were tears in Blume's eyes as she greeted me.

'This is a dream come true for me, Nicki. To know that Ernie's family grows again,' she said laughing, looking at my tummy. 'Excuse me. I hope you do not mind the joking, do you?' Her English was stilted but clear.

'Of course not,' I said. 'And anyway, we've come to tell Ernie that this baby is a girl.'

Ernie let out a delighted yell: 'Lovely! So you found out, then?'

'Yes,' Martin replied.

We gathered round Ernie's Shabbat table, all eyeing Blume from under our lowered eyes, then had a delicious piece of *challah*. Dad put an envelope down on the table next to him.

'Ernie, you baked this bread, didn't you?' I asked.

'We kneaded it together,' he answered, looking at Blume. How romantic.

'He showed me how to plait it, coat it with egg, then sprinkle it with sesame seeds,' Blume explained.

'It's just yummy!' Jake said. The meal was yummy, too – Ernie's creativity showed as much in his cooking as in his designing, as with the curry powder he had added to the chopped liver that time and, this evening, chicken with lemongrass.

'So – what are you going to see during your stay, Blume?' This was only the first of a stream of questions that were fired at her, all the way through dinner. She coped well. She was a handsome woman, well built but with a good figure. She was in a modern, cream striped trouser suit, with a patterned blouse under it. Her hair had obviously been blonde, now coloured a bit, it was cut in a smart bob. She wore just a touch of eye make-up and light lipstick.

I noticed her earrings: they were in the shape of the *Magen David*, the Jewish Star of David. She saw me looking and explained that one of her friends at the Holocaust survivors' group had given them to her. They had once belonged to one of the many family members who had perished in Auschwitz.

'They are so precious,' she said.

I liked her; she was obviously intelligent and fitted in to the family so easily. I watched her watching us and thought she had spotted something in Dad's behaviour. After all, it hadn't been long since they were together in Israel. Ernie, meanwhile, was full of energy; it suited him to have someone to fuss over.

We walked Dad back, on our way home. Martin was staying another night, as our appointment with Rabbi Lever was at lunchtime the next day.

Just as we reached his house, Dad said, 'Nicki, I meant to give you this. I brought it, but forgot.'

'What is it?' I asked.

'That letter.'

We were getting nowhere fast. 'Come on, Dad, what letter?'

'The missing letter from Freidl. I told you there was another one.'

'Of course.' Now it was me who was forgetting. 'Thanks, Dad.' He gave me the envelope, which just about fitted into my bag, then we saw him into his house and set off home.

'Isn't Blume nice?' Jake said.

'And Ernie shed ten years tonight; it's hard to think that he's over eighty.' We joked our way home, none of us mentioning concerns about Dad or ourselves.

As usual, Jake brought up the unspoken subject. 'Grandpa was quiet this evening. D'you think he's jealous of Blume or something?'

'Could be.'

'It's tough for him,' Martin commented. 'Israel lifted him, after losing Malkah, but now there's nothing to look forward to. Then Blume comes...'

Martin spent that evening writing in his study, occasionally coming to add a few brush strokes to the nursery walls with me. The next day, we left for the rabbi's just after lunch and Jake went off to the reform shul for his Bar Mitzvah lesson.

'The Taylor family's sucking up to rabbis all of a sudden,' joked Martin.

TWENTY

We went tentatively into the synagogue building. As we passed the open door of the secretary's office, she jumped up, welcomed us and gestured to the rabbi's study, down the corridor. Martin had remembered to wear his *kippah* and I wore an appropriate skirt, instead of my usual Sunday trousers. Rabbi Lever opened the door as we reached it and greeted us.

'Good to see you. How are you both? Do you want a drink? Water, or orange juice? Please, sit down.' He gestured to two rickety looking chairs facing his huge desk.

We asked for juice, which he poured for us, chatting all the while. He was dressed casually: under a navy jacket was an overworn Fair Isle sweater, with a shirt collar showing and no tie. He was a good-looking man who smiled a lot; it struck me as a shame he had begun to put on weight.

I looked around. His study had one bright centre light and the room was devoid of ornament. All that lined the walls were overfull bookshelves, bending under the weight of well-used, dusty tomes. Most but not all the titles were in Hebrew; I recognised the Talmud, which took up more than one whole shelf in numerous volumes. Where the carpeted floor, largely threadbare, met the walls, there were more books and papers, piled high.

His desk, however, was orderly: a photo of him with his wife and seven children stood with two wedding photographs and another three of their baby grandchildren. I had to remind myself how young the rabbi and his wife both were – late thirties or early forties, about the same as Martin and me, in fact. They were still an attractive couple; in the photo and whenever I saw them, they looked at each other like teenage lovers.

In front of him as he sat down was his opened appointment book and I recognised our two letters lying on it. We had each jotted down our problems and posted them to him, last week, as he had requested. He smiled at us benevolently.

'So, how is everyone, since your dear mother died?'

'We're coping, thanks, Rabbi,' I replied.

'Well, I've read both your letters, with all the background. How do you think I can help you?'

We said nothing, looking blank.

'By talking?' I suggested.

'But where to start?' he asked. He looked quite at ease with the challenge before him and his grey-blue eyes were what you noticed first in this man, though his hair and trimmed beard were black. The lightness of his eyes came as a surprise.

'I gather you've already seen one counsellor. I hope you don't get bamboozled by too much advice.' We smiled.

'Can I begin, then, since you've both gone quiet?' We nodded. 'Firstly, you know, don't you, that Jewish law accepts divorce – I mean, it accepts that it's sometimes unavoidable. Always did.'

'I did know that,' Martin said.

'You see, the earliest *written* contracts referred to in the Old Testament are one for marriage, one for divorce. We may be an ancient people but we were ahead of the times.'

'Intriguing, that,' I replied, more for something to say than anything.

'They were drawn up to protect people – particularly women, actually – from wrongdoers,' Rabbi Lever said. I hadn't contemplated divorce and nor had Martin. At least, I didn't think so.

'However,' he continued, 'even though divorce is allowed, the Midrash says that God weeps over every divorce.'

'So God's sending us on a guilt trip,' Martin said.

'Well, let's say He prefers that couples try to stay together,' the rabbi replied, looking serious. 'However, if you don't mind my saying, er, a woman who's recently lost her mum and who's pregnant is particularly vulnerable.'

'Point taken,' Martin said, blushing. I recalled John, the counsellor, saying the same thing.

'So many people hit marital problems soon after a bereavement or during a pregnancy in the best of marriages, so you've a double whammy,' Rabbi Lever added. 'On the other hand...' (We both smiled: his first *'on the other hand'*.) 'Maybe it was a bit unreasonable, Nicki, expecting Martin to come home for shivah? That was something you put in your letter.'

I was surprised by that and didn't know how to respond to his judgemental comment.

'Because he's a good son-in-law, I know that. Well, I know you both, unlike the other counsellor.'

'Do you know us *too* well?' I asked.

'I don't think so, only as Malkah and Joe's daughter and son-in-law. But let me go on.' I nodded. 'Let's look at the issues. Martin *was* away, but it wasn't easy for *him*, either, being so far from home, just then. Mm... can we put the shivah episode on the back burner, for now?'

'OK,' I replied. Martin looked smug. And I thought that shivah would have been important to the rabbi. I was wrong, obviously.

'You see, from what you've said, you expect a lot from each other. Maybe you like that in each other, that you both set high standards.'

'Mm,' was my response.

'Forbidding her from knowing the baby's sex,' said the rabbi, 'seems fairly harsh, yet on the other hand, Nicki, you didn't keep it secret, once you did find out.' He waited for a response but we were both concentrating on the *'other hands'*.

'So now what?' I said.

'Well, now we get to the tricky bits. Martin, you were away working, weren't you?'

'I said that in my letter,' he replied.

'Yes, but were you alone? I ask you "before God". I don't act vicariously in place of God, like a priest, but I want the truth.'

'Should you ask me that, Rabbi?' Martin was scowling.

'Don't be so shocked! We rabbis know all about life. So, were you?'

'I was away working. There's no one else.'

'And Nicki, I must be sure: this *is* Martin's baby, isn't it?'

The rabbi looked unembarrassed by the direction of his questioning but I felt myself blush as I replied: 'Of course!'

He continued: 'I believe you both, so I ask myself, how could such a crisis arise in so short a time? Let's look at Nicki's accidental use of David – and Martin's leaving home. There seems to be a lack of mutual trust here and, well, an immaturity, in a way.'

We felt like kids in the head teacher's study, though he was wise and more incisive than John.

'All this reminds me of a story – we rabbis have a story to illustrate everything, you know.'

'Like theatre in education, really,' Martin said, glibly.

Rabbi Lever took no notice and went on. 'This one's in the Book of Numbers. It's the Sotah – about the wayward wife.'

Martin looked at me, smiling as though we were about to watch a performance. I hoped he wasn't going to get the giggles.

The rabbi began his story. 'A man accused his wife of adultery. He had no proof and brought her in front of the sages, for them to punish her; he wanted to humiliate her, publicly. Those rabbis had asked around and knew that the man was controlling and enjoyed subjugating his wife. They told him his accusation abused both his wife and God, since God sanctifies marriage. "Go home. God will be the judge," they said, and off he went, with a flea in his ear.'

'Where's this leading?' I asked, since I could sense Martin shifting on his chair.

'For Martin to punish you, by leaving home, just because you let out a secret, was… how can I put it… ungodly – even if you don't believe in Him.'

'But…' I began. Neither of us could get a word in edgeways. He certainly didn't conform to a counsellor's practice of long silences, but I did find him interesting.

'Hear me out a minute. Martin, demanding that Nicki shouldn't know the baby's sex, then leaving her over her discovery of it was… well, how can I put it? Making a Mount Sinai out of a sand-dune: completely out of proportion.'

'Oh?' interrupted Martin for whom I now felt quite sorry, but the rabbi continued.

'You know that biblical phrase "an eye for an eye", all about making punishment and crime equivalent?'

'Kind of,' I replied.

'It's called Talionic Justice,' the rabbi explained.

'That's a new one to me,' Martin muttered.

'You know the song in *The Mikado*,' he said, humming the 'punishment fit the crime' chorus.

'Do you like Gilbert and Sullivan, then?' Martin asked, happy to find a light moment. The rabbi nodded. Martin continued, impatiently. 'Forgive me, Rabbi, but I'm lost. Where's this leading?'

'I was trying to illustrate the fact that, maybe, you overreacted to the baby/David issue. But it is a complex one – and I'm sorry, I've talked too much,' he said. We looked at each other in agreement.

'I have, haven't I? Oh dear. But, well, could I now see each of you alone for a few minutes? People often see things more clearly without the adversary present.'

'OK?' Martin asked, turning to me. I nodded. Rabbi Lever had astutely pinpointed the main elements of our argument. We had a lot to digest. And I'd always thought the rabbi a quiet man.

'Good. Nicki first, then, if I may? Martin, go for a walk round the block, or wait in the hall. Please tell my secretary when you are leaving – her door is always open. Rivkah's my chaperone as well as my secretary, you see. Come back in five to ten minutes.'

Rabbi Lever leant forward on his elbows and looked at me kindly, over his desk.

'Nicki, this is about David's and Martin's tears.'

'You enjoy being enigmatic, don't you, Rabbi?' I said.

'Maybe. There are many examples of tears and sadness in the Torah, as in life and, for some reason, your relationship with David makes Martin "cry". Not literally, perhaps, but it makes him feel insecure – unloved, maybe?'

'That's ridiculous!' I said.

'Is it? Isn't it doubly hard, his having no siblings and living with a *twin*? And your telling that twin the secret was an accident waiting to happen. It did cause bitter tears.'

'So? It's done. And I have apologised.'

'And there comes a time to wipe his tears away,' Rabbi Lever said.

By this time, the tears were mine; luckily a box of tissues lay conveniently near. I nodded as I wiped my eyes. *I should open a paper hankie business.*

The rabbi went on, 'Only you can relieve Martin's sadness over the David issue.'

'I told you. I apologised,' I protested, between sobs.

'Apologies are just words. He needs to feel that he's the centre of your universe – you see?' He smiled at me kindly. 'So. It's over to you.'

'Well... David and Martin had a chat, this week, so that may help. But the thing is, Martin's got to come home – or decide to live without me.'

'I hope to hear that from him, Nicki – that he's coming home.' Then he added, 'And I'm sure I don't need to remind you that people who've converted to Judaism never forget the sacrifices they made. Martin changed his life for you and he's been your rock.'

'But rocks don't budge,' I replied.

'There might be a little earth tremor, let's see. But only you can wipe away his tears. And then, get on with loving Jake and each other.'

'How d'you know we do?'

'What?'

'Love each other.'

'I see it a mile off,' he said, winking.

'I thought you expected us to want a divorce.'

'Why?' he asked.

'Because you began this meeting by talking about it.'

'That was just to acknowledge the possibility but it wasn't what I expected, by any means. Anyway, let's call Martin. You go and have a breath of air.'

'Thanks so much, Rabbi.'

I left and crumpled into a chair in the hall, then stood by the open front door, breathing deeply. Martin passed me and went back in. Eventually, I was called in to say goodbye.

As we were leaving, Rabbi Lever said, 'I want you both to be happy – if possible, with each other. If not, at least you've tried everything. But I've a feeling you'll be alright.' I raised my eyebrows.

'Off you go to Jake,' he continued. 'And please bring the baby to see me, as soon as you can after she's born. You could have her blessed here, in your dad's synagogue. He would love that. Me too.'

'Lovely idea!' I said. 'Thanks.'

Martin and he shook hands enthusiastically.

Rabbi Lever smiled a goodbye but then, at the outside door, he stopped us and asked how Dad was and whether we'd planned the unveiling. The unveiling of a tombstone takes place any time between a month and eleven months after a burial.

I replied, 'We must get on with it. Can you email me a list of available Sundays, please?'

'Sure,' he replied. I was taken aback by what he said next.

'I just wondered about Dad, because he hasn't been to shul for a couple of days. Since your mum died, he's come to recite *kaddish* every day – he isn't ill, is he?'

Martin thought quickly and said that Dad had left his walking stick behind at Ernie's and needed it to walk with. With that, we thanked him and left.

'Is he breaking confidentiality by telling us Dad hasn't been to shul?' I said.

'Not sure. Attending shul isn't a secret, like a private meeting, is it?' replied Martin. We were exhausted by the barrage of advice but spoke initially about Dad, with concerns spinning round my head – and we needed to push Dad to plan the unveiling. On the way home, we walked into a nearby park and sat on a bench.

'Biddy benches already,' I said, letting out an audible sigh.

'He was brilliant,' Martin said.

'He did go on a bit. I felt like a naughty schoolgirl.'

'I've never spent much time with an orthodox rabbi; I hadn't expected him to be so... practical. He got right to the nub of the problem, even if he did prattle on.' Martin started to tell me what the rabbi had said while I was out of the room.

'You don't *have* to tell me,' I said. But he did.

'He asked me whether I really had the grounds to erase our marriage (his words). I thought he blamed me for everything. What he did blame me for was for preventing you from knowing the gender and for walking out. He said it wasn't justified.' I waited for him to go on, looking at the various people in the park who didn't seem to have a care in the world, unlike us. That's how I felt at that time. It seemed so unfair that we had so many problems; everyone else seemed to just get on with life, like the people playing with their kids in the park. And like Great-Grandma Freidl.

Martin went on. 'He said that nothing surprised him about human behaviour. He said that although we're unique, our problems aren't.'

'Fair enough.'

'And he stated the obvious.'

'Which was?'

'That only the two of us can sort this out.'

'And can we?'

'I thought so, at the time.'

'And now?'

'Less so. I know the twin thing is still an issue.'

'What did he say about that?'

'What everyone says. No one can separate siblings – and that I must just accept it.' Martin looked embarrassed. 'Also, *he* thinks that I want to go back home but daren't ask.'

'And do you?'

'I'm not sure. Don't we have to apologise first?'

'Well...'

'He said that apologies can't be conditional – that you can't say, "I'll say sorry if." It needs to be a "sorry" that closes the chapter.'

'Difficult.'

'I have upset you *and* while you're pregnant – nasty me.' He put his arm round my shoulder.

I put my head on it and snuggled closer, partly, I admit, to feel warmer. 'Was that the apology, then?'

'Did you take it as one?' Martin asked.

'Kind of,' I answered.

'Thanks.' With that, I relaxed into his shoulder and thought back to another time, when I was nine and was meant to give a big apology – and I didn't, which got me a big telling off from Mum and Dad.

'Nicki, you didn't hear me – what are you dreaming about?' Martin said, bringing me back to the present.

'Another time I didn't apologise, when I should have done,' I said, looking up at him.

'What happened?'

'I was in big trouble,' I replied, 'with my parents. I don't like trouble, you know. Somehow people think I like conflict but I hate it; I just like honesty, which is different. And I specially don't like conflict with *you*. But I *have* apologised for telling David our secret.'

'I know – and it's OK to love your brother. I've always known you're close but it knocks me off balance sometimes… maybe cos I'm an only child.'

'Probably,' I replied.

'Can I come home, then?'

'Shall we give it the rest of this week?' I couldn't even say why I said that. Instinct, perhaps.

'Hey? But you wanted me to come home.'

'I do, but just let everything settle. My head's buzzing and – I'm afraid of something going wrong. Know what I mean?' I asked.

'Not sure. You are enigmatic, Nicki.'

I wanted him to come home because he *wanted* to, not because he'd been told to. 'Let's breathe a bit,' I said. 'Oh gosh!'

'What now?'

'What about Dad? Do you think he's got…?'

'Nicki, hold on. He just missed shul, that's all. More Mount Sinais out of sand-dunes?' With that, he kissed me on the nose. He hadn't done that for ages.

'Poor Nicki, you've had a basinful – no Mum, Dad ageing, a baby, a pre-teenager and an idiot of a husband... a bit much. Try speaking to Ernie first – about Dad, I mean.'

'Will do.' I stroked my nose where he'd kissed it, then smoothed his hair, gently, where the breeze had blown it out of place. Holding the back of his neck, I drew his head close to mine and we kissed gently and were wolf-whistled by two kids on their skateboards, passing by.

We went home and as we went inside, we saw a note from Jake on the board, saying he was at a friend's and to text him when we were back. Since he didn't say, I wondered who he was with and what they were doing. I worried about whether his generation overused the internet.

Still, we left it a while before calling him. I'd listened to so much but at that moment, Dad bothered me more than anything. I went straight to the computer and clicked on an 'Ask the Doctor' site. I typed in: 'memory loss in old age'. *Now who was overusing the internet?*

A text from Jake came, asking if I was back. I texted 'yes' and moved away from the computer. What a guy Rabbi Lever was. Fancy having the guts to ask the questions he did! Martin had to be telling the truth, surely?

The phone rang.

How do I find a peaceful moment? I should be thinking seriously about the rabbi's advice.

It was Blume. I wasn't familiar with her voice, yet, but it was lovely to hear from her. She wanted to meet up, to go shopping, have a chat – just the two of us. I suggested Wednesday, as I had a non-teaching session at the end of the afternoon.

'I won't have time to go shopping but we can have a coffee,' I said.

'That will be good,' she replied. 'Wednesday afternoon. Where?'

'Outside M&S and I'll take you to a nice place.'

That phone call meant that I hadn't switched off the computer when Jake arrived home. In he came and, peering at the screen, said, 'Now who's an internet addict?'

'Hey!'

'Well, why were you looking at it, Mum?'

'Just reading something... anyway, it's going off now.' Luckily, Jake had other things on his mind.

'How's Dad? I thought he'd be coming home properly. Have you had another row?' I assured him that we hadn't. Then he told me how, after his Bar Mitzvah lesson, he'd gone out with Ernie and Blume, while Martin and I were at Rabbi Lever's.

'They're a great pair. D'you think there's anything, you know, in it? Couldn't be – you know, I mean – could they be *partners*, at their age?'

'Could be, there's no age limit,' I replied, laughing.

'She can talk about anything. She's done so much and she seems so youthful. Must be hard to be German and discover your past, d'you reckon?'

'Hm? What did you say? Sorry, Jake, I was miles away.' I couldn't stop thinking about Dad. 'Sorry.'

'Let's have something to eat.'

Jake offered to make supper and created a good scrambled egg, with bits of smoked salmon in it. While he was cooking, I quizzed him about the friend he visited. He was evasive.

'Oh, you wouldn't know her, but she lives near Ernie, actually. Mum! Don't look like that, just cos it's a girl.'

I asked no more questions. For the time being.

TWENTY-ONE

Freidl's missing letter was nearly forgotten, again. I eventually remembered which bag I had put it in and asked Ernie to come over, when Martin was around. I could tell Dad about it after we'd seen it.

'This one is handwritten,' Martin said. 'Wonder why?' He began to read it.

Dear Malkah,

This part of my story is another piece of the jigsaw which you will be able to fit in to my life-picture quite easily, I think. When I decided to reveal this bit, I couldn't bring myself to share it with the lady who transcribed other letters for me, so I wrote it myself.

Please forgive the spiders that crawl across the page! And any spelling or grammar mistakes. Even when I was younger, my written English never came up to my spoken English; now, it's worse still.

I never really got over the shame of this episode. It stayed with me the whole of my life so I entrusted this particular letter to Joe – he can decide the right time to let you read it, if at all.

'What now?' Jake said. Martin read on.

Suffragette activity varied, as I am sure you know. Some of it was simple, passive action like giving out leaflets and just making people aware. Those women who instigated violent action and vandalism were, for the most part, members of the radical political organisation, WSPU (Women's Society for Political Union).

There were many strands to the suffrage movement and although the main issue was fighting for the vote (of course!) they were also fighting for equal rights in all aspects of life, like owning land or property, equal pay for equal work and equality in education. There was even a Jewish League for Women's Suffrage, which tried to revolutionise internal synagogue politics. I never related to that, somehow, it seemed too insular.

We were always prepared for hostile reactions, like the one Lydia Becker received when she gave a speech in Manchester, once. She was before my time, but she was active on the Manchester School Board, arguing for equal education. Once, while giving a speech, she was heckled by a man who said that if women became as educated as men, 'Who will be there to bake the cakes and cook our meals?'

I felt for women like Lydia Becker and, even if I didn't take part in physical violence or vandalism, I empathised with the views of those who did. And I paid the price.

It was just before the war and my marriage to Jacob. Baby Malkah and I were living with Uncle Isaac. A group was organised to go to a protest meeting in London. That was a long journey in those days, so I asked for time off from work and organised for Jacob to stay with the baby in the evening. If I was delayed, he would take the baby to his home for the night.

Among the group were a couple of the more strident of the 'Sisters' but I was used to them and some were good friends of mine. The camaraderie between us was incredible and something it is hard to describe to other people. I have no way of knowing whether that kind of relationship is stronger among women than men, but I suspect so.

'What's coming?' Jake asked.

'Sh,' I replied. Martin shrugged and continued.

We were due to march on the head office of a government building in Whitehall, where we would stand, silently, for three hours, holding the banner. Then we would come home, travelling through the night. At one point, a couple of men came out of an adjoining building, shouting offensive things at us, saying that we weren't proper women; that we looked more like men: 'Disgusting!' I think you can work out what they meant. And I'm sure some of the protesters were lesbian but first and foremost we were comrades, women fighting together.

Suddenly something just went 'pop' and out of nowhere, stones and bits of bricks were being thrown at the windows and doors of both offices. More stones were somehow handed to the rest of us. I did nothing to stop them. And, caught up in the frenzy of the moment, I probably threw something as well. Whether I did or not doesn't matter.

'Great-Grandma, the vandal! I was right,' said Jake.

Within minutes, a fire engine arrived and parked at the end of the street as did police on horseback, waving truncheons. Firemen encircled us, holding the hoses menacingly, though they were not, at that point, squirting water. We were shoved along, bodily, to the nearest police station, followed by the menacing fire engine. We were treated like a load of cattle – or worse – and the names the police called us were little better than those of the earlier cat-callers.

It was a devastating night; we were crowded into cells where the conditions were far from sanitary. Until the Women's Movement, it had not been commonplace for crowds of women to be put in police cells. I was scared but we were in it together.

'Oh my God!' I gasped.

However, we could not contact anyone back home and I was worried about the baby. I also feared for Jacob's reaction but, as I said, we had made those contingency plans.

In fact, we sent the bus driver straight back to Manchester, so that he could give the news to anyone awaiting our return. Not many women had babies to worry about, but we covered a very varied age range. Anyway, I did not expect to be treated differently. The night in that cell is not worth describing, for you can well imagine it, but it was for the cause and I thought a prison sentence was sure to be our fate.

In the morning, a solicitor came in to represent us and to tell us we would be held until the hearing, or until bail was found. Out of the blue, my name was called out. Wrongly pronounced, of course: 'Frydelle Leaveye'. I went into the interview room, alone, petrified as to why I had been singled out.

I was told I could leave – go home – because someone had put up the bail for my release. And the police had also received a telegram for a money order, with which to buy a bus ticket back to Manchester. I was shocked and asked who else was being released. I'll never forget his words.

'Aren't you the lucky one!' The police officer smirked as he said this. He told me all my friends there would end up in jail.

Lucky? It was the opposite. How could I go home and leave them? They would never speak to me again. I'd be safe but cast out. I couldn't work out how this had happened, and they wouldn't tell me who had put up the bail. Of course, none of the police officers could understand why I was so unhappy. I begged to stay.

Then they were sure I was crazy. They suspected that suffragettes were not of sound mind at the best of times. I told them I had to stay with my sisters, that I could not desert them. But to no avail. I was made to go home, as surely as my friends were made to go to jail.

Martin stopped reading, open mouthed.

'Was she heroic? Or crazy?'

'Bit of both,' Jake replied.

'Poor woman,' Ernie said, as Martin continued.

I sobbed my heart out. I felt desolate, despairing, knowing that I had to leave but that once I did, none of the girls would have anything to do with me again. I was ashamed. I suppose you will think me mad, too, as you read this, but I couldn't live with myself. I later learnt that Uncle Isaac had paid the bail and I hardly spoke to him after I tried and failed to make him understand.

To this day I regret falling out with the man who had helped me so much. They say you should not bite the hand that feeds you. But he just would not see that he made it seem as though my struggle had been worthless and that money was the way out. He also could not see that in one action he had made me lose some of my closest friends. But I had to move on regardless and that, too, was hard.

'Oh. So I was right. She did cut off from him,' I observed. 'I was suspicious when I read that they didn't choose him as Malkah's godfather.'

'Poor Isaac,' Ernie commented. 'Such a good guy and look what he got.'

'Suffragette zeal... unbreakable, y'see,' Martin said. 'They were real martyrs.'

'And Freidl didn't want to be an exception,' I added. 'I can relate to that.'

'Cos you're a woman?' Jake asked.

'Maybe.'

'It'll add drama to the play, Dad. The scene in the cell... all that. I can just see it.' Jake seemed to be inside the stage set.

Martin read on.

Naturally, Uncle Isaac was heartbroken, feeling that I was ungrateful. He was right to an extent, but it was a matter of principle. We could not reach a compromise, which is why Jacob and I married very soon after that, during the war instead of after it. We would not live together till we married, and wanted to be with the baby: you, Malkah. I think I fell into a depression, as you would now call it, feeling such guilt for failing my co-suffragettes. And, in a way, for casting Isaac aside.

One good thing was that suffragette action was halted once the war started and strangely, that helped me cope – that and Jacob, who was remarkable. He tried to persuade me to make up with Uncle Isaac but I couldn't. It took many, many years for that to happen. I needed to work off my guilt; luckily, the War Effort gave me the opportunity, so I helped in any way I could.

I do not want to suggest that the First World War was in any way a positive thing; it was dreadful, terrible. But it saved my sanity, as I was quickly put to work sewing: making uniforms, in fact. And in between, with Jacob's help, I was bringing up you, Malkah, the easiest and most pleasant baby in the world.

The memory of that episode never fully left me, and I only felt whole again so many years later, when we took Ernie, our little boy-stranger, into our home. The opportunity to give something back, helped to ease my conscience, since I think Jacob, Malkah and I managed to make him fairly happy.

Ernie looked down and, tearful, said, 'Fairly? Very happy.' Jake put his arm round him.

'What a woman. What a life,' Martin said. 'Let's just finish the letter.'

I am so very tired from writing this by hand, but once again, I feel my shame is assuaged, so I can die happy. God bless you, Malkah, and whoever else reads this. I hope you can all understand me and still love me, whatever I did.

Your ever loving Mother.

We were stunned but I, for one, understood how she must have felt, letting the side down – all that. So we were left to use the history the best way we could. Martin's play seemed the perfect vehicle and he decided to envisage the row between Freidl and Isaac. With changed names it could work.

'I don't feel bad if I am creating something I didn't witness,' he said, 'and it really is at the core of the feminist struggle. Isaac's attitude is universal, and it means that the play touches on wider women's issues, not simply those of the suffragettes.'

'Exactly. It's about what people – in this case women – will sacrifice for their cause,' I said.

'But it's about men's attitude to women, too,' Jake said.

'I wonder how long it took for the general public to hear about the torture they suffered in jail – when they were force-fed... they were seriously physically abused, you know. Wonder how Isaac would have reacted to that?' I added.

'How d'you know about it?' Martin asked.

'I heard some archival interviews on radio, a while back, when surviving suffragettes told how they still suffered the after-effects of force-feeding.'

'Yuk,' said Jake.

'Well, I've got a lot of writing to do, folks!' said Martin as he left the room.

TWENTY-TWO

Being back at school after my rest break was more disconcerting than going back after Mum died. I didn't feel quite fit enough – nor was I on top of my lesson preparation. Since my pregnancy was now obvious, the kids were actually caring but I had to regain control. By the time I came to my weekly 'design' lesson, I felt stronger.

It combined art with maths; the children enjoyed designing something both functional and attractive. It brought out strengths in unexpected children and the end point was to create a scale model of a bedsit they'd designed, in an open shoe-box.

After work, I texted Ernie. Finding him in, I went straight round, having texted Jake to tell him where I was. Blume opened the door – it was lovely to see her smiling face; that relationship was unbelievable. I explained about our concerns over Dad, of which they were aware.

'You can't *make* him see a doctor,' Blume said.

'That's why I came round. How do we broach it?'

'He's not himself,' Ernie said, 'but it varies – today, he seemed fine.'

Ernie and Blume offered to go round to Dad's, pretending they wanted to discuss the unveiling date, which genuinely needed to be fixed. I didn't want it just before the baby's due date and also, David had to be there. It would take some organising so, in between, Ernie would try to suggest a medical check-up.

'Leave it with us.' They were so good. Before they left, we chatted about the missing letter.

'What a heritage you have, Nicki,' Blume said.

'A lot to live up to, isn't it? I haven't achieved half as much as Freidl,' I said.

'That's ridiculous, Nicki!'

Blume pulled Ernie out of his chair. 'Let's go to Joe's, Ernie, come on.'

Wednesday came and with it, my meeting with Blume. I was happy with my school routine and with the children's work. After school, I picked Blume up at M&S and took her to a coffee place. Jake called on my mobile.

'Hi, love – everything OK?'

'Sort of,' he said, 'only I was meant to go to my Bar Mitzvah lesson with Ernie and he didn't come. He isn't at home either. Can I call and say I can't make it?'

'Poor you. Of course – he went round to Dad's. I'll call the rabbi to tell him you can't make it. I'll be home in about an hour.' One missed Bar Mitzvah lesson wouldn't harm; however, I had to get to grips with Jake's routine. Suffragette rallies had nothing on family chaos. *Except the risk of jail.*

When I finally sat down with Blume, my head was so full of Jake, Dad and everything, I couldn't relax. She went to get coffee and two Danish pastries.

'Here,' she said, 'enjoy!'

'Thanks so much. Blume, this is lovely. I feel I've known you all my life. What do you think of... everything? Ernie, Manchester... things?'

'I feel completely at home, with Ernie – and in Manchester. I'm used to city life, and I feel comfortable with you all. You are under a lot of pressures, Nicki. Sorry, is that too personal?'

'Let's leave me out of this, OK? How long will you be staying for?'

'I haven't decided. Ernie says I can stay as long as I like. I have leave from the centre in Haifa for a month. After that, we'll see.' There was definitely an extra sparkle as she grinned. 'After my first husband died, I never imagined meeting anyone else. Let alone someone like Ernie,' she said, blushing.

'So it *is* more than just a friendship, then.' I said. 'Aha! Anyway, how about meeting up, the four of us, one Sunday? Mind you, Martin has a lot to do, to finish his play, what with funding and staging.'

'Can you tell me about it?'

I described quite a lot for her, but time raced on. 'Actually Blume, what d'you think about Dad?'

'I think we watch and wait. It may just be the stress from all his life changes. I know you are worried but let's see.'

'I must get back to Jake now, sorry.' We kissed goodbye. 'Good to be with you, Blume. Thanks.'

'For what?'

'For being here, I suppose.'

She walked off, back to Ernie's.

At home, my weird plants, animals and birds took life on the wall of the nursery, around the tree trunks, with aerial roots sprouting from the branches. A stream ran along the bottom, over the skirting board, and the heads of pink spotted alligators peered out of the water. It had turned out exactly as I wanted. Unlike the rest of my life.

On Thursday evening, Martin phoned while I was painting.

'Can I come back home for good, tomorrow – please?'

'Y'know, I've longed for this and now, I... I'm scared.'

'Of my coming home? Oh.'

'What if things go wrong again – or –'

'Look Nicki, none of this should have happened. We're not meant to be –'

'What?'

'Apart – or do you like being without me?'

'No. You know that. But can you cope with the David stuff?'

'I'll try. I've been a bit paranoid – but he phoned me again, today, y'know.'

'He phoned you again?'

'Yes. About Dad. He'd called him and was a bit worried. We had a good chat.'

'Oh.'

'Now *you're* jealous!' Martin said. 'You don't know what else we talked about, though.' He was teasing. It had been a long time since he'd teased or joked.

'So tell me.'

'He's coming over. He wants to see Dad for himself, he thinks he's more depressed than confused. You know, he does some bereavement counselling and says we often underestimate how much bereavement can affect people.'

'I can relate to that,' I said. 'So we can choose a date for the unveiling during his visit, then.'

'Exactly. That's what he said. Nothing's booked yet. And *if* my play's ready by then, that could fit, too.'

'Course! He came to all your plays at uni.'

'I think I need more on Freidl's family... But, listen, please can I come home?'

'See you Friday afternoon,' I said. 'Can't wait.'

'Love you,' Martin blew a kiss, over the phone. 'I never didn't, actually.'

'"Never didn't"? A double negative! You always did. I know, me too. See you.' He could probably 'hear' me smiling. I had never stopped loving *him*, either.

I carried on painting the mural: the material for the curtains had been forgotten, so I ordered blinds.

Jake came bounding in. 'I just got a text from Dad! He's coming home!'

'I would have told you, you know,' I said, ruffling his hair and giving him a hug, before he wriggled his way out of my paint-daubed hand.

'And Uncle David's coming over, too, soon,' I told him.

'He didn't tell me that – mean thing!'

'He'll get repetitive strain injury, texting so much. That goes for you, too.'

'Ah, but our generation is growing a mutating thumb – it'll become a wider and wider joint for text strength: survival of the fittest, you know? So, if you don't text, your fingers turn into tentacles,' he said, giggling.

He was funny; I hoped the laughter would last. I wanted finally to get rid of my nagging fear that, with an independent, suffragette grandma, that fiery streak might make me the Bambergs' first-ever single mum. Since our relationship crisis began, that's all I thought about.

Next morning, Dad called before I left for school: not a good start to the day. He moaned about Ernie and Blume, about the unveiling and having to see the doctor.

'I'm fit as a fiddle!' he said.

'I know, but does the doctor know how you're coping, since Mum died? I think Ernie's right, just to have a check-up.' I waited with bated breath.

'Oh, OK. Can Ernie or Martin take me? Don't want Blume interfering,' he said.

'Whatever... Fine. I'll ask Ernie to fix the appointment and sort it with you. Do you need a shop for tonight?'

'Stop fussing,' he replied.

'OK But, hey, Martin's coming home on Friday – so come and see us on Shabbat afternoon.'

'Will do,' he replied.

'Speak soon, bye.' I texted Ernie: one hurdle jumped.

The rest of the week rushed by with teaching, Jake, and gearing myself up psychologically for the homecoming. I'd even got out of the habit of cooking properly. Jake and I had snacked most of the time, even in front of the TV – a family 'no-no' usually – and I used lots more microwave meals. That Lydia Baker would have approved!

On the Friday afternoon, I was adding a couple of butterflies to the mural, with lemon and lilac spotted wings, when I heard Martin shout 'hello'. He was earlier than expected. He ran upstairs and we hugged, kissed and hugged again. My bump was in the way but we managed.

'Come on, wipe that paint off your hands and have a Happy Hour with me!' Martin said.

'D'you like the mural?' I asked.

'It's great – fantastic!'

'D'you think I can make a second career of it?' I asked.

'Maybe. But just come downstairs!' Martin sat me down on the sofa while he poured a drink for himself and sparkling water for me.

'Put a drop of white Martini in the water, please,' I said. 'A drop can't harm.' With that, Martin brought in a bowl of crisps and we clinked glasses. *'L'chaim!'* we said. 'To life!'

TWENTY-THREE

'Welcome home,' I said.

'Feels good.'

We sat there for a while and I asked about the play. Martin said he needed to do more research on Freidl's Romanian family and hoped Dad could help.

'Why? With the latest letter, you don't need any more,' I said. 'There's so much drama there: protest marches, the police abuses, cells, all that,' I said. 'And the friction with Isaac: it would be feminist argument an audience would really get into. Or use dramatic licence and have her go to jail!' I suggested.

'Good point, about Freidl's argument with Uncle Isaac,' Martin said. 'I'll think about it. But I want more about her family in Romania.'

'I suppose they lost touch, though,' I said.

'Well, I'll start an internet search. Jake might help.'

'Jake might, might he?' Jake had crept in after slipping silently through the back door. I wondered how he'd put down all his clutter so quietly. He ran at Martin and squeezed his long, lanky frame between us, forgetting that he was now five-foot-four and I was fairly chunky.

'Hey! Move over someone,' I said.

Jake said he'd love to help with research for the play. After a while, Martin picked up the phone to Ernie.

'Martin! Glad you're home,' he said. In the course of their

conversation, they planned a foursome outing for us, him and Blume.

Later, Martin called Dad, who seemed better than the previous week. He complained that he'd been bullied into a doctor's appointment, but Martin skilfully changed the subject by asking about Freidl's family.

'Freidl talked about her sister a bit, but, I mean, none of them came to our wedding. If they'd been in touch, they would have. I'll look through my papers again – they need tidying.'

'Thanks. Can I help? There may be some clues,' Martin asked.

'Why not today?' Dad replied.

'Done!' And Jake said he'd go to help, too.

After lunch, they went off and I put my feet up; my ankles looked a bit swollen, so I lay along the sofa. Then the phone rang.

'Hello, stranger.'

'Ros, sorry I've been out of contact. All my fault, but I've had to be off work, then Martin and I have been resolving stuff, now I'm back at work, etcetera.'

'No worries. Are you OK – you two?'

'Absolutely, Martin's back home and the nursery's… Oh! You haven't seen it. Come over, the two of you, tomorrow evening – and Martin can tell you about his play. '

'Love to. See you then. Just for coffee – don't start cooking.'

'I won't, I have to keep my feet up as much as possible.'

'Is your blood pressure up?' Ros asked.

'It fluctuates, so it's checked every week, now.'

'Oh. Well, see you tomorrow.'

I looked forward to a comfortable evening with the four of us. I could catch up with how Gill was getting on – among other things. Every so often I sent her some seed packets or bulbs. I always received a note written by her supervisor, signed in childlike writing by Gill. I was also longing to show Ros and Howard the mural.

Martin was home for good, then. There was so much else to think about, it happened without a fanfare. Neither of us knew what to think of first, though it should have been us and Jake. We were relieved when Ernie called with the good news that the doctor wasn't overly concerned about Dad, pointing to the bereavement as the main cause of Dad's anxiety and even his apparent forgetfulness. We were to watch and wait. Blume's words exactly. Perhaps I could relax, now.

How was it that nearly a hundred years ago, my grandmother was able to plough her own furrow, yet I was constantly entangled with everyone, leaving no space for myself?

'Ros and Howard are coming for coffee tomorrow evening,' I told Martin.

'For goodness sake, can't we be alone?' he asked.

'I'm sorry, but we haven't seen them for ages – maybe it'll feel more normal, having visitors? Particularly them.'

'Hm –'

'You're right, I didn't think… But I don't fancy putting them off, now.'

'Not to worry,' he said, before coming to see the nursery. That put a smile on his face. He suggested I create a website to advertise my 'skills'. He was serious and went straight to the computer to try out some trade names. We tried Murals4U – no good, it existed already. We'd just thought of another one when the phone interrupted us. It was Jake.

'Dad left me at Grandpa's looking through his papers and said he'd pick me up in half an hour. That was an hour ago – I think everyone's going bonkers!'

'Gosh, Jake, sorry. He'll be right there,' I replied. How awful. We'd both forgotten. Poor kid.

'We've relied too much on his good nature, lately – need to keep a careful eye on him,' I said.

'You're right.'

Once home, Jake stormed up the stairs angrily and shut himself in his bedroom, playing loud music. It went quiet once he began listening through earphones, but he remained incommunicado. Martin raised his eyebrows to me, shrugged and nodded his head in Jake's direction, his whole body a question mark. I beckoned him into the kitchen, where we started to prepare supper.

I closed the door. Martin told me Jake had hardly spoken to him and nothing he said could bring him round.

'Funny, I thought he'd be really happy I've come home again. I flatter myself, obviously!'

'Poor you. But life's been pretty difficult for him, and even Ernie can't give him undivided attention. Mind you, he's round a lot with a new friend, too: a girl.'

'So?' Martin asked.

'Nothing. Just... he's been too good to be true for a kid of his age.'

'Seems all that's about to change.' We heard banging from Jake's room.

I went up and knocked, but Jake didn't open the door. We left him to cool off. Soon after, a text arrived on my mobile. It was from Edna, Martin's mum. She said that Jake had just sent her a message, asking if he could stay with her in the summer holidays. It was fine with her but she wanted to check with us, so Martin called her.

'You mean he just asked you? He never mentioned it. How odd!' he said. 'Of course he can come but we'll talk it over. He's into silence, at the moment, big time.'

'Aha,' said Edna, 'he's at that age. Well, let me know.'

We gave up patiently waiting for Jake to reappear – we always do – and shouted to him. Of course, he didn't hear us with earphones in his ears, so I went to carry on painting, leaving Martin banging on his door.

'OK, I'm coming.' He peered round the half-open door at Martin. 'Yeah, what d'you want?'

'Just to talk,' said Martin tentatively.

'What about?'

'Dunno, really. Anything.'

'Oh. Is that all?' replied Jake, shutting him out.

'Er... well I'll be in the nursery when you want.' Martin came into the nursery and, saying nothing, gestured to me to go downstairs and leave him doing the painting. I went down and turned on the radio, so Jake would know I wasn't around, if he came to Martin. It was good to offload onto Martin again.

Martin came down alone and told me Jake was enjoying looking for more on Freidl's family.

'I peeped, slyly, at the computer screen, which Jake quickly turned off,' Martin told me. 'He said he'd been looking at family-tree websites, but it didn't look like a family-tree site, Nicki. I'm not sure what it was but I felt uneasy. What do we do? We've always trusted him. D'you think his computer is as confidential as his diary?'

'I suppose it is... honestly, it never rains but it pours. I can't take much more.'

'Much more what?' Martin asked.

'Other people's stress, that's what!' I screamed. 'What am I meant to think of first? Us? Dad? Jake? The baby? God, I think being a suffragette was less stressful than all this. Freidl only had to think of herself,' I sulked.

'Yeah, right. No parents, no family, sure. She only took on someone else's child – children! Come off it, Nicki. At least we're together,' Martin said. I sat down at the kitchen table, where he joined me. He took a can of tonic from the fridge, poured a tonic for me and for himself, a G&T.

'Here's to the future!' He clinked my glass.

'Can't I have a drink?' said Jake, suddenly appearing. 'Trish's mum lets her. *And* she leaves the key in the door of their drinks cupboard.'

'Good for Trish's mum,' I said. 'Who's Trish, anyway?'

'My new best mate. She's in the year above but we always chat before footie.' *Of course, unisex football.*

'She's friends with Damian, in my year and we hang about in a crowd together.'

I had to be as nonchalant as Jake: 'That's the good thing about co-ed schooling, having friends of the opposite sex. Can you imagine being at my all-girls school?'

'You bet!'

'You know what I mean.'

'Or my all-boys one!' chipped in Martin.

I asked whether he'd found anything about Freidl's family that could help the play; there was very little.

'Thing is, even with the internet, we only have Freidl's maiden name and Levy is *not* the most unusual name. And if her sister married she'd have another surname anyway. Nightmare.'

'That changing your surname thing,' Jake said. 'What d'you reckon, Mum? Did you stop being "yourself" when you changed it?' I hadn't really thought twice about it, but, now, I realised how it must be nice to retain your birth identity.

'There are all kinds of websites that can help find people, you know,' Martin said. He had seen an opportunity to broach our worries about the internet but was less than subtle: 'You do know how to protect your identity on these sites, don't you? So you don't get loads of spam – or worse?'

'Course. You create a new email address and a new user name.'

Martin nodded. So that was that – and Jake knew exactly what we were on about.

My clinic check-up came and so some kind of normality had returned, with Martin home and Jake a bit calmer. My scan showed a kicking baby, which was exciting, but the midwife said she wasn't quite as big as she'd like. I felt hot all over.

'Meaning?'

'Meaning she is "small for dates", as they call it in the trade,' said the midwife, trying to sound reassuring.

'But I thought babies shouldn't be big,' Martin commented.

'We're not talking about big or small, exactly, Mr Taylor. Rather, about the rate of growth, month on month. Look – here's a graph.' She showed us the rate at which a baby should grow in utero and, clearly, ours had slowed down. She took my blood pressure, which had gone up a bit more.

'You know, these things put together spell out the need for more rest, Mrs Taylor. I'd like you to stay off work for a month, while we monitor you. If things improve, fine, if not, you'll be off work until the birth, if it's up to me. I'll make you an appointment with the consultant obstetrician, OK?'

I was scared and my pulse raced.

'Was that the kindest way to put it?' Martin asked, in a fairly aggressive tone. I nudged him. 'Seriously, was it? Couldn't you sugar the pill a bit?'

'It's alright, Martin. The midwife – Jean – is just being careful. It's her job,' I responded, trying to break the tension.

'I think you were far too abrupt, Jean, sorry. I really do.' The poor midwife wasn't actually thrown off balance at all.

'My job is to protect the unborn baby,' she said, 'and of course, the mother, too. If you don't like my handling of the case, you can request another midwife.'

Good on her, I thought and I told Martin that I was happy with Jean, so we said goodbye and left. Martin was seething, but so was I... with him.

'Surely there should be some compassion, some way of allaying fears, something human...?' he said. I put my arm through his, squeezed it and told him to calm down.

Once home, I emailed school to say I'd be off work and attached my lesson plans for the next month – that would almost take us up to the summer holidays. At least I could be busy with the nursery and help with Martin's play. As long as the baby was OK. And at last, we emailed David with suggested dates for the unveiling.

When we got back, Jake was waving a sheet of paper at us.

'Look – I've been searching for people with the name Levy and Jewish Romanian roots.'

'Great – and I'll be able to help you, soon. I'll be off work for a while.'

'Why? What's wrong?' he asked.

'Nothing really. It's preventative. To give me and the baby a rest.'

TWENTY-FOUR

The phone rang. It was Ros, sounding distraught. 'It's Gill.'

'What?'

'Well... you know she lives in sheltered housing – almost independent, kind of? Anyway, she felt ill but couldn't describe it, so her care worker took her to hospital. Seems a nasty fly bite, maybe a horsefly from gardening, got infected – she didn't realise how bad it was... she doesn't notice things like that and now...'

'What?'

'She's got septicaemia. She's on life-support and...' Ros tailed off, in tears.

'I'm coming round,' I said, without thinking.

'I'm at home. Mum and Dad are with her.'

'See you in ten minutes.' *Should I have been driving round? How much was I meant to be resting?* Martin said he'd take me and we left as soon as I'd taken some of my vegetable soup from the freezer for Ros. When we got there, Martin stayed in the car till he knew what was going on.

Ros fell into my arms; she made the shoulder of my blouse damp with tears. I realised I'd soon get used to that feeling again, with a baby over my shoulder.

'Go into the living room,' I said, guiding her onto the settee, lifting her feet onto it. I went to make her a hot drink – I knew I would find what I needed, in the exact spot as always. I brought her a mug of her favourite milky coffee and she told me everything.

'Mum and Dad have had no respite, you know, even though Gill's been living away for a few years. There's never a day without some problem or other. Anyway, the hospital rules say two people, max, in intensive care. I'll take over from one of them in an hour or so.'

She reached for my hand, as I sat down next her. 'Thanks, Nicki.'

'For what?'

'For being here.'

'And haven't you always been there for me? I'm around more, now, actually – the baby's small for dates –'

'You shouldn't have rushed!'

'Yes, I should.' Her phone rang. I picked it up and handed it to her.

'Oh, no! Oh my God, you poor things...' she cried. 'You mean you had to decide to... Mum, I'll be over right away – I know you have – Martin or Nicki can bring me. Rabbi Lever? Yes I'll tell him. Of course, I'll find his number. Mum, wait, I...'

Ros turned to me, still holding the phone.

'Gill's – Mum and Dad had to let the doctors switch off her life-support,' she said, sobbing. 'How can parents be expected to do that?'

The doorbell rang and Martin came in, wondering why I'd been so long.

'Why have – is Gill worse? Oh no!' he said, seeing us crumpled together on the sofa.

'I've got to get to the hospital but Mum and Dad have my car. They...' Ros began, sobbing.

'I'll run you there,' Martin said, 'Nicki can stay here and do your phoning.'

'I will sit with the... with Gill. I'll stay till someone takes over, even if I'm there all night,' Ros said.

So I was to contact Rabbi Lever and he would call the *Chevra*

Kaddisha, volunteers who step in at a moment's notice at times like this.

'Oh! Howard – doesn't know – he's away on business,' said Ros. 'How could I...? Will you tell him, he's in New York... He does know Gill's in hospital.' She scrawled down his phone number, along with some others and the code for the house alarm, then gave me a spare key.

'I can't believe what I'm doing!' she said, sobbing softly. 'Is it true, d'you think?' I hugged her goodbye.

Calling through the car window, Martin shouted, 'Don't forget to tell Jake, Nicki – I'll call when I can. And sit down, while you're phoning.' He blew me a kiss.

I phoned Rabbi Lever with the news and he said he would go down to the hospital, but it was too late for a burial that day. *A bit easier on the family, then.*

'Leave it with me, Nicki. I can sit with the body till the team gets organised.' I thanked him and called Howard in New York. Poor guy – not the easiest phone call I've ever made. He had looked after a lot of Gill's needs since marrying Ros and had a good rapport with her – or as good as anyone could.

Her relationships with people never progressed in adulthood; nothing seemed to change, except her body. She clearly would have been a very beautiful girl in the normal course of things, with thick auburn hair and olive skin, but her awkward gait and ungainly movements detracted from her appearance.

After phoning all the people on Ros's list, I eventually called Jake – who was initially angry that we hadn't called earlier. After clearing up Ros's unusually messy kitchen, I sat down and waited. How sad it all was, how awful. By the time Martin came back for me, everything was in hand.

'This funeral arranging stuff – it's like a well-oiled machine. The rabbi calls the Chevra, they sort out a rota to sit with the body, prepare it for burial, help the family with the paperwork, inform the cemetery... So organised,' I said. 'How are Ros's parents?'

'Bereft.'

'Stupid question, sorry.'

'Mm – they said no one understands that a child with special needs gives something special to the parents. Poor things. When I left, Rabbi Lever was chatting to them and Ros. He calmed them a bit and discussed details for the funeral.'

'Awful, awful,' I said.

'He was talking over his eulogy. He does know them all well, which helps. Shul members will bring over prayer books and low chairs for the mourners to the shivah house; others will bring a meal for the family.'

'So there'll be nothing for them to do except... think of Gill,' I said. The funeral was set for 11.30 the next morning. Life was certainly unpredictable.

Rabbi Lever addressed the crowd in the *Ohel*, the special little room at the cemetery. There were many friends and family members, including staff and residents from the sheltered housing. Ros's parents looked even more frail than usual. Losing a child is so dreadful.

'Gill was a girl of special talents,' the rabbi began. 'She saw life and this world differently from the rest of us – so she brought something special to all who knew her.' I stood just behind Ros and squeezed her hand as we wept, silently. Martin had one arm round her and the other round me. Howard was on a flight home but wouldn't arrive till evening prayers.

The rabbi continued: 'In Gill's home village, she was known as "The Head Gardener" – she was gifted with anything green. Like Prince Charles, she thought that speaking to plants made them grow better. And they did! So, although it's not customary at a Jewish funeral, I asked Gill's parents to bring some flowers from her very own garden, to commemorate her talent. It's May, so they've brought some lilies of the valley – you can probably smell them. Let us all inhale their sweetness and remember the beauty and sweetness that was Gill's.'

His words were so meaningful; there wasn't a dry eye in the Ohel as he proceeded with the usual service, including her elderly father's frail voice reciting kaddish. That traditional prayer sounds, in itself, mournful – or perhaps that's because of its associations. I realised that Ros was accompanying him. Women don't always recite it, but Rabbi Lever encouraged her and it gave her father much-needed support.

Before we went to the graveside, the rabbi announced that prayers, at Gill's parents' flat, commenced that evening and would finish the following Tuesday morning. On the last night, they would be held at the sheltered housing village.

The only thing that lightened the leaden atmosphere was that the sun came out, after days of rain, just as we went outside to the graveside; it caught the little beads on Ros's hat, making them glisten, and caused people's wet cheeks to glow. Maybe sadness could shed its own kind of light.

The family stuck the lilies of the valley into the fresh pile of soil, after everyone had thrown their spadeful of earth into the grave. With each thud, we shivered, despite the sunshine.

We had to dash from the funeral to Jake. Life was frenzied – and I was meant to be resting. Martin took me home, telling me in no uncertain terms to rest until evening when we would go to Gill's parents' together.

Martin, at a shivah house? Interesting. As I opened the front door, Jake came bounding down the stairs – or rather, thudding.

'Hello there, darling!' I should have known better than to be sarcastic.

'For goodness sake, Mum. I've been waiting for *anyone* to be here to talk to!' He was entitled to be cross.

'OK, I get it,' I said, 'and poor Dad has had to go back to the office for a few hours. Life's mad, but it's out of our hands. I must sit down.' I put my feet up on the sofa.

Jake stood over me, hands on hips. 'So phone him and get him home, OK?'

TWENTY-FIVE

'What's so urgent?' I asked Jake.

'Why isn't Dad a proper Jew?'

'Say that again!'

'You heard.'

'He is.'

'No. He's not. He's reform. And you, Ernie and Dad are orthodox. Proper Jews. Officially, I am, too – cos you're my mum. But Dad's different. It's not fair!'

'Excuse me! What's this "proper" or "not proper"? Don't ever say that. We don't look down on anyone in this family. What started this?'

'Trish and I were –'

'Aha. It's something to do with Trish again, then. Does she not consider us "proper"?'

'Mum! Stop that. You know nothing about her. She's a mate. She's so bright, she's a school year ahead of her age. We've been looking on websites about identities.'

I was afraid of what was coming next; talk of websites makes me jittery.

'She's adopted and wanted to know more about her birth identity. She doesn't know much about her birth parents. I was on a Jewish genealogy website and she just wondered whether one or other of her parents could be Jewish.'

I was so relieved. 'And are they?' I asked.

'Doesn't seem like it. Her adoptive ones aren't, so she isn't, really, but she – well, she's dark haired and stuff… So, anyway, there's loads of stuff about Jewish identity and one bit was about conversion. It said, "People who convert 'reform' are not proper Jews."'

'Written by a far-right rabbi, no doubt,' I said.

'Whatever…'

'Look. You know there are differences between reform and orthodox. But we need to talk about it properly, with Dad.'

'So get him!' Jake replied.

'I told you – he'll be back this evening but then, we've got the shivah for Gill.'

'Y'see. Never any time,' Jake mumbled.

'You're right – and you know what? We're both exhausted. We need time together as well. Hm… we'll be back by 8.30 – why not come with us, then we could all go for a pickled meat sandwich? Just the three of us, eating and talking.'

'Just the three of us? And all the Jews of Manchester in there as well, all staring and gossiping. Yeah, right.'

'Fair point. So we'll buy some to take away and talk here, with all phones switched off.' I hoped that would do it. Grudgingly, Jake agreed.

Martin looked drained when he came in. What a twenty-four hours! And he didn't know what else was in store.

'God, I'm whacked.'

'Well, there's more to come,' I said and told him briefly about Jake, who was upstairs, changing for the evening. Martin stretched out on his favourite chair, not really absorbing what I'd said.

'You OK to drive to Sue's?' he asked.

Evening prayers were due to start at 7.30. We parked on the next road but, at 7.20, people were struggling to find parking places right outside; cars going in both directions blocked the short cul-de-sac. I hoped someone had warned the neighbours.

It was equally difficult to get through the front door – if people didn't chat on the way in, it would have been easier.

We squeezed into the lift, full to over-capacity ('Doris is only tiny', 'Just let him in, he's only twelve'), with people left downstairs, grumbling that they'd arrived first. They could have used the stairs. Were people impatient because they were anxious, visiting the bereaved? I watched Martin and Jake's strained faces as we went into the room – so, Jake took after his dad.

Ros and her parents, seated on their low chairs, were pleased to see us when, eventually, someone made a space in front of them so we could talk.

Her dad, taking Martin's hand in both of his, said, 'We couldn't have managed without you last night, at the hospital, thanks.'

'No thanks needed,' said Martin, smiling in acknowledgement, as he hugged them all. 'Rabbi Lever spoke well today, didn't he?' he added. Despite his reticence on these occasions, Martin still knew the right thing to say.

Ros nodded. 'Mm.' We hugged. They fussed over Jake, who looked quite a man in his green T-shirt with a checked over-shirt and cream chinos. Then Sue, Ros's mum, squeezed something into my hand.

'What's this?' It was a packet of sweetpea seeds.

'It's for you, it was in Gill's drawer, in her room. You taught her how seeds become flowers, when you were little and came to play, and gardening became her passion. Please, plant them and remember her.' I thanked her and read the packet.

'These are the perennial kind – lovely! You'll come and see them, next summer,' I said. 'So, is Rabbi Lever speaking again, tonight?'

'No, he's teaching, so anyone who wants to, can say something,' Ros said.

People carried on pouring into the room, backing up into

the hall and even the kitchen, where gifts of food containers and cakes piled up on the table. A freshly baked honey cake teetered on the top of one pile, so the frozen pies and boxes of soup underneath looked unstable. A small trickle of chocolate mousse was seeping out of a foil dish in a second pile, like lava flowing down the sides of a volcano. Its sickly-sweet smell mingled with that of honey cake, stew, soup and the coffee which was brewing.

A cousin of Ros's was trying to organise all the food, putting some in the freezer, some in the fridge and cutting up cake for later. The family wouldn't have to prepare any meals for the week – or beyond. It was still something to wonder at, this outpouring of kindness.

I went in to the sitting room and sat on a chair someone had kept for me. Martin and Jake were in the thick of it, standing near the family. Prayers were recited, psalms chanted and Ros again helped her father say kaddish. There was shuffling as people tried to create some space round the family who, by then, must have found it hard to breathe, though at one point, Martin took the initiative and opened a window. Ros asked everyone to be quiet.

Two people were ready to speak – through the crowd, I saw enough to realise they both had Down's syndrome. They read falteringly, in unison, from a crumpled piece of paper: 'We are Gill's best friends. We love her. She's the best.' They lived at the same sheltered housing. They cried, silently, as did many there – including Martin, I noticed. No other speeches about Gill could match that one.

After the service, people lined up in a disorderly queue to see the family again, before they left. No one knew which way the crowd was moving and as usual, people stayed leaning over the mourners for far too long. We had to be patient, because each visitor meant well.

As we left, Martin said, 'That was special.' A man of surprises.

'Chaotic, though,' I said.

'That's OK,' he replied. 'All that chaos ties us to life, not death – it's good, that.' Hang on a minute, Martin playing Spinoza?

'And it was good she had friends,' Jake said.

'Mm.' We all fell silent. We made for the deli, then home – which could prove more tense than the evening so far.

'Let's go to the last night prayers at Gill's sheltered housing.' That was Martin speaking? 'I wonder how it's done, there.'

'Maybe,' I said, 'if we've any time or energy left, by then?'

TWENTY-SIX

'So... come on, then, what's the problem?' Martin asked, looking straight at Jake, once we'd put the sandwiches and pickles on plates. 'Seems like a biggy. We can talk till I can't stay awake any longer – it's been quite a day.'

Jake looked down and took an extra big bite of his pickled meat sandwich, through which he attempted to talk – unintelligibly. He obviously didn't know how to start, so I did.

'Jake's upset, because –'

'Nicki, don't speak for him. Jake, just get it off your mind.'

Jake blushed. 'People say that reform converts aren't proper Jews. So why didn't you convert orthodox, so we'd all be the same?'

I was shocked that he would say this to Martin's face. I interrupted: 'That's a bit...'

'Nicki, shush. It's his Bar Mitzvah year and he wants to know. I can handle it.' Poor Martin, having to bare his soul to his own child. A reasoned debate is a very Jewish way of doing things, yet I tried to keep quiet.

Martin explained that when we decided to marry, we talked endlessly about whether he'd convert, and if so, how.

'First, I had to realise that I'd no longer be a Christian – a big first step, y'know.'

'That's obvious,' Jake replied.

'It may be, now. But even though I was Christian in name only, converting meant leaving lots behind.'

'Like what?'

'Mum and Dad, for starters. My whole childhood, really.'

'Did they cut you off?' Jake looked concerned for his father.

'No, but it wasn't easy.'

'Were they as hostile as Mum's parents?'

'Not hostile – they knew we were happy – but they worried about how I'd change. Anyway, I read a lot, talked with different rabbis, your grandma and grandpa – and Freidl, too.'

'Was she a battleaxe?' Jake asked.

'Quite the opposite,' Martin said. 'She was great. Funny. Y'know, Nicki, Rabbi Lever wasn't here, then. If he had been, I might well have gone the orthodox route. I like his approach.'

'That's history now, love,' I said, taking his hand across the table.

Jake went on, 'What kind of Christian were you?'

'Lapsed! But, seriously, we went to a Unitarian Chapel – when we went to church at all. We only went there because it was on our street. And y'know what? Some people at my school told me I wasn't really Christian –'

'OMG!' Jake interrupted.

'True. That's what they said about Unitarians. Everyone's judgemental, y'see. I didn't know how to argue the case, then. But let's get to your mum and me.'

'Did Mum *make* you...?'

'What?

'Convert.'

'Not exactly. But the main thing was that I knew that her Jewishness, or Judaism, would pass to our children.'

'So you could take the easy way and go with reform.'

'That's rude!' I said, wanting to put a stop to the whole discussion, but Martin answered.

'It wasn't an easy route at all, but it did take less time. The "easiness" was that I didn't have to live with an orthodox family for a year, even though you do learn how to live a Jewish life that way. But I learnt lots from Mum's family and –'

'Did you have to have the snip, or were you circumcised already?'

'Both. Once as a baby and then for the conversion,' replied Martin. Now he was blushing. 'That was not easy.'

'S'pose not.' Jake replied.

'Look. I don't mind having this out – really, it's good – but can we carry on tomorrow?'

'You're chickening out.'

'Jake, enough,' I said.

'Only joking.'

'We'll carry on, but I don't know when. OK? I'm shattered,' Martin reasoned. 'It'll all take time, too.'

'OK.' With that, Jake made to go up to his homework and bed.

'Night, Jake.' I kissed him goodnight and Martin hugged him.

'Thanks, Dad.' Jake went upstairs.

'That was tough,' I said.

'It had to come.'

I wondered whether this was *too* transparent an argument to have with your child.

'I'm whacked. You must be, too.'

'Come on, bedtime for my daughter!' Martin smiled as he pushed me out of the kitchen, stroking my pregnant tum. 'It hasn't exactly been the kind of restful day the midwife ordered!'

The next evening, the religion discussion continued.

'Where were we up to? Martin asked.

'Not sure,' said Jake. 'I get what you said, yesterday, but it's my Bar Mitzvah that's bugging me.'

'Well it would, for anyone,' Martin replied.

'I'm not *anyone* – I'm mixed up –'

'About...?'

'About where I belong in all this... shul stuff.'

'Meaning?'

'I want my Bar Mitzvah in Grandpa's shul.'

'Hang on. That's a new spanner in the works.'

They talked well into the night, focusing on the choice of synagogue for the ceremony. The celebration party wasn't the issue. Earlier, Jake was happy when we suggested having it in Israel. But we'd shelved that plan for now, because of the new baby on the horizon.

He knew that Martin, having converted at the reform shul, couldn't be directly involved during the ceremony at the orthodox shul: Rabbi Lever's synagogue and the one attended by Dad, Ernie and, previously, Mum. However, everyone could be involved if the Bar Mitzvah were at the reform shul.

'Look,' Martin said. 'We can go back to Plan A and rethink Jerusalem – dependent on how old the baby is then. That's one idea. The thing is, who makes the compromise?'

'Dunno.'

'Well, at the reform shul, I'll be by your side; at the other shul we'll all still be there, but Grandpa would stand by your side, instead of me.'

'It's rubbish! You're my Dad! It's bonkers. Not fair...' Jake tailed off, trying his pre-teen best not to cry. I agreed.

'Life's not fair, a lot of the time,' Martin piped up, 'but you have it a lot fairer than many –'

'Oh yeah!'

'Yes. You have Grandpa and Great-Uncle Ernie, who can play my part, for that few minutes, if you want to be in their shul.'

I was amazed that Martin would even contemplate sitting on the sidelines; I so wanted him to be at the centre of things.

'Listen, Jake,' said Martin. 'If the baby is early, we can shift everything over to Israel, even with only a few months' notice.

But we couldn't finalise anything until the baby was here and healthy. You know which portion of the Torah you will be reciting. The complex stuff, you have to sort out for yourself. Agreed?'

'I'm still thinking. And – oh, I meant to tell you, I do want to go to Grandma Taylor's for a few days. In the hols, remember? You suggested it a while ago. She said it's fine.'

I pretended I hadn't already heard about it. 'You asked her?'

'Yes – we chat from time to time.'

'Good,' Martin said. 'The country air is great. Maybe it'll help you.'

'Hm.'

We were absolutely exhausted, again. This discussion was far harder than the one we had with my parents when Martin and I decided to marry. I had thought nothing could be harder than that. In bed that night, we decided we needed a break, even just for a weekend.

'Let's take off to the Lakes for a couple of nights,' I said. 'Blume wanted to go there with Ernie. What if they came, too? And we couldn't leave Jake behind in the circumstances, I suppose.'

'Just the two of us, *please*. Why not while Jake is with Mum? Night.' Martin was almost asleep already.

'Love you. You've been a star with everyone,' I whispered, as I kissed him on the ear. With his back to me and half asleep, he bent his arm back and stroked my shoulders, breasts and belly. I stroked him, too – firmly, on the back of his neck, trying to soothe him, and down his arms. I was tempted to stroke his buttocks and thighs but left off, as we both needed sleep.

'Don't stop there,' he whispered, as he guided my hand back. He turned us both over, with my back to his front, and stroked me between my legs. I expected him to be too tired – was there no limit to this man's energy? We made gentle love that way – my belly was now a bit in the way if we faced each other – but

I curled my arm behind my head to run my fingers through his hair. He nuzzled the back and sides of my head, licking my ears. It felt good.

'I'm well and truly back,' he said.

'So I noticed. Night.'

Are we reconciled, so easily?

TWENTY-SEVEN

Blume and Ernie became an item – her two weeks became a month and after that, she just stayed. Ernie was rejuvenated and we liked having her around. One weekend, they went to Germany to collect some of Blume's belongings. There was no property to sell as she had never owned a home there, just rented. In Israel, she had stayed in a guesthouse, so anything she took there had accompanied her to England.

She fitted in, she made Ernie happy and somehow, she reinvigorated the family. No one could substitute for Mum, but in some ways she was a kind of mother figure. People we knew were fascinated by my natural friendship with her and I was fascinated by hers with Ernie. They held hands a lot, kissed every so often, and Ernie's arm was round Blume whenever possible. You could tell by the way they looked into each other's eyes that this was a full-blown romance.

While I was off work and Martin was back in the routine of writing and working, Blume came round often, to help with the nursery. She wasn't artistic but was happy to do anything. What she did do well, was sew – she offered to make the blinds, but she had no sewing machine.

Freidl's old machine – which Mum used – would still be around somewhere in Dad's house, so we went over to look. Dad was pleased we were coming but, naturally, he wanted to chat. His house was looking more orderly; we had hired a cleaning agency for him – even though Blume had wanted to take this on herself. I left Dad chatting to Blume over a cup of tea and went upstairs to the little spare room where I hoped to find the sewing machine. It was a good job we weren't looking for the old treadle version Freidl once used; we'd never have got that home.

I could barely open the door of the box room: it held a lot more than boxes. I tried to concentrate my search because if I wasn't careful I'd be there for weeks. I peeped at the photo albums, papers and scraps of fabric: *That was from the skirt Mum made me, for…? And Freidl's dress for my wedding was made of that!*

I'd never finish. If there was fabric, there had to be a sewing machine. I spotted it under some box files, behind an old chest of drawers which contained enough for a whole haberdashery. I foraged in that chest: I could use any little bits of braid or ribbon for a collage for the baby, so I stuffed them all into an old plastic bag. Blume would help me extricate the machine from its prison. Dad called from downstairs.

'Nicki! Are you alright? You've been ages.'

I went onto the landing: 'I'm fine, Dad. You know what it's like in there. I'll help you clear it out sometime.'

'Oh no you won't.'

'OK. Blume, can you help me?' She came up and we managed to slide the machine out of its hiding place and took off its heavy wooden case. She carried that gingerly downstairs but I couldn't lift the machine itself. Even though it was electric, it was very heavy. Blume took that down as well.

'Dad, just a word. Can we find a date for Mum's unveiling, d'you think? Now we know you're OK, we have to arrange it.'

'As far ahead as possible. That's all. I don't fancy going back to the cemetery too soon. I was thinking of December or January.'

'I think it will work better for the family if it's this summer.'

'Oh alright, you sort it out with David then,' Dad mumbled.

'We'll do our best.'

'We'll be off. Thanks.' Blume had hauled the machine into the boot of my car.

'Thanks for coming,' he said, hugging us both. 'You make a good pair.'

Blume carted the case into the house, putting it down heavily on the hall table.

'Phew! That case is so heavy,' I said. 'It was before the days of plastic.'

Before I knew it, Blume had wiped down the sewing machine, found a packet of needles inside the case and tried it out on a fabric scrap she fished out of the plastic bag. It still worked.

'It will need oiling, though,' she said.

She planned out the blinds on the fabric roll, checking the pattern match, but she needed some thread and new needles. I took her to the only haberdasher's left in the neighbourhood, the next day, while I went for my midwife check-up. It was the same midwife as before and she was fairly reassuring about the baby.

'A good strong heartbeat, your blood pressure is fine, but I'm afraid the baby is still not growing at the rate I'd like – it's growing only marginally faster than when I saw you last. Are you really resting?'

'I'm trying.'

'Next week, you see Mrs Robertson, the consultant. She'll look into everything in more detail. For now, carry on as before, only more so. You are on folic acid, aren't you?

'Yes.'

'Good. I'd tell your school that you'll need another two weeks on top of the month.'

'Oh.'

'Sorry.'

'I will rest. But what if the baby still doesn't grow? Then what?' I asked.

'It'll mean hospital bed rest and an early delivery. You see, at the moment, the baby doesn't find the uterus or placenta very user-friendly. Keep on with your folic acid and we'll see.'

I couldn't see how we'd plan anything at all, with all this. Everything else paled into insignificance.

At the shops, Blume got into the car, looked at me and asked, 'What did she say?'

I told her everything.

'Babies take over your life even before they're born,' she said. She was so wise, with no children of her own.

'Nicki, can I help with anything?' she asked. 'With the unveiling, perhaps? I don't have to be Jewish to bake, or make tea for people, do I?' She was smiling.

'Of course not, but it's...'

'That's settled, then. What else?'

I told her we needed to check a date with everyone concerned, see the stonemason and, later on, announce the date in the papers. She said she'd do all that.

'And we could have the reception at Ernie's. I'll check with him and Joe,' she added, seeing my look.

So Blume took a weight off my mind – but was she taking over? It seemed we thought alike.

'Can I offer some more? Or am I being, perhaps, pushing?'

'What do you mean?' It was the first time her stilted English didn't quite make sense.

'I can help more – but not if I am being pushing,' she said again.

'The pram, do you mean? Pushing the pram? Oh, no! You mean "pushy",' I laughed.

'I have many nieces and nephews. When they were little I did a lot with them. They're grown up now, but I would love to help with the new baby. Ernie and I can be your babysitters; you'll never have to worry about that.'

'But Jake can babysit.'

'He'll be out having fun.'

She was right, but perhaps she *could* become too 'pushing'.

'Thanks, Blume. It's great to know you'll be around.' I hugged her. 'You aren't pushing at all!'

Martin received her offer far more keenly than I. He thought it would be great to have a local grandma figure.

'Martin, we don't know where the Bar Mitzvah will be, yet. Which synagogue, which country even!'

'Stop worrying. For now, the date's the Shabbat before Pesach.'

'Sounds wonderful,' I said. 'So I'll wait till you've finished the "big discussion".'

'It's more like a party political debate,' Martin said.

Even though I was off work, I didn't seem to have a head for sorting things. The less I did, the less I could concentrate. And I'd neglected my teaching colleagues completely, so I emailed school. Later that day, emails came back from friends there, worried about me, so I invited them round to catch up.

I left Blume to sort out the unveiling and the nursery blinds. She set up a table for the sewing machine in the nursery, checking her measurements as she went along. She was stitching away when Ros arrived the next day, so they met when Ros came up to see the nursery. But Ros couldn't grasp the relationship.

Once we were back downstairs and Blume was sewing again, Ros said, 'Hang on. She's German and is living with your uncle, and he was a child refugee from Nazi Germany? How d'you know what her family did in the war? What if she was in the Hitler Youth or –'

'Hang on! It's so amazing,' I said, and I told her the whole Lanzig story. Naturally, she was dumbfounded – and moved.

But eventually she had to leave. 'Hope your life's getting back on track,' she said as she did so.

'Maybe,' I said.

I decided to have a proper rest in bed. I left the bedroom

door open, so that Blume could shout if she needed anything. It didn't take her long. I had just taken off my shoes and climbed onto the bed, when she came in, waving something. It was an empty envelope, old and torn.

The writing on it was faded but mostly legible. How could we deal with yet another piece of the past? It had dropped out of a compartment in the sewing-machine case where attachments were stored. The handwriting was obviously not English, but typically European – yet we could make out that it was addressed to Grandma Freidl. The stamp, now a collectable item, was damaged but was clearly from Romania. It was addressed to Freidl Levy and from someone called Miriam M Something.

'That's Freidl's sister's name,' I said. 'Miriam Malkah!' The surname certainly wasn't Levy. It looked like 'Fainaro'; I quickly briefed Blume on the background to this.

'This is so exciting,' I said. 'So, her sister must have married – strange name. Is there an address on the back? … There *was* some correspondence, then.' This was a big find.

Blume helped decipher the place name in the sender address, as it looked a bit like German handwriting. She brought me the laptop so, with the help of the internet and the bits we could decipher, we made it out to be Str. 1 Decembrie, Botosani, which was in North East Romania.

'Str. will be short for street, something like *strade*, *strasse*,' I said, 'and the website says that Botosani had a large Jewish community.'

We kept on looking and learned that Fainaro was a common name in the older, Sephardic Jewish community. It meant miller or flour-maker, a bit like the French *farine*.

When Jake came in from school, he wondered whether I was ill, being in bed.

'I'm fine – but look at this!' I shouted.

At that, Blume said she'd go home so Jake could have time with me.

'Love and hugs to Ernie,' I said, as she left. 'Let's sort out an evening with you both.'

'I will,' she replied.

'So, Jake, this is a big clue to Great-Grandma Freidl's family,' I said, handing him the old envelope.

'Can't read that,' he grumbled, though I told him what I had discovered. I thought he'd be excited by it, considering the envelope was about a hundred years old. He looked miserable and tired and I offered to make him a snack; he declined and went to his room.

Pre-teen angst hung over the house like an unseen spider's web, waiting to cling to you in hidden corners. I took the laptop into the living room, sat down and continued to search the web, just googling the name and address in Romania. The phone rang.

'Good to hear you, Ernie, it's been ages.'

'Not to worry, Blume's spoken for me, I suppose,' he said.

'Is she back?' I asked.

'No. She's shopping.'

'So – do you mind?'

'Mind what?' Ernie asked.

'That she has taken over… things. Did I sense something in your voice, before? … Whoops! I've gone too far.'

'You can never go too far for me, Nicki. I understood what you asked me. I don't mind really, it's just new for me, that's all. I am fond of her. We're fond of each other.'

'And I like her, too.'

'Good. She could overcrowd you, it's the German way, but she genuinely loves us all. It's nothing short of a miracle –'

'My thoughts exactly,' I said. 'So, when can we get together?' I broke off as I heard Jake whistling as he came downstairs. The air had cleared, then. 'Ernie, I must go for now, sorry, but what about coming here next Friday night?'

'Could we meet, just the two of us, like we used to?' Ernie asked.

'Of course. It'll have to be here. But wouldn't that upset Blume?'

'Not at all. I'll come round for coffee tomorrow, then, if that's alright.'

'OK.' Jake was trying to interrupt me by flapping his arms around. 'Just stop that and wait! No, Ernie, I was talking to Jake, sorry. See you tomorrow.'

'No problem, bye,' Ernie said.

'Jake. Calm down!'

'Listen, Mum. Trish is on her way round. She's a whizz at using the internet and I told her about the letter – I mean envelope...'

'Well, blow me! I thought you weren't interested in it,' I replied.

'What? Oh, that. Sorry, I was mad about something else,' Jake said.

'Which was...?'

'Nothing.'

'Didn't look like nothing.'

'Just leave it, Mum, OK?'

I left it. Five minutes later the doorbell rang.

'I'll get it – it'll be Trish,' Jake called.

Into the house walked a divine being. In striped tights, her long, colt-like legs eventually met her tiny skirt; a droopy open-weave tunic hung loosely round her non-existent hips.

She kicked off her floppy boots as soon as she came in and held out a porcelain hand, saying, 'Hello, you must be Jake's mum. I'm Trish.'

'Nice to meet you, Trish,' I said, impressed by her good manners and unable to take my eyes off her. She had fair but rosy skin and wide-spaced, green eyes. A few dark curls cascaded over her forehead and ears, escaping from the rest, which was caught up nonchalantly in a top knot. She undid and rewrapped the shiny bobble at least twice in the time it took to introduce ourselves. As she smiled, dimples appeared and her eyes sparkled.

'Er, can I get you a drink or something?' I faltered, unusually lost for words.

'Not to worry, Mum, I'll make us a smoothie. We'll take it up to my room so we can use my computer,' Jake said.

'Alright, I'll just get on then…' I mumbled, having nothing to get on with and feeling useless.

'Thanks, Mrs Taylor,' Trish said, as they went into the kitchen together.

So it was that the polite and beautiful Trish entered our lives. What a sweetie! But they were in his room – a room with a bed in it. And dangerous websites. What a new world they inhabited. I flopped onto the sofa, from where I began to text Ros, to explain why we hadn't managed to go to another night of prayers – Martin and I were both completely exhausted.

At that moment there was a ping and a text appeared from David. Like me, he'd heard from Blume about the unveiling.

'BLUME'S A BLUMING GOOD ORGANISER! ALL LOOKS FINE. WILL COME WITH BABY. WILL MARTIN'S PLAY BE READY THEN? CALL YOU SOONEST. X'

Well, good for Blume. She could push all she liked! The unveiling was close to mine and David's birthday, so we could have a celebration of sorts while he was here.

I thought it was time I called Ros, who answered rather – well – not like herself. It was obvious that she'd expected us to go to another night of prayers. I understood that and began to explain why we hadn't. But she didn't leave me room in the conversation to do so.

'Look, Nicki, we're all busy. I feel so alone. I know there's Howard but – well – Gill's all I had.'

She was alluding to their having no children – something we'd rarely touched on in recent years. Should I now feel guilty, for having Jake's problems and a pregnancy?

'Ros, you're right to be upset, but I've been told to rest: that's a priority. And then there's a little aggro with Jake that I won't bore you with. As well as worrying about Dad, he's been a bit off colour, so I –'

'You know, Nicki, I can't get into all that right now.'

'Fair enough. I haven't come up trumps for you but I wanted to explain why.'

'Well, for now, you get on with your busy little life and let me know when you can spare some time for me. OK?'

'OK, but I did call you, remember. I'll call again next week.'

'Fine. Bye.' And she rang off. I had failed her.

I put my feet up on the sofa and tried to be selfish, for the sake of the baby. As I dozed, an image of our crowded calendar kept taking up my relaxation space. I couldn't remember how the friendship between Ros and me had survived her childlessness and the subsequent difference in our lifestyles, but it had and I'd always thought there was no place for envy between really close friends.

I stayed lying down and concentrated on our baby. I smiled to myself. I realised I couldn't settle comfortably on the sofa any more. I wrapped my arms round the baby, who seemed to respond by wriggling nicely. Wriggling nicely is not exactly what twelve-year-old boys do – what an age gap! She seemed fine, though, I thought.

A girl… wouldn't have minded a boy at all – but this could be fun. Hope she's OK.

We'd have to talk about names, eventually, but there was too much other stuff floating around for that, now. For myself, if Martin agreed, I knew I'd call her after Freidl, since David had already called his son after my mum, Malkah.

Hm… a name beginning with F – that's a start. Got it! Fleur! That will recall Grandma's flower, and also Blume and the Lanzigs. Lucky that her *name means flower. What about Fleur and Taylor*

– 229 –

together though? Hm, not too good. Flora, then, Flora Taylor. That's better. And her second name can be after Martin's mum, who will be thrilled. So – what? Edwina, Edina, Edana, Elana? Flora Edina Taylor? Mm. Nice. Or maybe...

TWENTY-EIGHT

'Wake up, Nicki,' Martin whispered, kissing my cheek.

'I wasn't asleep. What's the time?'

'Half five.'

'Then I dozed off for an hour! Wow – is Trish still up there with Jake?'

'No idea,' Martin said. 'I'll see.' I mouthed to him how lovely she was and he went up the stairs noisily, whistling as he went. I followed him; he knocked before he went in.

'Dad, there's no need to knock.'

'I always do. Anyway, hi – I gather you are Trish,' he said, as nonchalantly as he could. She stood up and shook his hand to say 'hello'. No friend of Jake's had ever done that; even the nicest kids usually grunted without looking up.

'JT and I are having a websites adventure,' she said, grinning.

'Adventure? Meaning...?' Martin asked.

'You know, Dad, on the genealogy ones... looking for relatives of Malkah Fainaro.'

'Who is – ?'

'Grandma's namesake: Miriam Malkah, Freidl's sister – you know?'

'No I don't, sorry,' Martin said. I filled him in on the recent find.

'That's fascinating.'

After a bit, Trish said she was leaving.

'Please can we give you supper?' I asked.

'Very nice of you, but no. Mum prefers me to eat with her.'

'D'you want a lift home?' Martin said.

'I'm fine. It's light enough for me to get home OK,' she replied.

'Another time, then,' I said, warming to this delightful girl, who smiled in response. She tapped Jake on the shoulder, as he carried on surfing the web.

He didn't get up, just half-turned his head: 'Seeya, then.'

Martin went to see her out but she went downstairs on her own, shouting up from the front door, 'Bye, everyone!'

There was something very appealing about Trish and I felt guilty for my initial scepticism.

'She's a really nice girl, Jake.'

I thought that would please him but he replied with his usual, 'Cool, Mum.'

Martin looked like the cat who'd licked the cream, beaming. The Trish effect – or so I thought. As I went down, he stayed upstairs and talked to Jake.

I left them to it, thinking that they might continue the identity debate, and spent a while reading the minutes from the school governors' meeting, but the altercation with Ros weighed on my mind. It was up to her to patch it up. Martin and Jake came down to the kitchen.

'We carried on our Judaism discussion,' said Martin.

'And?'

'There probably isn't a perfect solution.'

'I reckon you two are nearer to a solution than anyone else in the Jewish world.' They both smiled and I ladled out bowls of vegetable soup.

'We're getting there,' I said. 'And what about your play, love, how's that doing?'

As he answered, I wondered whether we were tying up all the loose ends. Jake, meanwhile, was continuing to research the Fainaro family.

'You know, there is an archive of all kinds of things at Central Ref,' I said. 'Not on computer but on microfiche.'

'What's Central Ref, and what's micro-thingy?' Jake asked.

'Oh come on, Jake, you know Central Reference Library – the big round building in St Peter's Square. We've taken you to plays there.'

'Oh, OK. But the theatre's in the basement. I've never seen the actual library.'

'You're deprived then.' I told him of the many happy hours I spent there revising for exams – which was more about looking at the boys on the next table than any books.

'I'll take you there one day,' said Martin.

'Take him? There's the metro tram, now. He can take himself in the holidays, or go with Trish.'

'Will do,' Jake said, smiling.

'And when you go into the main, round hall, look for the saying that runs round the edge of the ceiling,' I told him. 'We spent our time swivelling round to read it, when we were really trying to spot the boys at the furthest side of the massive room, and seeing whether our voices would echo clearly enough for them to hear us whispering. A day researching at Central Ref is a Manchester rite of passage, even if you do no research at all.'

Martin was working on a scene in the play depicting Freidl and Uncle Isaac's big row.

'The thing is, suffragettes acted more on principle than emotion –'

'Like anyone fighting for a cause,' I said.

'But Freidl chose to forget how much Isaac had done for her,' Jake suggested.

'Exactly,' Martin replied.

'I don't think she *chose* to… but she and Isaac had no common ground,' I said.

'Could make a great scene. But… Listen. There's more work

news. There's a lot of expense coming up for us. It was worrying, but now...'

'Now, what?' I asked.

'Spit it out, Dad.'

'Well – we may not need to.'

'Not need to what?'

'Worry.'

'Meaning?' I was lost.

'I'm in line for... a promotion – another job – I –'

'What? Out of the blue?' I asked.

'Yes and no.'

'Well, that clarifies it, thanks.' I passed round the shepherd's pie.

'Hang on, Nicki. So much is going online and before long, most books will be published digitally.'

'But that's bad news for you, isn't it?'

'Wait a sec!' Martin explained that the company wanted someone to take on the running of a digital division – an entirely new section. After that, there could well be a merger with another company.

'Sounds great,' Jake said.

'We have to get in quickly, there's lots of competition.'

'Could you get it, Dad? Because of your computer skills?'

'Maybe.' Martin seemed reticent in spite of his smile. I could tell there was more to it.

'There's a "but" isn't there?' I asked.

'Yes. A big "but".'

'Go on, go on!' Jake said, with the enthusiasm of youth. But I was afraid of what would come next.

'We'd have to move.' I looked hard at Martin as he spoke. 'To London. Or maybe the States.'

Jake punched the air.

The tension that followed was almost tangible – just as we were enjoying our meal. For a moment, I thought Martin was joking: he'd applied for a new job without telling me? We'd only just recovered from major crises. This seemed unbelievable. Was I being unreasonable yet again? I didn't think so and tried to think of anything other than the topic of conversation.

'Hello?' Martin leant over the table and looked me straight in the eye. 'Anybody home?'

I looked up and realised he was grinning, showing no anxiety whatever. Jake was practising his American drawl, 'Howdee folks!' followed closely by his Cockney impersonation: 'The rine in Spine falls minely in –' I wasn't amused.

'Doll...?' Martin tried again. 'Aren't you excited? There's a big increase in salary. Life will be brilliant – a whole new start!'

'But we're OK as we are – we've just settled down. How could you think I'd be excited? We can't move, now. There's the new baby, my job, Jake's school, his Bar Mitzvah, Dad, Ernie...'

'Hold on! Don't bring the whole family into it, for goodness sake! Let me tell you about the job, first. You should be pleased Catherine asked me to apply. D'you want to know about it at all?'

'Mum, at least let's listen!'

'Don't interfere,' I said, as I summed up my recollection of this Catherine, his managing director. Smart, attractive, very slim, the last time I met her, a couple of years ago. My pregnant shape suddenly felt grotesque.

'Not fair. It's my life too,' Jake said.

'So tell us,' I said and I tried to pay attention.

Martin explained about the digital division which was the only way for publishers to keep going and also keep their public reading.

'But how come this is the first I've heard of it?' My mind raced through our other conversations to find clues.

'We began discussions before Hong Kong and it was the general talking point at the conference.' Why 'we'? I wondered.

'But it wasn't a good time to throw it at you, when I got home,' he said.

I was not feeling charitable. 'Now isn't much better.'

'I can't help that. Emails and calls have been flying to and fro ever since,' Martin went on. 'I've had a couple of meetings with the top brass. They prefer someone from inside the company to take on the initial set-up –'

'And they want you because of your computer know-how, when you ran those arts festivals, years back?'

'Partly, yes.'

He had been very successful – quite unusual in the arts world – and broke records at various fringe festivals in Southern England – usually notorious money-losers. He could combine his techno skills with his eye for new writing talent in this new department. Maybe Catherine would move, too? His colleague's name suddenly reared its head again. I was becoming paranoid.

'But you're on short-time working, now, so I assumed the business wasn't buoyant,' I said.

'In general terms it's tough, but if the new section takes off, we'll be ready to merge with another company to strengthen our skills. But we've got to move fast.'

'Why did you give up that arts festival stuff, Dad? Jake asked.

'He wanted to come back to Manchester,' I said.

'To be with your mum,' Martin added, smiling. 'Those jobs were all London-based and we didn't want to live in London, then.'

'Ironic. Do we, now? And what did you mean by "London or maybe the US?" There's a heck of a difference.'

'There's bound to be a link with the US. They're way ahead of the game and it may be an American company we merge with. Even if I'm based in London, I'd have to go there a lot. Look – for now, the management will put my name forward.'

'The management', the euphemism for 'Catherine', rang in my ears as I cleared the empty plates, delaying my response.

We finished dinner in silence. Martin eventually broke it.

'I'm sorry it's upset you – but it's an amazing opportunity, love.'

'Hear, hear!' Jake said.

I was on eggshells. I was pleased for Martin but I couldn't see us starting a new life without any of the family support system. And our relationship was still vulnerable.

'It's good you've been offered it.' I tried to sound conciliatory. 'But...?'

'You already know the "buts". It'd be painful to leave Manchester – even though I'm not madly attached to my own job.'

'Oh God, sorry. But I did think of that, I –'

'Well... but to be honest, kids in a classroom don't differ that much.'

'No, really, I did think of you. I thought in London you'd have a good chance of setting up a mural-painting business. I mean it,' Martin said.

'There'll be loads of posh people wanting their darlings to have pretty nurseries,' chipped in Jake.

'Could be,' I continued. 'Look – the other big "but" is my dad. If David lived here, it'd be different. But I can't expect Ernie to take on all my – all our – responsibilities.'

'D'you think I haven't thought of that? You underestimate me sometimes, Nicki. We could take him with us.'

At that, I felt he overestimated *me*. 'Have him *live* with us? No way! Do the washing for three men? Thanks.'

'His house could fetch enough for a small flat – he could come with us but not *with* us.'

'But he couldn't move to the States at his age.'

'No. Only if we went to London.'

'So the States isn't a definite option?'

'It's not compulsory, no.'

I wondered if refusing the US made him less of a favourite.

The whole thing terrified me. 'I just don't know. We've got friends here, family, jobs – roots – and you'll be further from your mum, too.'

'I think it's wicked,' Jake said. 'I know lots of guys from London from youth group – met them at summer camp last year. They're cool.'

I watched Jake and, yes, he seemed to mean it. I wondered whether he had really thought about it carefully – and of leaving the beautiful Trish. But at his age, he'd go along with whatever happened. Perhaps he liked the thought of a bit more money coming in – a few more pairs of designer jeans?

Martin broke the silence. 'I'm really sorry we'll be leaving your mural.' *Was that all?* 'I know you could never take it with you, but it's so new...'

'And the rest,' I said.

'The rest of what?'

'Everything.'

Martin came round to me and put his hands gently on my shoulders. One look from his milk-chocolate eyes could have totally won me over, but I suddenly realised he didn't really know how my mind or my emotions worked. He was a picture of contentment and looked well – his angular cheekbones had filled out just a little.

'Look, I know what you feel, obviously,' he said, 'but try looking at the bigger picture. Let's let it rest for now – at least till after you've seen the obstetrician. If I do get the job, we won't move before the baby, anyway.'

'Oh. That helps. And the unveiling's in the summer, so that's OK. What about the Bar Mitzvah?'

'Well, if it's going to be in Israel, it won't make any difference where we're living. And y'know, Nic, about the family support network – you're the mainstay of the family. It may do you good to release the strings a bit.' He could be right again.

'Good one, Dad,' Jake added.

At that moment, in his ebullient mood, I saw Martin in Jake. He was maturing fast and, while he'd been a Bamberg as a little boy, this adolescent was rapidly becoming more of a Taylor – and so handsome.

Martin looked at him admiringly. All the in-depth discussions they'd had lately had brought them closer. They would probably stand together on the move.

'Let's see what the next week brings, OK?' I wasn't ready for compromise yet.

'OK. Fine with me,' said Martin, one arm round Jake's shoulder and the other round mine. 'We three are in it together, aren't we?' He squeezed my shoulder and kissed my ear. 'Well, four, actually.'

TWENTY-NINE

My meeting with Ernie had come at a good time.

'You look wonderful. Two weeks in a pregnancy makes such a difference,' he said, as we kissed. 'You look less drawn. But you're looking at me strangely. What's wrong?'

'Absolutely nothing,' I lied. We chatted about the unveiling, Jake, all that, before coming to what really mattered.

'How's Blume?' I asked.

'And how's Martin?' was his reply.

'You start.'

He looked embarrassed as he began to describe his misgivings about her rapid move into his life. I wasn't surprised but I was sorry for him. He still liked her, but he had difficulty finding 'space'.

'I like being on my own sometimes and she doesn't understand. She's an amazing housekeeper, but I don't need mothering – maybe it was too late to change.' Ernie's face dropped; wrinkles and lines appeared from nowhere.

'So – do you think you've made a mistake?' I wondered whether I'd gone too far. He simply shrugged. Poor, dear Ernie. What a shame, at this time in his – and Blume's – life. I couldn't think what to say. We sat there, miserably.

'I can't bring myself to tell her.'

'It depends *what* you tell her,' I said. 'I think she could handle it if you open a discussion. She's so eminently sensible. Maybe you could work out a way of living less on top of each other? I don't think you want to lose her altogether, do you?'

'No. You're right.'

'Then broach it carefully, OK?'

'Will do. Thanks Nicki.'

'So. What about this? Martin may have a job move.'

We talked for ages about that, until we'd finished our coffee. Ernie couldn't bear the idea of our moving away. I hadn't expected that. It was touching but made me feel worse.

'I'd miss you all,' he said.

'You and Blume could move to London as well, then,' I said. 'Or maybe have a pied-à-terre there. That would be a way of having space. For now, let's arrange that weekend away, the four of us, maybe while Jake is at Edna's? It could be good.'

'Sure,' Ernie replied, looking a little better.

'Just wait till I've seen the consultant again, though, OK?'

He wanted to know all about the issues of 'small-for-dates' and looked worried. I assured him I was in good hands and that there'd be no moving until after the baby.

'It's nearly lunchtime, Ernie, you'd better go. Blume will be worried about you.'

'That's just it. I wish she'd stop fussing.' With that, we hugged and he left. Life's not easy. As Grandma Freidl said, 'The most significant things in life are out of your control.'

Yet happy coincidences do happen: five minutes later, the doorbell rang. It was Ros.

Ernie called to me from his car, its engine running, in the drive. 'Look who I found!' he said – and promptly drove off.

'How…? What…?'

'Ernie spotted me on the street,' said Ros. 'We chatted a while and he told me you were lonely. Before I knew it, he offered to bring me round.'

'Oh. So… come in,' I said, bewildered.

'Oh, Nicki. How could you...?' I thought she was going to shout at me again.

'How could I what?'

'Ask me in, after...' She hugged me, crying.

I felt like joining in, but simply hugged her back, whispering, 'Forget it, OK?'

Ros didn't look well – thin, gaunt in fact, with dark rings under her eyes. There was no sparkle. She wasn't even dressed in her usual, snazzy way. This had to be more than just bereavement.

'I've missed you,' she said. 'You're such a good listener.'

'Not sure my family would agree with you,' I said, wistfully.

'What d'you mean?'

'Long story. What about you, though?' I asked.

She had problems at work. She went back to counselling soon after losing Gill – against the centre's advice – and a client had complained about her handling of his case. She had just come from a senior managers' meeting.

'Is your job threatened?' I asked, before telling her she'd find coffee in the Thermos.

'I did start back quite soon after losing Gill – I thought I could just "do my job".'

'And...?'

'It *was* too soon. I've got to take a month off work, now.' That didn't seem too bad.

'Well, we two can have fun, cos I can't go back to work, either, for a while.' I seriously liked the idea of being leisurely ladies, for once. 'If you want to fish in the fridge, you can make us a snack lunch. I've got to learn to be lazy.'

We had a good chat while we ate, till she had to leave. I felt and had always felt that Ros was the one person in the world who genuinely understood me. Well, her and Ernie, to be fair, so I supposed I was lucky to have them. However much Martin loved me, we seemed to have missed connections lately, and I ended up feeling it was all my fault.

'Nicki, that was good,' said Ros. 'The food and... seeing you again. Cheers.'

My rest time continued in that surreal, light-headed way that time off work dictates: rounds of meeting people for coffee, tea or lunch; cooking only occasionally. I didn't know what to do about the mural. The more I did, the more depressed I became. If we moved, we'd be leaving all the love I'd put into it.

Next day, when Dad called my mobile, it had to be bad news.

'Sorry to bother you Nicki, but it's about Ernie.'

'What about him?'

'Well, it's Blume, really.'

'Go on, go on!' Poor man – he was being as quick as he could.

'When he got home from seeing you, he found a note from Blume on the kitchen table, saying they needed to talk. You don't think she's gone off him, do you?'

'Poor Ernie. How is he?'

'He doesn't sound too bad, really, but I think he's covering up.'

'I'll call him later. But thanks for telling me.'

Martin came in. 'Come on Nicki, the appointment's in half an hour,' he reminded me. I wasn't ready because I wasn't looking forward to seeing Mrs Robertson. Martin and I chatted about the Ernie–Blume situation; if they were both uncertain, at least they would talk it over.

'Separations are the new togetherness in our family,' Martin said, pinching my thigh as he drove. I didn't reply, because I was thinking about the baby and the new job. Another separation? I really hoped they would work things out and stay together.

'By the way, the recruitment guy suggested that, if I do get this job, I could start by commuting, weekly.'

The idea of being alone with a new baby – and Jake – did

not appeal. 'Let's get this appointment over. Please? So you *are* applying, then?'

'I couldn't not.'

'But – living on your own all week – what kind of a life is that? For you, I mean.'

'Lots of people do it. It may be the only option.'

'It's so much the wrong time,' I said, with a nagging fear that Catherine had something to do with it.

'Come on, we're here. Deep breaths and in we go.' He took my hand as we got out of the car. 'Deep breaths and in' reminded me of the time we tried scuba diving: going into the deep, deep ocean, when I began to panic. Then, as now, I was sure I was drowning. At that moment, I saw big-toothed sharks and a bright pink octopus. I was trapped between underwater grasses and Martin's voice floated around me, on the surface of the water.

'Come on, love. You'll be fine! Stand up a bit more but lean on me. You're alright.'

The next thing I knew, I was sitting on a chair in the waiting room of the obstetrician's clinic, feeling very odd. I'd fainted, but somehow Martin had held me upright till we got inside. A nurse brought me a glass of water, which I drank but immediately threw up. If I hadn't felt so ghastly I'd have died of embarrassment.

'Looks like coffee to me,' said Martin, calm as ever. Someone kindly mopped up after me and gave Martin a cool, damp cloth with which he bathed my face and cooled my brow. 'Poor you. I think you're a bit feverish. I don't think it was a panic.'

The consultant, Mrs Robertson, found I had only a slight fever and thought it was nothing to do with the pregnancy. She examined me and scanned the foetus, then used a tape measure with some charts. A graph appeared on the monitor opposite, on which she plotted the growth of the baby.

'She is quite healthy but still not growing fast enough. This old-fashioned tape-measure trick is almost as good as the scans, to be honest.'

'Meaning?' Martin said.

'The number of centimetres from pubis to the fundus – here.' She pointed to the top of my womb. 'It's usually the same as the number of weeks into the pregnancy, believe it or not. It's quite a way off, at the moment.'

I thought I'd throw up again. Martin held my hand and put his arm round my waist, to help me off the examination couch.

'So what happens now?' I asked, sure they could both hear my heart pounding, as well as the baby's.

'More serious resting, I'm afraid.'

'And then...?'

'We keep the baby healthy for as long as we can, in utero, but have her out of there as soon as independent life is viable. That's what we do. And when I say independent, that will most likely be in an incubator.'

'I hate the term "viable",' Martin said. I thought he was about to go on another rant, but he stayed calm.

'I'm sorry about that. It does say it all, though. It doesn't mean I don't think of your daughter as a person – I certainly do – but I have to present the facts.'

'Am I likely to go to term?' I asked.

'That's the only question I can answer with certainty: no,' she replied. 'The placenta has become hostile to the baby's growth, even though the uterus is still the best place for her, for now. Odd, isn't it?'

I felt awful and helpless, too. 'I've heard that before,' I whimpered. 'But it sounds so ghastly.'

Now I felt that my whole body, my womb – the most significant part of me – was as inefficient as the rest. Why was I such a failure?

'It would have been ghastly, years ago,' said the doctor, 'but not now, with all our knowledge and equipment. We will bring out a healthy baby because we keep such a careful eye on you both. For now, go home and go to bed till you feel stronger. Drink plenty. And afterwards, make sure to eat well. Are you a good cook, Mr Taylor?'

'Adequate,' Martin replied. I hardly heard any of that, I was swimming again.

'From now on, Nicki's time at home must be completely inactive – oh, and no driving, either. I don't like saying complete bed rest, if I can help it, but I'm afraid you won't be going back to work until after the baby's born.' Mrs Robertson's voice was quiet.

'Anything else?' Martin asked.

'Yes, I think your wife needs you to take her home. I'll see you in a month's time, unless you need me earlier.'

'Mm,' I mumbled as I slipped sideways off the chair. Martin half lifted me up and guided me out and along the eternal corridor. Then I felt a rush of air and a sense of speed. I came round in a wheelchair and before anyone would let me get into our car, Mrs Robertson appeared and took my blood pressure again.

'It's fine. Just get on home to your own bed, OK?'

Great – what a time to get ill.

At least Jake was off to his grandma's the next morning. When we arrived home, his rucksack and its future contents lay strewn across the hall and he was speaking to someone on his mobile.

'Speak soon, Mum's just back. Sure I will, bye! That was Trish – she sends love. Hey, Mum, what's up? You look awful.'

'Thanks for that, Jake,' I said, trying to smile. Then I saw my face in the hall mirror – it had found a new meaning for 'pale' – and I went to sit on the stairs. Martin hauled me up to bed, then he started to sort out Jake's plans for Rochdale, checking his bus tickets and reassuring him that my feeling ill was nothing sinister.

'Had I better not go, then?' I heard him ask. Martin told him he should go, and enjoy himself.

I managed to sip some water and closed my hot eyes. Martin put a damp flannel over my face to cool me down.

It was a feverish sleep: very heavy, yet fitful at the same time. At one point, I was woken by Martin replacing the damp cloth with some frozen peas wrapped in a tea towel.

'Saw this on *ER*,' he said. He took my temperature but again, it didn't register anything alarming. It was dark by then so, since it was early June, I knew it was late. Martin sat on the bed, stroking my belly through the bedding, looking anxious.

'Your pillow is soaked – I'll change the pillowcase. Take my pillow for now.' He lifted my head while he exchanged them and I couldn't wait to lie down again. 'But your temperature isn't up – it's probably just one of those things.'

I knew nothing until the next morning, when Jake came in to say goodbye.

'You sure you can manage?' he asked. I nodded. 'Well, when I get back, I'll tell you about the email Trish got through one of those "hunt your family" websites. We might have found one of Malkah Fainaro's relations.'

'It can wait, Jake.' Martin gestured. 'You go and have a good time with my mum. I've called a cab to take you to the bus station, because I don't want to leave the house, OK?'

'Cool. Cheers.' With that, he blew me a kiss and left.

'Call us when you arrive – see you in three days,' Martin shouted over the banister, as the front door banged shut. He went to watch Jake leave, through the window. The house was still and too quiet. I wished I felt like enjoying it.

Martin went into the study to write, leaving our bedroom door open. I didn't even feel well enough to worry about the job thing. I just let it all drift round my mind. When I fell asleep again I had some fantastical dreams. I was surrounded by the weird-coloured animals of my mural, running naked through a kind of forest with Jake and Dad, then switching, nightmare-like, to a familiar place where policemen were shouting to us to get dressed. We were outside Central Ref, but in London's Leicester Square as well. I was screaming at them, when I woke, perspiring so much that the pillow was wet again.

'What's up, love?' Martin ran in as he heard my scream.

'I was dreaming,' I said, weakly. 'Can I have a fresh glass of water, please?'

I sat up gingerly and drank the water, feeling slightly better.

'What were you dreaming about – or nightmaring – is that a verb?'

'I was running naked through a forest – it was like the nursery mural actually.'

'Sounds good to me,' Martin replied, winking. 'So what made you scream – was I chasing you?'

'We ended up in London. Nude, in Leicester Square!'

Martin laughed. 'Aha. So London is giving you nightmares already, is it?'

'The weird bit was that we were outside Central Ref too!'

Martin chuckled. He sat down on the bed, stroking my arm. 'Look, I have to apply for the job, you know.'

'I realise that, I really do, but…'

'The worst possible scenario is that I end up unemployed and unemployable, when digital publishing and e-readers kick in. And don't kid yourself that there's a career in writing plays.'

'I know.' I lay back on the bed. It was far easier talking about his career without Jake interrupting. 'Meanwhile, can I try to eat something?'

Martin left and came back with a tray of edible bits and pieces to coax my tastebuds. I was cooler and listened to the radio while I nibbled at the food. Martin wrote for the rest of the afternoon and, later, Jake called to say he'd arrived. Edna came on the phone, sounding delighted that he was there. I rested more peacefully after that.

In the evening I went downstairs with Martin, feeling like an old woman but glad, at least, that the baby was kicking merrily. Martin had had a good afternoon's writing – he'd started on the last act and had begun to apply for funding.

THIRTY

Once that bug left me, my enforced rest at home meant that I was like blotting paper to the news snippets from visitors and phone calls. The weather was better and warm enough, on some days, to sit on a chaise longue outside, with the papers and my mobile phone.

I thought the baby was growing, and my blood pressure remained stable so the health visitor was satisfied. The fact that, from time to time, I was painting in the nursery was kept from her, but Martin had taken up the kitchen stool and I only painted what I could reach while sitting down. Anything higher, Martin did for me. I concentrated on details like the monkey's silver eye and the crocodile's beaded tail, by mixing glue in with the paint and sticking sequins to the wall.

In the meantime, the lives of family and friends circled uneventfully around me and I was simply a spectator. From my seated or supine position, I dished out advice and offered a listening ear to all and sundry. I really turned into a dangerous gossip, since all I could do was listen to people when they came or phoned.

Ernie came round about Blume. After she left that note, they had met for a weekend together in London. That is where she had gone when she left, to see some old friends. She and Ernie had thrashed out their problems and realised they wanted to stay together. Blume found London exciting, so they were considering spending more time there, in this friend's underused apartment. A change of scenery every so often would probably resolve things.

'So, how do you feel?' I asked him as he sat on a chaise longue by me in the garden and we drank lemon tea together.

'You know, I'm fine. I'd hate to lose her altogether. We both feel better from talking. Yet when she's in London, she misses the family. And, for as long as we're fit enough, we'll take lots of holidays, mainly in Israel. So she won't lose touch with her group and I can keep tabs on the Lanzig quest. When are you moving to London, Nicki?'

'Martin still hasn't had his first interview,' I said, 'but his play is going really well – a couple of local theatres are biting – which is good, cos it's a real Northern story. Now it's the fundraising bandwagon,' I added, trying to buoy him up. 'Hey! Have you seen the nursery lately?'

'No – let me see.' He went up and waved wildly to me from its window, with a thumbs-up. When he came back out with Martin, they were giggling like children. Martin was waving a piece of paper – I was terrified it was about the job.

'That Oldham theatre,' Martin began, 'they want to put it on as a work in progress, inviting potential backers...'

'Fantastic! Well done, you. When?'

'They'd like it to end off the summer season in their studio theatre – the one they use for new stuff.'

'Could it be when David's here for the unveiling?' I asked.

'Could be – I'll get back in touch.'

The play became the talking point, which was great. Resting always seems attractive but this doing nothing was mind-crushing. The bigger my belly grew, the more my brain shrank. I tried to keep up with good books, radio, avoid numbing daytime TV, but still my remaining grey matter turned to marshmallow.

Except, of course, when I put Catherine into the picture. Or when the health visitor was due – then all the latent tension surfaced until she had taken my blood pressure and declared it fine. I was worried about my unborn daughter, but somehow, worrying in overdrive blanked out my senses. A kind of negative response. Sometimes I cheered myself up by reading through girls' names lists – how intellectual was that? 'Flora Edina' went over like a lead balloon when I tried it out on Martin.

Thankfully, Jake came back from Rochdale full of beans. He and his grandma had taken long walks across the moors every day, dropping in to a country pub for a quick lunch. They'd talked a lot and Jake told Martin that his grandma had helped 'sort his head out about the Bar Mitzvah stuff'.

'Either we have it in Israel, or we have it at the reform shul, so Dad can be properly with me,' Jake said, with a satisfied grin.

'Good one,' I said, as Martin hugged Jake's shoulders, obviously touched. 'And you know what? There are complications over women at the Western Wall.'

'What?' Jake was shocked. 'How come?'

'Well, by the Temple, there's a separation between the men's section and the women's that's too high to see over.'

'How long have you known?' Martin asked.

'A while. But let's drop it, for now.'

'Blinking marvellous! At the orthodox shul here, Dad wouldn't be comfortable; Mum wouldn't like it at the reform shul and in Israel, we couldn't even stand together. What a mess,' said Jake. 'I'll go and recite my Bar Mitzvah portion standing on my head, in a park.' We both looked at him.

Jake was grinning. 'Didn't you two ever see that *Bar Mitzvah Boy* play on TV? I found it on a repeats channel.'

'The Jack Rosenthal play?' Martin asked.

'Maybe. It's very funny. This kid gets so fed up with all the hassle, he storms off to a park and recites it there.'

'Standing on his head?' I asked, recalling it dimly.

'Yep! Good idea, don't you think?' Jake winked.

'Might be the best idea yet,' Martin said, as he gave Jake a hug.

My next scan came up. It showed, yet again, that the baby had grown only just enough. The doctor was at the point of deciding how long the babe could live successfully in utero but gave me another month.

Some days were lightened by visits, often from Trish, who had sensitivity beyond her years. She brought me a pile of magazines.

'I know you usually read good books, but I bet you love rubbish, sometimes,' she said, smiling as she plonked them all down on my ever-shrinking lap.

'Great idea, Trish! Thanks.'

She then looked serious and asked me how I was. 'You don't mind my asking, do you?' she said.

'Not at all – but it's complicated. The baby is well but not growing fast enough and when she's born she'll have to be in an incubator,' I explained.

'Oh.' A bit bemused, she scuttled off with Jake. After a while they both came back outside.

'We've got something to show you,' Jake said.

We went inside, where they showed me all the emails about Miriam Malkah Fainaro, née Levy, sister of Grandma Freidl. Older than Freidl, she would have died long ago; they hoped any remaining relatives could fill in some details.

'But look, here,' said Jake. 'It seems as though they lived at or in the synagogue. Doesn't make sense!'

'It could do, perhaps their father was the caretaker or even the *chazzan*,' I suggested.

'Could be,' Trish said, 'we never thought of that.'

People had answered Jake and Trish's emails, either called Fainaro or with that as their maiden name. Quite a few said they were related to a Miriam or a Freidl. So who was the genuine article?

'Look, Mum, here – there are only two people with connections to both names: two guys, living in Buenos Aires, apparently sons of a brother who was born after Freidl left Romania. That's feasible, even though Freidl was a teenager, because they had massive families in those days. Anyway, these guys prefer to write – or speak – in Spanish. English isn't even their *second* language. Now Trish's mum speaks Spanish. D'you mind if she does the Spanish emailing?'

'Do you?' Trish asked.

'Course not,' I replied.

We gave Trish the questions her mum should ask and when Martin came home from work, he was excited about the play again and carried on writing. I carried on sitting, lying and dreaming. The future was out of our hands, as Freidl would have told me. The lack of tension became stressful, like living in a vacuum. How crazy is that? But nothing to worry about *is* unnatural. If Martin succeeded through to the next round of interviews, we'd still have to wait and see what happened.

One day Martin said he had a surprise. He wouldn't tell me what it was but bundled me into the car, drove into the warehouse district of Cheetham Hill and drew up outside a long, corrugated iron building. He took my arm to prevent my tripping on the rough stones around the place and took me into a darkened space.

'Sit here, my darling, and watch this special rehearsal of my play. Abracadabra!'

The lights went up and I realised I was in the centre of a short row of chairs in front of a makeshift stage. This was Martin's rehearsal room.

He squatted behind me and whispered, 'You are my first audience.' He sat on the floor and the lights went down.

There was a screen as a backdrop and the music began. It was like that old-fashioned piano music that accompanied silent movies. On the screen was a silent, flickering projection of women against railings with 'Votes for Women!' banners held high. There were subtitles: 'Listen to us! Support us. You know it's right, women need the vote. YOU need us!'

Then the screen showed women being herded by old-fashioned policemen with truncheons and high hats – pushed down a street where a sign said: 'To Holloway'.

Alongside this screening with its atmospheric music and slogans, I spotted a lone woman at the side of the stage, standing under a representation of a gas lamp. She wasn't in costume but in black, as were all the actors, to exaggerate the gloom.

'I am Freya Fainaro and this is my story.' The initial impact was stunning. The lighting gradually came up but never became really bright. Nor did the clothes of the characters – it was like a film played in black and white. And it was mesmerising.

I put out my hand behind me to find Martin and squeezed his arm in delighted approval. The first Freya disappeared into the wings and the young Freya emerged, as if from the gangplank of the ship that now swayed on the screen. It wasn't long before she tripped over that fateful bundle. As she realised it was a baby, even I gasped.

The action was interspersed with Freya's letters, read offstage by the first actress. Jacob came over, correctly, as the most *sympathique* person imaginable, taking on Freya and her 'find' without batting an eyelid. I almost dreaded the scene between the young woman and her uncle as she returned from that awful rally in London, but it did begin well. Martin waved to his co-director to stop the action there, though, as he thought it was not polished enough.

'What d'you think so far?'

'I think it is marvellous – far better than I could ever have imagined – and I love the screen, the subtitles, the reference to silent movies. I also like the slightly foreign but Manchester accent. I have no criticisms at all. Not one!'

'Now I am worried about you,' Martin said. 'Do you feel OK?'

I had never been to his rehearsals without comment, at

his previous productions, but this was truly fantastic. I was so proud.

The next day, when I was at my most languid, Dad phoned. Always a reason for my pulse to race.

'We never talked about that extra letter you know,' he said. 'Can I pop round? Ernie will drop me off.' He arrived ten minutes later. I wasn't sure who was forgetful, him or me. How could we have taken Friedl's letter and not told him what was in it?

'So, tell me,' he began. I told him all about the arrests, the bail and Freidl and Isaac's estrangement. Dad shook his head.

'You know, I could imagine something like that. Freidl was my mother-in-law, don't forget. I loved her and – more than that – I admired her –'

'But?'

'But she was so tough, so determined, so...'

'Strong principled?' I suggested.

'Exactly. I mean, to be a suffragette she had to be, I know. But Isaac hadn't only given her a home, he took her baby in, too. And it wasn't even hers!'

'I know, Dad. Did she ever talk about her uncle Isaac, mention him at all?'

'I'm just thinking. She did, once or twice but not, well, not that you'd have known he was her only blood relative in this country.'

'So you never met him?'

'No. I knew he died very young... not sure who told me.'

'He probably thought of her as a daughter, not having married himself and everything,' I said. It was a sad chapter in Freidl's life. Dad looked crestfallen.

'Don't let it get to you. It's history, now,' I said.

'You're right. Oh – that'll be Ernie's car horn. He told me not to tire you. What a story.'

'But Freidl was a brilliant mother to Mum – and to Ernie,

remember,' I said. 'Maybe Uncle Isaac *was* in the wrong.'

Dad left and at least now I had something to think of in my brainless haze. The good thing was that David's forthcoming trip would cover all the family events, since Martin had persuaded the theatre to stage the play at that time. It would be shown on the Thursday and the Saturday – the night before the unveiling. It all worked out well except that I would probably not be allowed to attend at all.

That was five weeks away and still the baby stubbornly refused to grow enough. Her heartbeat and all other vital signs were fine but we were nearing the time when a Caesarean would be fixed. I supposed that if all the family was over then, it could be a best-case scenario.

One day, Ernie called to say that Blume wanted to come round; she still wanted to help organise the 'big weekend'. She was heaven-sent – she took lists from Martin: whom to invite to the play launch, how to finalise everything for the unveiling. She emailed all this to David and arranged for him to sleep at Dad's and eat at Ernie's.

She came round, bringing a whole meal. The starter was pickled herring with apple in sour cream – a traditional German dish I adored. She offered to stay with me on the big weekend, if I had to stay away from all the events.

Martin received an interview date in London – he'd done well to get that far. He went for the day, so Dad and Ernie came round to keep me company. We had such a fun time, playing board games in the garden. Odd, how anxious moments can turn into good ones. When Martin called to say the interview went well, I tried to sound pleased.

I went for another scan with Mrs Robertson. Things were much the same and she said, 'The time has come to talk about the big question.'

'You mean: when to have the baby out?' I asked.

'Exactly. We have decisions to make. There's a fine balance

between leaving well alone and giving the placenta one last chance to do its work, or on the other hand, having that tiny baby girl out and safely in one of our lovely, cosy incubators.'

That sounded so sweet if it weren't so scary. I began to cry quietly; the consultant handed me her box of paper hankies. Then I giggled. She must have thought me quite mad, but I was thinking of all the different paper hankies I'd used in recent months – I was an emotional mess.

'Sorry,' I said.

'Don't be. You've been very strong so far. It's so difficult for us, too. We want to put mothers' minds at ease, yet in these cases we can't really do that.'

'Well, I leave it to you, obviously.'

'And I must go on experience, facts and gut instinct. Let's look at the calendar. You know, however tiny the babe, we have the best facilities here, even for lung problems – we've discussed those, haven't we?'

I nodded.

'OK, I want to bring you in a month from now and give you bed rest here for a week. You'll both be safe and cared for, here. And then we'll perform a Caesarean the first week in August.' Mrs Robertson looked at me. 'Why are you shocked?'

'It's the timing. Can I call my dad in?'

With Martin at work that day, Dad had come with me by taxi, and was waiting in the corridor.

'Sure – but what's wrong, now?' She went to the door and beckoned Dad into the room. He did his usual 'jovial self' act. Playing Daddy again – I liked it.

'Well I never! It's a long time since I came to a room like this – there weren't many lady doctors then, you know,' he said, as he shook her hand. He looked at me, sat down beside me, took my hand and asked, 'Nicki, love, is it the baby? What's wrong?'

'Nothing, Dad. Well, not really, but...'

Mrs Robertson took over, explaining everything. 'Your

daughter is upset about the week I've chosen to induce the baby.'

'Dad, it's the same week as the play *and* the unveiling – I won't be at either of them. And what about my birthday with David?'

'So... we can *all* celebrate with a new baby! What could be better?'

'But what about Martin? It's his first staged play for twenty years!'

'Look Mrs Taylor, we can fine-tune the dates, one day to either side, that isn't crucial,' said the doctor. 'What is crucial is to have you in here, with my wonderful staff looking after you, a month from now. You tell me the dates your husband can't be here and we'll try our best, OK?'

'That'll be just fine, won't it, Nicki?' Dad said, enjoying his fatherly role.

'Mm.'

'What we want is a healthy baby,' he said, talking as though I were a little girl myself. I liked it.

'Dad, she'll be in an incubator for quite a while after she's born, you know?'

'I'm not daft. And where d'you think you and David started your lives?'

'Of course, we were tiny, weren't we?'

'You know, Doctor,' he said, turning to her, 'I could hold a twin in the palm of each hand, they were so small. No heavier than a bag of sugar, each one!' he said.

'They did well, then, didn't they?' she answered.

'It was their mother that did it,' he went on. 'No one could have been as dedicated, no one. My Malkah gave them her milk through a dripper – brought it to the hospital every day...' he tailed off, tears in his eyes. I was worried that he'd go on with our whole life story.

'Dad, we'll tell Mrs Robertson more, another time, OK?' I

turned to her and explained that Mum had died only recently.

'I am sorry. But I love hearing about births in other times. Lovely to meet you,' she said to Dad, shaking his hand.

Dad and I left and, pragmatic as ever, he said we'd just deal with the inevitable. He tried to persuade me to let fate take over and he was right, because *'nothing of real consequence is of our own making'*.

THIRTY-ONE

Preview announcements for Martin's play appeared in the local press, while Jake and Trish kept up their emails to the Fainaro family, hoping for some revelations. Martin made it to the second interview – another mixed blessing.

Most of the time, the cocoon of pregnancy I inhabited cushioned me from anxiety. That is, until one afternoon, in that dreamy doze that engulfed me at times, I had a thought that woke me as nothing else would. I had never asked Martin the fidelity question that Rabbi Lever posed.

Suddenly, I wondered whether there was a connection between his trip to Hong Kong and his decision to apply for this job – had Catherine been there, too? Maybe that was why he was so keen. Or maybe it was my twisted mind. As I shook myself awake, I knew it would destroy me to become the suspicious wife and that these thoughts could spiral out of control.

All the dates were set, but I had to see Mum's grave somehow. Martin asked Rabbi Lever, who agreed to allow him to take me before my due date. So we went, just the two of us, to the empty cemetery, and along to where a little sheet was covering a gravestone. I leant on Martin as I read the simple inscription and suddenly pictured and heard Mum as I had hardly done since she died. Had I forgotten her? Maybe I had blanked her out until I had time and space.

I remembered my first funeral, when David and I were considered old enough: it was Grandpa Jacob's brother's funeral. In the slow drive to the cemetery that day, Mum gave us her 'tears' lecture. She told us that we could expect people to be crying, that that is how people dealt with loss. But she also told us to try our hardest, throughout our lives, not to cry 'too much'.

'What d'you mean, Mum?' I asked.

'I never cry,' declared David, at which I dug him in the ribs.

Mum explained that whether we laugh or cry, there can be a limit. She said that people eventually lose sympathy for those who sob uncontrollably.

'I don't get it,' I said. 'How can anyone help it?'

'Trust me, they can, and it's just something to keep in mind, my darlings,' she said, hugging us both, one arm round each of us, with a tear trickling down her cheek.

'But Mummy, look at you!' David said.

'Yes, I know, I had to learn the hard way. I was once told off for my crying, in front of grown-ups, and I can't forget it,' she replied, but she didn't expand on the episode.

Martin's voice brought me back to the present. 'She understood you like no one else.'

'But she did seem harsh, sometimes,' I sniffled into his shoulder, which was wet by now.

'She was a good mum y'know,' he said, 'but she was bringing you up to be independent. She had a modern approach to parenting.'

'Meaning?'

'Meaning that it is a parent's job to prepare you for the nasty world out there. She loved you as well.'

'I never doubted it,' I replied.

'I know.'

'Maybe I've been angry that she left us.'

'Probably. But she loved us all.'

'Mm. She didn't always show it, though.'

'She didn't need to,' Martin assured me.

'Oh God! I think my...'

My waters broke. Just then. Just there. I felt that my whole body was crying, pouring, emptying onto my mother's grave. Martin steered me to a bench where I crumpled. He ran to get the grave attendant to open the double gates for us and drove the car down the path between the graves.

He guided me into the back of the car gently, strapping me loosely but allowing my knees up on the seat. He drove swiftly but carefully round corners and over bumps.

'I think this is really... spiritual, y'know,' he said.

'Spiritual?'

'Yeah... you starting in labour by your mum's side and everything. Well, it's definitely poetic,' he said.

'Glad you think so. Go and write a poem then!' I replied.

As Martin took me into hospital I was strangely relieved, but watching him closely. Could this caring, gentle man be capable of leading a double life?

'Why are you looking at me like that?' he asked, kissing me as we went onto the ward. I just shrugged my shoulders.

'You've been very good to me, that's all.' He kissed me again. On the nose this time.

The staff were lovely, very caring and the ward of other mums-to-be was a fun place, really. After Martin left, we all talked non-stop about our pregnancies, our lives, everything – nothing was taboo and woman-talk was a great leveller. I was the only woman on the ward with a husband – almost a pariah.

'How long d'you say you've been married?' 'To the same guy?' 'Bet he's gorgeous, then.' The comments from bed to bed came thick and fast.

I was carefully monitored, kept fairly quiet, with no visitors except the family. It was an experience for Jake to come to the ward, where women waddled around in various stages of pregnancy, their dressing gowns open if they wore them at all.

Even though the waters had broken, I didn't go into labour immediately. Just before visiting time, I felt a kiss on my cheek.

'David! Wow! You're here already!'

'We kept the time of my flight a surprise. So – sis, good to see you!' He bent down and we hugged; the last time had been at Mum's funeral. A lifetime away. As he stood up, he gestured to the ward's corridor window. 'Look!'

There in the corridor was Blume, holding the most adorable baby, jumping in her arms, smiling. Of course, it was Malachi – I'd almost forgotten. Blume looked very comfortable in her role and took the baby's hand to make him wave.

'He looks just like Hannah,' I said. 'Gorgeous! I'd love to hold him.'

'No babies allowed in the ward. When you've had your baby you can cuddle him in the day room.'

I blew kisses to Malachi. We chatted about all kinds of things for the few minutes we had together.

'I'll be here again,' said David. 'But, hey, isn't Blume great? I couldn't imagine how easy she is to get on with. Or how happy Ernie is, he's a changed man. So,we've got a hectic time ahead – but you've only one thing to think of. Not the play, not the unveiling, only this baby girl of yours, OK?'

'OK.'

'Love you, Nic.' We kissed goodbye. I sighed and fell deeply asleep. It seemed only minutes later that I was woken by Martin, flapping something over my face which I thought was a fan.

'Hey, what's that?' I asked, as we kissed.

'It's the programme for the play,' he replied. 'What d'you think?'

The cover was edged in purple, with images of suffragette banners swathed across the corners; at the top was an old, brownish photo of a group of suffragettes. Underneath, in classic loopy handwriting, was the title – *On the Soapbox* – followed by, 'a play in three acts by Martin Taylor'.

'Exciting, hey?' he said, grinning.

'Fantastic,' I said. 'Of course, the soapbox at Speakers' Corner, in Platt Fields.'

'Yes. Here – look inside,' Martin urged me.

Freidl had become Freya Fainaro, heading the *Dramatis Personae* – Martin wouldn't use Freidl's real name, or anyone else's. Act Three was called 'The Shame'. It was the scene when Isaac paid off Grandma's jail sentence; Isaac was called Avram in the play. At the very bottom, after a brief history of the story, was the following:

'Dedicated to the memory of Malkah Bamberg, beloved daughter of a suffragette.' And I cried – controlled, happy tears, especially for Mum.

'The play's had good previews in the press, everyone likes the idea.'

'I'm sure they do,' I said, wiping my eyes. 'That dedication is lovely, Martin.'

'Good,' he said. 'My co-director's got the play well in hand now. Don't worry about tomorrow. I'll come straight to the hospital after the unveiling and I'll be here when you go in for the Caesarean to see you come out with our beautiful baby girl.' With that, he hugged me, leaving the programme on the table by the bed. There was no mention of the job or the interview. We kissed goodbye. As I waved him off, everything was still in the air – although Flora Edina would definitely arrive soon, whatever Martin thought of the names.

The nurse came in. 'The foetal heart's racing a bit,' she said. 'I'll buzz the consultant. I'm not sure if Mrs Robertson is on duty yet, but if not it'll be Mr Chance. Lovely guy. And he doesn't take any.'

'Doesn't take any what? Oh – sorry, I get it,' I said, suddenly tuning in as she left me. My pulse raced – could that change the foetal heart rate?

The blood-pressure machine, ready strapped to my arm,

beeped and the nurse came back quickly. She held my hand, saying, 'Bit worried, are you, Nicki?'

I just nodded. At that moment a doctor came briskly into the ward, followed by Martin.

'They wouldn't let me go,' he said, quietly.

Proffering his hand, the doctor introduced himself as Mr Chance.

'Hello there! Looks like we'll soon get to meet this little girl, then,' he said, while scanning the monitors and feeling my abdomen.

'Well, the Caesarean was planned for tomorrow, anyway,' I said. 'Will you let me go into labour myself, now?'

He sat down at the foot of the bed. 'In normal circumstances, we'd leave things for a while: watch and wait, y'know.'

'But…?' I said.

'But… these are not normal circumstances. The baby is small, the waters have broken and your blood pressure is up. All those put together give me every possible reason for performing the Caesar now.' He was calming although firm.

'Oh,' I said, my hand already fishing around for the tissue box on the bedside table.

'Is that any worse than tomorrow, really?' asked the doctor, looking concerned. 'It won't be so much different. It'll take us about quarter of an hour to get sorted.'

'It's just that… Oh God!' I drifted off, wiping my eyes and nose.

'Shall I get theatre ready, then?' Mr Chance said, patting my leg through the sheets in that consultoid way. I nodded, thinking of an entirely different kind of theatre.

'OK then. Nurse Janet here will start all the pre-op prep very soon, and I'll see you in theatre. Cheer up, your worries are nearly over!' And off he strode.

Martin popped out of the ward to tell the family he was not coming straight home. When he returned, he told me Blume wanted to reassure me that all the food and drink was ready for the next day.

'She said to tell you you'll love her kuchen, made to your mum's recipe.'

'Thank her for me later, will you, love?'

I closed my eyes and thought of Mum. I could picture her properly again; I could see her, with her twinkly smile, sitting so straight and sewing. I could picture her long fingers, nails always painted, guiding fabric through the sewing machine with a pin between her teeth.

I began to whisper my own kaddish for her, as the nurses came and lifted me onto the trolley, which they then wheeled speedily out of the ward.

'Saying a little prayer are you, love? Lots of people do that, y'know,' one of the nurses observed.

'Kind of – I was thinking of Mum,' I told them.

'Calling the baby after her, are you?'

'No, I'm not actually –'

At that moment, Martin leant over the trolley and kissed me, stroking my hand. He couldn't love anyone else, could he?

'See you later,' I said, as we disappeared into theatre.

In what seemed like minutes, but was in fact half an hour, I was conscious, if muzzy. A tiny bundle was handed to me by the same nurse who had seen me onto the trolley, with a warning that the cuddle was to be a very short one.

As Martin bent over to peep at the tiny face, I managed to whisper, 'I'm going to call her after a flower.'

Acknowledgements

My thanks are due to:

My late mother, who always told me to write a book; my husband, whose patience knows no bounds; my sons, their wives and children for their loving support; my rabbi for his friendly and worldly advice on certain Jewish issues; my three readers, for their time and opinions; Manchester's Womanswrite group, for their honesty; Helen, my publisher, for her good-natured attention to detail; and all the people I have ever met whose experiences may have unwittingly embroidered the story.

The book is a work of fiction. Whilst I have met survivors of the Kindertransport and also know that my own grandmother was a suffragette, everything about the women's suffrage movement or the escape from Nazi Germany is fictional, apart from well-documented dates, people or places.